THE CRONE OF ARCANE CINDERS

IRIS BEAGLEHOLE

1

DELIA

*D*elia shuddered as she held the phone. "What is it, Gilly? Whatever it is, you can tell me."

She'd been waiting for her daughter to reveal the big secret. It had been months of strange behaviour at this point. She didn't want to push it.

But she really did want to know what, in the name of all the Goddesses, was going on.

"Perhaps you could come outside," said Gillian. "I'm here with the kids."

"You're out front?" said Delia, rushing out without putting her coat on, into the cold night air.

"Nana!" Two adorable grandchildren burst upon her the moment she was out the door.

"Where's your mum, my loves?"

"In the car," said Merryn.

"Right, you two, run inside and tell Auntie Kitty to get you something delicious."

"Yay!" said Keyne. "I want something delicious!"

"And even more delicious!" said Merryn. "All the delicious things! I want all of them!"

"Very well then," said Delia, hugging the children and relinquishing them to the warmth of the house. She stepped out with some trepidation towards Gilly's car parked on the street outside her cottage, having the sense that whatever this conversation was going to be, it wasn't for the ears of all those inside the house. She could see Gillian's face illuminated by the soft streetlights. She looked pensive.

Delia opened the passenger side door and got in, closing it gently behind her. She turned towards her daughter.

Gillian's lip trembled. "I saw that there were people in your house. I was hoping to catch you alone."

"We're alone now," said Delia. "To what do I owe the honour of this surprise visit?"

"I'm so sorry, Mum."

"Nonsense," said Delia. "You never have to apologise for visiting your own mother." Delia put her hand on Gillian's shoulder. "You can tell me anything, you know that."

"I suppose I do know that. Especially after..." Gillian's voice trailed off.

"After finding out that I'm a witch?" said Delia with a slight cackle. Gillian's face remained tense.

"I suppose it's not funny right now," Delia offered. "Are you having problems with the paranormal?"

"You might say that," said Gillian, her voice heavy.

"You know, they say the apple doesn't fall far from the tree," said Delia. "No, I'm going to stop guessing now. Just going to be quiet till you tell me."

Gillian took a deep breath. "Well, everything was normal up until a few months ago, and then everything changed."

Delia nodded slowly.

Gillian took a shuddering breath. "I woke up one day and I was different."

Gilly's tone was cold.

Delia simply waited, having committed to her own silence, but she wanted to ask a million questions.

Different how? What was it? What happened? Something hurt my child...how can I get revenge? How can I get justice? How can I protect this person who I love so very much?

"I might as well just tell you, Mum," said Gillian finally. She rested her head on the steering wheel, let out a moan, then some words that sounded strangely like "umpire."

Delia's brow furrowed. Was Gillian having an affair with an umpire? Was she trying to become one? This didn't sound particularly paranormal until the dreaded realisation sank into her belly.

"Vampire." the word formed in her mouth and she spoke it aloud.

Gillian trembled and sat back, tears streaming down her face. They were blood red.

Delia shook herself. "How could this have happened?"

Gillian shook her head. "I really don't know exactly what happened."

"What do you mean, you don't know?"

"I can't remember any details. Nobody knows who *made* me and nobody knows why."

"Why didn't you come to me?" Delia asked. "I've got connections in the magical world. I could have protected you from the vampires."

Gillian shook her head. "No, Mum, no, you couldn't have. Besides, you didn't even know you were a witch back then, and the vampires are looking after me."

"Don't tell me you've joined some kind of blood cult," said Delia. It was a half-joke, but the other half was deathly serious, so to speak.

"I...I don't know anything much about them, but—" said Delia. "Aren't vampires are some kind of magical monsters...?"

Gillian recoiled.

Delia reached out again. "I don't think that you're a monster, love. You couldn't be. But have you tried maybe reversing it?"

Gillian looked her dead in the eye. "You mean, have I tried simply *not* being a vampire?" Fangs protruded from her mouth.

Delia pulled back.

"I'm not going to eat you, Mum," said Gilly, somewhat crossly. "But this is a strange situation for me, and I'd appreciate you not giving me advice on something you know nothing about. I can't not be a vampire. I just am. It's eternal...It's eternal life, which is a lot to get your head around."

Delia shook her head. "It's starting to make some sense now," she said as a wave of grief washed over her.

What had Gillian lost? The ability to walk in sunlight? The ability to eat Italian food with all that garlic? Perhaps the ability to eat at all? It was a lot to get her head around when she knew so little about it all. She couldn't tell what was real compared to what was just in the books and films. But her daughter had been acting so strangely – she hadn't seen her in the daylight for quite some time. Gilly had eaten food, but it was her own special food that she brought to Christmas, and not the beautifully prepared meal that Delia and Kitty had slaved over for hours.

Delia had believed the story that it was some kind of health problem plaguing her daughter...and perhaps it was – just in a more magical way than she'd anticipated.

Delia sighed. "And here I was thinking it was a miracle that you took that witch stuff so lightly."

"Oh, Mum," said Gillian. "I really need you to be here for me."

"And I will be," said Delia. "I'm always here for you, even if this is hard for me and I have to go through my own process about it."

Gillian squinted at her. "What do you mean?"

"I'm not going to make my emotional reactions your problem. It's a really weird situation, though."

"Tell me about it!" said Gillian, rolling her eyes.

Delia reached over, pulling her daughter into an awkward hug as close as she possibly could get in between the car seats.

Gillian sighed and sobbed a little, and Delia regretted wearing her favourite cream silk shirt, but only for a moment, because some things were more important than blood stains...like supporting your crying vampire daughter.

"I didn't know how to tell you," Gillian said between sobs.

"Does this mean you drink blood now?" Delia asked, feeling that her daughter's fangs were uncomfortably close to her clavicle at this particular moment.

"That's partly why I've stayed away," said Gillian. "I didn't want to put you or anyone else at risk. The blood cravings are very strong at first."

"The children are safe?" Delia asked. "I mean, you haven't tried to—"

"Of course not! Actually...I mean, at first they were – oh, I hate to even admit this – things were not so in control when it all happened, but this wonderful vampire family swooped in and looked after us. They do this for new vampires sometimes. They protected the children and enchanted them so that their blood would not appeal to me at all, so that we could stay connected, even if I can't spend much time with them outside."

"This was the move to Burkenswood," said Delia as the pieces began to fall into place in her mind. Gillian nodded. "And the new job. That was a lie?"

"No," said Gillian. "I needed something to be getting on with. Fortunately, some of these vampires are lawyers, and they set me up."

Delia smiled. "You and I are so similar in that way – we need our work to be getting on with to feel grounded. Even joining this local theatre troupe has given me such a feeling of satisfaction. I didn't anticipate it could come from community theatre, and yet somehow I feel more satisfied than I have in years."

"I'm so happy for you," said Gillian. "I...I wish I could say the same, but I feel like so many things are still unresolved for me."

"It's a mystery, isn't it?" said Delia. "I need to know more about vampires so that I don't keep putting my foot in my mouth. What dangerous things do I need to avoid?"

Gillian shook her head. "I'll see if I can get you an information pack."

Delia sighed. "Thank you." She paused. "Wait a minute," she said, squinting at her daughter. "Your new vampire lawyer friends..."

Gillian's shoulders sagged a little. "Yes, I must come clean about that. Your lawyer, Perseus Burk, is an ancient vampire."

Delia shook her head, a wave of confusion wafting through her mind as she pictured the ornate office of her lawyer and his reserved but witty manner. "He does a good job of hiding it, I suppose, and he looks so young."

"Well, there's got to be some perks with being undead," said Gillian with a shrug.

"Undead? Undead? What does that mean?" said Delia.

"I suppose I'm going to find out," said Gillian.

"Do you..." Delia started. "I mean, this is probably an insensitive question, but do you..."

"Do I...eat people?" Gillian offered.

Delia's gut clenched in discomfort. "Ah, yeah, do you? Is it rude to ask that?"

Gillian shook her head. "I don't eat people, Mum. There's

blood-enchanted food, and I...at first, I required some human blood from a blood bank...just to help me adapt. Animal blood can be fine too, and in the long term, I won't need any human blood at all."

Delia nodded. That part sounded almost reasonable. She shook herself for thinking so. "Isn't it kind of gross?" she asked. "Is that insensitive too?"

"No, it's not insensitive," Gillian said with a laugh. "It tastes amazing. It tastes like blissful ambrosia." She sighed.

"Well, perhaps I'll keep my clavicle away from you after all," said Delia in a theatrical tone.

Gillian roared with laughter. There was a warmth in the air that hadn't been present before, and perhaps hadn't been felt between them for a long time.

Gillian smiled at her mother. "It's so good to tell you this. And your clavicle's safe with me."

Delia grinned. "It's going to take me some adjusting, but you know that I love you so unconditionally, my darling. You're my only child, and you are everything to me. Whatever transition you're going through, I'm here for you, and I wish you could have told me before."

"I know," said Gillian. "I know."

"Perhaps you weren't ready, and I can respect that," Delia added.

"And you have respected that," said Gillian. "You haven't probed too much. You've given me space, and that was exactly what I needed. It's been a very strange time in my life, and you've looked after the kids—"

"Of course I've had the kids," said Delia. "Anytime. You know I love you, know I love them so much."

"I know, and they love you too, and that's been helpful, because the change has been tricky on them. They don't quite understand what's going on."

Delia nodded. "And you don't want them to either, do you? After all, this stuff is the stuff of nightmares."

Gillian frowned. "Of course I don't want them to be scared of their own mother."

"And is it a nightmare?" Delia asked. "Are you scared?"

"I'm terrified," Gillian admitted. "But it's not totally a nightmare. It's also been thrilling and amazing and powerful, and I'd love to tell you all about it, but not right now."

Delia nodded. "Not right now."

"I was wondering..." said Gillian, "if the kids could stay with you just for a night or two? I packed their things. They're really excited. It was a bit of a rushed decision, and I didn't know if you'd be busy, so I thought I'd just—"

"Just show up?" said Delia with a smile. "You are welcome to show up on my doorstep anytime, you know that. And of course they can stay as long as they like. Kitty and I will take very good care of them."

"It's not too dangerous with all your magical stuff?" said Gillian.

Delia shook her head. "No. I gather we're in a calm patch, for now. Where will you be?"

"I've got some work to do," Gillian said effusively.

"Maybe you'll be able to tell me about it someday," said Delia.

"Maybe I will, especially since you've been such a good sport about all of this. I kind of knew you would be – that's why I felt safe in not telling you as long as I did, because I knew that when I was ready it would be okay, you wouldn't hold it against me that it took me so long. I was still scared to say anything, of course, because this whole situation is outrageous, but I do trust you, Mum, and I love you so much."

"Isn't it funny?" said Delia. "Isn't it funny that we both stumbled into this magical world at the same time?"

"They say there are no coincidences, just different levels of synchronicity," said Gillian. "But I must admit, it is rather odd."

Delia sighed. "And now I've got a bone to pick with my lawyer about not revealing his identity to me."

"Would it have made it any better if he had?" Gillian asked.

Delia chuckled. "I suppose it would have made things an awful lot stranger."

2

DELIA

*D*elia had to leave. Delia had to go back into the house. It seemed like a strange transition indeed. She gave her daughter one more big hug, promising to be there for her no matter what, as she had thousands of times before over the time that she'd been a parent.

Yet, as she opened the car door, the icy chill of the still winter air bit at her skin, at the cold red tears Gilly had left on her cheek, that must contain...real blood.

She walked the steps back towards her cottage, shivering, not entirely from the cold, but a sense of doom set in deep in her bones, a heaviness, a slowness.

Her house was still full of people celebrating the latest victory of the Crones. She longed for silence, for escape, and yet the grandchildren being here was so very good. And Kitty being here to look after them was excellent.

She wanted to clear the house of everyone else, except for

one person or maybe two...Her head was still cloudy. Who did she need right at that moment, aside from the children and Kitty?

She opened the door and Declan was there.

"Delia," he said softly, gently, deeply, as if he knew. Delia searched his face for a moment, the weathered lines that bore so much wisdom and experience, much more than his appearance could ever give away.

"I don't know what it is," he said, "but I felt something, something in you, something shifted just now. There's a chill."

Delia nodded. "Can you stay tonight?"

"Of course," said Declan. "What do you need?"

She took a deep breath and her shoulders relaxed a little. "I'm ready for some quiet. Could you let everyone know? Kitty can put the children to bed, and I'll come and see them when they're tucked in, and I need to talk to Marjie."

He reached out and gently put his hand on her shoulder. "Consider it done."

"Thank you," said Delia, feeling supported despite the wobble in her being. He stepped out of the way, and Delia caught sight of Marjie across the room, sipping her hot chocolate as she smiled merrily, but her expression cooled as she met Delia's eyes.

"Can I talk to you for a minute?" Delia asked.

Marjie nodded, and Delia led the way up to her room, where it would be quiet, feeling no guilt at all about abandoning her guests, because there was nothing really to be guilty for. There was nothing really to do except put one foot in front of the other right now.

"That was Gilly who called," said Delia as she closed the door, shutting out the sounds from below.

Marjie sat down in the armchair next to the bed. "I figured as much," she said. "My intuition is rather powerful these days."

"Of course it is," said Delia, feeling a headache coming on as she pinched the bridge of her nose and sat down on the bed.

"You can lie down if you want, dear," said Marjie. "That might help."

Delia wanted to resist the advice, but sitting up did seem like a rather heavy burden on top of everything. She let herself fall back against the pillows. She was vaguely aware of a soft padding sound. Moments later, Torin pressed against her legs, his steady familiar presence offering wordless comfort. She buried her fingers in his warm fur, grateful for his uncomplicated support.

Delia found herself spiralling through emotions. She turned her attention back to Marjie. "You knew, and you didn't tell me."

Marjie flinched just slightly. "I did not know exactly. But I had some suspicions, and I didn't want to pry into your daughter's life. But I suspected, given she's been working with the Burks, that she had some kind of tie to their world."

"You knew about *them*? Of course you did!" said Delia. "I feel like such a fool. Why didn't you tell me my daughter was working for vampires!?"

Marjie shook her head sadly. "It simply is not done. You must understand." Marjie sighed. "When Rosemary first came to Myrtlewood, we had a similar problem, and she found out that the property lawyer settling her grandmother's estate happened to be a vampire."

"Oh?" said Delia.

"Yes, she felt so betrayed that I hadn't let her know. She assumed that they were dangerous."

"Aren't they?" Delia asked. "Aren't vampires dangerous? And I take it that her property lawyer was also Perseus?"

"Yes..." Marjie said.

"And now they're happily entwined in some great romance, I gather," said Delia. "So I suppose vampires can't be all bad."

Marjie seemed to send out a wave of warmth, caring, and empathy. Part of Delia wanted to resist it, feeling that she might be manipulated by this incredibly powerful water witch, but she trusted Marjie implicitly, and so she let herself be soothed by the warmth.

"Thank you for that."

"You can feel it?" said Marjie. "That's wonderful. It's something I've been working on recently."

Delia sighed. "Thank you...I...I feel like I've lost my daughter, and yet she's still here, and I don't know how to grapple with all of that." A wave of grief passed right through her whole body.

"Just let yourself feel it, my love," said Marjie.

Delia nodded. "But it's so much..."

"Emotion often is, and yet, if we don't feel it, it gets stuck within us. Feeling it helps us to open up and helps it to move along. Emotions need to move."

"Of course they do," said Delia. "I used to teach that to my actors. I used to teach them how to channel the emotion right through them from their characters and let it release."

"So do that now," said Marjie. "Do that for yourself."

"It's not quite the same because I'm not playing a role," Delia said, her voice breaking a little bit, vulnerable, jagged, fragile.

"Oh, my love," said Marjie. "We are all playing our roles, even when they are so genuinely part of our lives. Are we not?"

"I suppose," Delia said, letting out a slight sob. The tears came. "I do feel betrayed by you, by everyone, by life."

"Yes, you do," said Marjie. "And I invite you to feel that too. I would be in a right tiff if I were in your position. I'd be dreadfully upset that someone who's supposed to be a friend of mine had withheld vital information. But you see, there's so much fear around certain magical beings, and it causes so much destruction that we in this community try to respect their boundaries so that they can reveal their identity if and when they choose, as long as they are respecting our humanity, our mortality, our blood and so on. So I couldn't have told you about Perseus Burk, not without inviting a whole lot of gossip and speculation and fear into our lives, and especially into yours."

"The vampires aren't all that bad..." Delia muttered. "I'm glad you're telling me that, because that is a relief."

"Right," said Marjie. "Vampires are not all bad, but they're not entirely good either. They are shadowy beings. That is part of who they are. They invite the darkness into themselves. They need it to survive. That's how I see it."

"Thank you," said Delia, and she sighed and surrendered further into her bed. She blinked up at the ceiling. "I need to know more about vampires."

"Of course you do, dear," said Marjie. "And I can only tell you so much because they are rather secretive beings, but I don't think all the mythos is very accurate."

"I gather that," said Delia, "given that I've seen Gillian eat food that looked like a salad."

"Blood enchanted," said Marjie.

"Blood enchanted? Gillian mentioned that but I can't fathom what it means."

"Yes, well..." Marjie began. "Blood enchantment is a special technical skill. It's part of how witches and vampires can exist symbiotically. You see, vampires don't have to feed on humans. When I have vampire customers, I simply blood enchant everything that I serve them, and they can consume it without being violently ill."

"How convenient," said Delia, raising an eyebrow.

"Convenient indeed," said Marjie. "And I can tell now – I can tell when somebody's a vampire. They have a particular aura to them, a stillness. It's quite peaceful, really, for somebody like me."

"Oh, really? How odd," said Delia. She wriggled around so that she could pull the covers over her and tuck herself into bed. Torin stirred and moved up closer to her so she could pat him. It was soothing.

"Yes, dear. I can always feel when you're upset, too. For instance, when you got that call, I felt it."

"You felt a chill? Declan said he felt that, too."

"He's tuned into you, isn't he?" said Marjie, leaning forward in the chair. "And that's a beautiful thing."

Delia looked at Marjie. "It must be hard to feel everything."

"It can be rather overwhelming for me when people get stressed," Marjie admitted. "Or angry. I do my best to shield myself against the harmful feelings. But with vampires, I don't have to try."

"But that presents another conundrum, doesn't it?" said Delia. "That means you can't tell what's going on with them. They have an emotional invisibility. Hey – is that mirror thing true?"

"Oh no," said Marjie. "I'm sure that's something the ancient vampires made up just to fool people. But don't assume they're all charlatans. I must reassure you that Perseus Burk and his family are among the most respected beings in our community. They have integrity, even if they have an interesting take on the world."

"Interesting?"

"You can't tell so much with Perseus, because he's rather the white sheep of the family. But if you ever meet his mother, Azalea, you'll see it. She has a darkness in her that is so beautifully delightful, like she revels in all kinds of things that mere mortals would shudder and run away from."

"Sounds kinky," said Delia with a giggle.

"That's it!" said Marjie. "That's how I'd describe a lot of vampires, actually, if I was being perfectly honest."

Delia shook her head. "That's certainly something I don't want to think about in relation to my daughter."

"I don't blame you," Marjie muttered, and they both began to chuckle, and their chuckling turned into cackling, and before Delia knew it, the tears in her eyes were those of genuine laughter, and she felt a warm wave of gratitude for her good friend and for having this support.

"Thank you so much, Marjie. I'm tired now. I think I need to sleep."

"Of course you do, dear, and you can call on me tomorrow. I'll be at the house, or I can pop in to see you, whichever suits you most."

"Thank you, Marjie. Thank you for that offer."

"And of course, if you prefer some space right now, that is also fine."

"I think talking is helpful, but we'll see," said Delia. "Oh, poor Gilly."

"Poor Gilly, indeed," Marjie echoed.

Delia shed more tears as her own empathy overtook her. "She has so much on her shoulders right now and I wish I could save her from it all, but I can't. I don't even know how to help."

"I'm sure you're already helping more than you know," said Marjie sagely.

Delia groaned. "And she still doesn't know the full story about her father!"

"There, there," said Marjie, getting up and patting Delia

gently on her hand as it rested on the blankets. "Perhaps we can leave the 'your father is a leader of an ancient patriarchal magical cult' conversation for another, less volatile time."

Delia blew out an audible breath. "Yes, let's leave that one for now. We have enough to be getting on with, what with all this crone stuff...like finding my grimoire and the fire dragon and the sisterhood and..."

"One thing at a time, my dear," Marjie coaxed. "Deep slow breaths, sleep, and plenty of tea. That's what you need. And I'll not have a word out of your mouth about coffee. Not at this time of day."

Delia giggled at that, feeling suddenly like a small child watching a pantomime. "Goodnight, Marjie. Thank you for being here."

"Of course, my dear. Anything for a good friend."

Marjie slipped out of the room with a gentle goodbye, and Delia lay there in silence for a moment as the house stilled. She heard footsteps on the stairs, Kitty's voice and the children as they went up to bed and bedtime stories were read to them. Almost silent, stealthy movements downstairs that gave her another feeling of warmth and safety that helped to soothe that chill still deep in her bones, and the heaviness was slowly lifting, knowing that Declan was here.

Gradually, she got up to brush her teeth and she popped in to see the children and kiss them good night as they were slowly drifting into their dreams.

"Will we stay with you forever, Nana?" said Keyne.

"You can stay as long as you like, my dears, until your mother needs you back."

"Mum could stay here too," said Merryn. "We could all be together, all the people we love."

Delia smiled. "It would be a lovely thing, wouldn't it? All to be together sometime. Maybe we will soon. We could even have a nice holiday together somewhere really beautiful." She sighed as she said good night and left the room.

She slipped into her nightgown and tiptoed downstairs, still feeling that she would be visibly shaken, and her reflection in the mirror certainly had not been her best as she'd washed her face and put on her night cream, but it didn't matter. Nothing like that mattered with Declan. He was here for her, and she only had to walk several steps down before he met her on the staircase and held her. She let herself sink into him, her head resting on his chest.

"That was so unexpected," she said, "and I don't even know what to say about it."

"Let me hold you," said Declan.

Delia let out a small, soft sigh. "I would like that more than anything in the world right now."

He gently picked her up and carried her up the stairs. He nestled her into bed, shedding the outer layers of his clothing, getting in beside her, smelling clean somehow, despite his ruggedness and the wood smoke wilderness scent of him. He wrapped his arms around her, not needing anything from her, just providing the solace and solidity and support of his presence. Delia sank into a deep and peaceful sleep.

3

BENEDICT

Father Benedict, the Crimson Shepherd – Chosen of the Almighty – sat in the centre elevated table in the dining hall, his presence a dark gravity well pulling at everything around him. The air crackled. Power coursed through him like black lightning. His satisfaction at the immaculate state of his domain was tempered only by the constant thrum of rage that never quite left him these days.

The hall stretched before him, every surface gleaming with perfection. Rows of monks, soldiers, and servants ate in perfect silence, their spoons lifting in an almost mechanical unison that pleased him. The imprisoned Elders, stripped of their former authority, sat hunched at the lowest table, accepting their new station with appropriate humility. Their fear flavoured the air like a holy wine to be poured as an offering at the feet of the Almighty.

Benedict studied the bowl before him – simple barley soup with three precisely cut pieces of carrot, two chunks of potato, and exactly ten brown lentils visible in the broth. A single slice of dark bread sat beside it, unbuttered. Such humble fare befitted a true servant of the Almighty, unlike the wasteful feasts the Elders had once enjoyed. He lifted his spoon with deliberate grace, watching the ripples disturb the surface of his soup. The taste was appropriately bland. All senses should be reserved for reverence, not spilled hedonistically into sacrilegious wastage.

"Cleric Mateas," he called out, his voice carrying easily across the silent hall. The trembling figure of the new Cleric nearly dropped his spoon at the sound of his name. Benedict allowed himself a small smile at the man's fear – so much more appropriate than his predecessor's rebellious spirit.

Cleric Mateas was a thin, reedy man with a perpetually damp upper lip and hands that never seemed to know what to do with themselves. Though relatively young for his position, anxiety had already carved deep lines around his watery blue eyes.

Mateas rose from his seat, wobbling slightly as he hurried forward. His plain brown robes were impeccably pressed, as Benedict demanded, though his tonsure needed slight adjustment – a detail Benedict filed away for later correction. The man prostrated himself before Benedict's table, forehead touching the cold stone floor.

"Yes, Shepherd...er, Chosen of the Almighty?" Mateas' voice quavered.

"Shepherd will suffice in this instance," Benedict said,

savouring another spoonful of soup. "What news of our wayward tracker?"

The memory of the enchanted sword plunging into the tracker's heart on that windswept beach brought a warmth that the bland soup couldn't provide, but he needed confirmation.

"We believe him to be vanquished, Sir—Shepherd," Mateas stammered, still prone on the floor. A monk at a nearby table knocked over his water cup, and the sound echoed like thunder in the silent hall. Benedict's power lashed out automatically, the dark tendrils of the Almighty's might forcing the monk's hand to right the cup while simultaneously drawing the spilled water back into it. The monk's face went white.

"Belief is not enough, unless it is faith in the Almighty," Benedict scolded.

"There is no evidence he survived, sir." Mateas trembled. "Our oracles have been scrying as you instructed. It's highly unlikely he survived your extremely well-executed attack."

"I am but a servant of the Almighty, you need not praise me." Benedict replied, but he allowed himself a small swell of joy at this apparent victory before turning to the other matter at hand. "And the former Cleric."

Mateas bristled. "Err...the former Cleric still remains at large. Which leads us to the impression that he is likely to be in—"

Benedict's rage flared before Mateas could finish. The Almighty's power responded instantly, making the wall sconces flicker and sending tremors through the ancient stones of the compound. Several monks dropped their spoons, the clatter accompanied by barely supressed gasps.

"Myrtlewood," Benedict snarled, rising from his seat.

The very name of that festering town filled his mouth with bile. A cesspool of unsanctioned magic, ruled by women who had no right to wield such power.

His mind flashed unbidden to Delia, to his decades of tiresome self-sacrifice in the field playing her supportive husband...to the disappointment of the girl-child she'd borne him. Gillian – now an adult with children of her own, including a boy who should have been Benedict's proper heir, if not for the feminine distortions that surely poisoned him.

He had kept careful watch over them all, of course. The reports of Gillian's infection with vampirism had reached him quickly. A plague that made her a potentially powerful weapon, but one too well-protected by the Burk family to be worth pursuing directly. But young Keyne...perhaps the boy could be moulded, purified of his mother's taint. Or perhaps it was time for Benedict to start anew, to create fresh spawn unmarred by the impurities that had resulted in his first child being female. All of this would have to wait.

A clatter interrupted his thoughts. A monk near the back of the hall scampered to pick up the pieces of the plate he had dropped in shattering Benedict's reverie. The unfortunate man froze as Benedict's power seized him, lifting him several inches off the ground.

"I apologise, Shepherd! Please, I meant no—" The monk's

words cut off as the power squeezed slightly, just enough to remind everyone present of their place.

Benedict released him after a moment, letting him collapse back into his seat. These displays of power were necessary, but they were mere distractions from his true purpose. His gaze swept the hall, taking in the terror-stricken faces of his followers. The Almighty's power surged through him again, stronger than ever, making the very foundations of the compound shudder.

This time would be different. This time, the crones would not stand in his way. This time, armed with the Almighty's might, he would ride the great beast to victory, and Myrtlewood would burn. But first, there was a traitor to be dealt with.

"Mateas. Prepare the strategy chamber. It's time we discussed the next stage of our strategy."

"Y-yes, Shepherd." Mateas scrambled to his feet, nearly tripping over his own robes in his haste to comply.

Benedict returned to his seat, lifting another spoonful of soup to his mouth, perfectly room-temperature now so as to be as little of an indulgence as possible.

His lips pressed together in the knowledge that at least order had been restored to the compound, but it was only the beginning. Soon, that order would spread beyond these walls, and all those who opposed the Almighty's will would kneel or be destroyed.

4

MARJIE

Marjie appreciated the warmth of the late winter sun as it streamed through Thorn Manor's windows and across the scarred oak table where she sat with her old family grimoire. She had only been in possession of the book for a few weeks but already it felt like an extension of herself.

Steam rose from her third cup of cardamom tea, curling in the sunbeams while she studied the water dragon's crystal. The beautiful blue stone lay stubbornly inert beside a bowl of apples, its facets catching light but offering nothing more.

The kitchen was her favourite room in Thorn Manor, of course – all worn flagstones and exposed beams – and since she'd been invited to live here there were always fragrant herbs hanging from the ceiling in neat bundles.

The hearth was currently home to a gently bubbling pot of soup that Rosemary had started earlier. The room smelled of onions and thyme, overlaid with the sharper scent of the oranges that young Athena was slicing for a salad.

As water crone, Marjie should have been able to sense something from the crystal. Her empathic abilities had grown so strong lately that sometimes the feelings of others overwhelmed her – joy, sorrow, anger washing over her like waves, and she'd been learning to build careful shields.

She could feel Rosemary's quiet contentment as she chopped vegetables, Athena's underlying melancholy despite her attempts at cheerfulness. And yet this crystal, this supposedly powerful magical artifact they'd retrieved from the ocean's depths at such cost, remained as emotionally blank as a fresh cup of distilled water!

"You'd think," she muttered, reaching out with her power once again, "with everything I can feel now, you'd at least give me a hint." The crystal sat mutely beautiful between her tea cup and the bowl of apples, its secrets locked away. Marjie sighed and pressed her fingers to her temples. The kitchen's warmth and familiar scents usually soothed her, but today her frustration simmered like the soup.

"It will come eventually, Marjie," Rosemary said from the kitchen, before turning back to Athena, her mind shifting quickly, as if usually did, to a totally different topic. "Are you sure about going to the fae realm now?" she asked Athena, laying down her knife to reach for more carrots from the basket by the sink.

"I think I need to, Mum. I need to get away," Athena replied, her hands stilling on the orange she was sectioning. Marjie felt the girl's uncertainty flutter beneath her words.

"Besides, you know that time works differently there and Queen Aine promises I'll be back before school starts. I just... I need to get away for a bit. Everything just feels so...heavy"

Marjie closed her grimoire, its leather binding warm from the sun. She'd been monitoring Athena's emotional state for some weeks now, watching the girl struggle with the horrors unleashed at Samhain, and then with Elise's disappearance into the underworld. The weight of Athena's grief pressed against her empathic senses, heavy as the iron skillet hanging by the hearth.

"My dear," Marjie said, rising to refill their teacups, "a holiday before Imbolc sounds perfectly reasonable. You've had such a difficult year." She let her own calm seep into the room like tea steeping, a gentle counter to Athena's turmoil. The ceramic was warm against her palms as she crossed back to her seat at the table.

Athena looked up from the oranges, her eyes glistening slightly. "I just miss her so much. And everything feels so hard lately." The knife trembled slightly in her hand.

"Of course it does," Rosemary said softly, leaving her chopping to wrap an arm around the girl's shoulders. Her maternal love radiated, warm and golden as sunlight. "I can see that you need this break. The fae realm will do you good."

"Who would have thought?" Athena said with a watery smile, leaning into Rosemary's embrace. "Me, visiting my grandmother in the fae realm who happens to be the queen...Sometimes I can hardly believe this is my life now." A small bubble of wonder rose through the girl's sadness, and Marjie cherished it, hoping it would grow.

"Life has a way of surprising us all," Marjie agreed, breathing in the mingled scents of citrus and herbs. The soup bubbled softly, marking time like a liquid clock.

Her thoughts returned to the stubborn crystal, of all the mysteries still unfolding around them. The water magic that now flowed through her veins had changed everything she thought she knew about herself, about what was possible.

Rosemary began to ladle out the soup, and Athena buttered toast from the bread Marjie baked just that morning.

Lunch was almost served when the doorbell's chime interrupted her thoughts, followed by a wave of such intense emotional turmoil that Marjie had to strengthen her shields. She answered it to find Delia appeared, a storm of grief, anger, confusion, and love so tangled together that it made Marjie's head spin.

Rosemary and Athena exchanged glances as Marjie led her dear friend into the kitchen. "We'll just take our lunch outside," Rosemary said tactfully, putting two bowls of soup onto a tray. "Such a lovely day for it."

As they slipped out towards the garden door, Marjie gestured for Delia to sit at the table. "Tea?"

"Something stronger, if you have it," Delia replied. The raw edge in her voice matched the jagged edges of her emotions.

Marjie reached behind the porcelain for a special blend she kept for moments of emotional turmoil, one designed to soothe and ground without dulling feeling entirely. As she prepared it, she carefully adjusted her empathic shields – she needed to stay open enough to help her friend while protecting herself from being overwhelmed.

She served Delia a bowl of soup without offering it first, because soup was always good for a troubled heart or a weary soul and Delia certainly carried both afflictions.

"How are the children settling in?" Marjie asked as she brought the tray over, though she could feel Delia's love for her grandkids shining like a beacon through her darker emotions.

"They're wonderful. As usual..." Delia's voice cracked slightly, her feelings fracturing and reforming. "I keep going around in circles...maybe if I just understand more about vampires, about what Gilly's going through..."

"Understanding helps," Marjie agreed, pouring the tea and setting out a plate of lavender shortbread for good measure. "But it won't change the fact that you're grieving."

"Grieving? She's not dead!" Delia snapped, anger flaring hot and bright, then immediately deflated into a well of sadness. "I suppose she is, in a way...I'm sorry. I just...one minute I'm angry, the next I'm bargaining with myself about how it might not be so bad, then I'm right back to feeling like I've lost her completely."

"You haven't lost her," Marjie said gently, picking up the spoon and handing it to Delia who took a sip, as if in a trance, and then, upon tasting the herby broth, began to eat and eat. Alternating every second mouthful with a sip of tea, after a moment, her shoulders relaxed and the bowl was soon emptied.

Marjie patted her friend gently on the shoulder. "She's changed, yes, but she's still Gilly."

"Is she though?" said Delia. "Is she really? It seems like her, but it's so...different. She's been so distant. Everything I thought I knew about vampires...I mean, does she even have a soul?"

"Of course she does, my love. We are all made of soul and spirit. Some twisted creatures cannot even tell this about themselves and that is always tragic, but Gillian is not like that. She's still herself. Only...a bit different."

Delia nodded slowly.

Marjie wrapped her hands around her own teacup, letting its warmth centre her before explaining further. "Most of what mortals think they know about vampires is nonsense," she said, watching Delia's aura shift and swirl. "Holy water is just water to them. Crosses have no effect as they're beings far older than Christianity – I've met a few who swear they were around to see Jesus leading the charge into the Piscean era! They're powerful beings, yes, but not the monsters of legend."

A shadow passed across the kitchen as clouds briefly dimmed the sun. In that moment of relative darkness, Marjie felt even more acutely the blank spots in her understanding, like the crystal's silence multiplied. She really didn't know much about vampires, nor did she completely trust them, with the exception of a few wonderful friends, but that was true of any magical beings, come to think of it...

Delia gripped her own cup and Marjie could sense determination threading through her turbulent emotions. The shortbread remained untouched. "I'm going to talk to Perseus Burk. He owes me some answers. At least I have the children close..."

Marjie hesitated, her fingertips tingling with intuitive warning. Something about this whole situation nagged at her awareness – a darkness at the edges she couldn't quite grasp. A seemingly random vampire transformation, the Burk family's involvement, the timing of it all...The same kind of blankness she felt from the crystal seemed to surround certain aspects of these events, spots where her usually reliable emotional sense went quiet. She trusted Perseus, of course. He was family now, but why had they swooped in like this?

She left her questions unspoken because Delia had enough on her plate.

She pushed the shortbread closer to Delia and refilled her cup.

A swift gust of air interrupted her, setting the hanging herbs swaying.

A woman materialised in the middle of the kitchen, directly between the oak table and the hearth. Her purple-streaked hair was swept up in an elegant French roll, and her signature purple pinstriped suit was as immaculate as ever.

"Juniper!" said Marjie. "To what do we owe this surprise visit?"

The space around Juniper tingled with magical energy.

Juniper's eyes fixed on Delia. "Ah, there you are!" she exclaimed. "I have an update for you."

5

DELIA

$\mathcal{D}$elia blinked as she recognised the surprise guest who'd just materialised in the kitchen of Thorn Manor who now brandished a folder towards her like a sword.

She'd momentarily forgotten all about the contractor and mage who she'd asked to look into her family records, hoping to find some clue to locating the grimoire she needed. All the other crones had theirs now.

Delia had the misfortune, of course, of coming from a powerful magical family she knew almost nothing about.

The Bracewells apparently wielded much influence in the magical world, and while she'd enjoyed getting to know her cousin Elamina – as icy and snobbish as she seemed – the whole situation was rather impenetrable. It felt a world away from her present concerns;

Delia fumbled for a moment. "I haven't even looked at the last stack of files you sent me. I've been...occupied."

Juniper shrugged. "That's fine. You're the one paying me. You can do what you like." She flashed a charming smile. "Besides, I know what it's like to be overloaded with challenge after challenge, especially in the magical world. Can get rather a lot, right?" There was a sassy edge to her tone that Delia appreciated. She wished that she embodied that kind of strength in this moment when she felt more swampy than anything else.

"But it must be important if you've arrived here like this?" Marjie prompted.

"Well, I did think you'd want to know about this," said Juniper, casually taking a seat next to them at the table and helping herself to some of the lavender shortbread that Delia still hadn't touched.

"Out with it, then," said Marjie, beaming, as though this new development was a welcome respite from Delia's emotional state – which it probably was. Delia felt a surge of gratitude towards Marjie, who had taken care of her so well, even if she had withheld quite a few things for the sake of some kind of integrity or honour that Delia couldn't quite fathom.

Delia leaned forward in her chair. "Yes, out with it, Juniper. I'm dying to know what was so important you had to suddenly find me here."

"Gosh, you must be powerful, dear," said Marjie, pouring a cup of tea for Juniper. "Thorn Manor has enormous defences."

"I often find that magical defences are not too hard to get through with my teleportation as long as I have good intentions," Juniper mused. "So I try my best to always have good intentions." She winked. "And my intention today is to let you know about some new details. I had a bit of time in between other jobs, and I went through some of the records in Glastonbury that relate to Myrtlewood. Quite a few passages had been deleted from the records, which was incredibly suspicious. I had to triangulate who had accessed them at different times, and some of what I uncovered was rather recent. The person in question had used an alias and disguised her own magical signature, but at one point she'd gotten rather sloppy."

"Which person in question is this?" Delia asked.

"Well, I suspect it was your cousin," said Juniper.

"Elamina?" Delia asked, feeling a chill down her spine. She really wanted to trust the snobbish and confident younger woman who she had just started to get to know.

"That's what I thought at first," Juniper said. "But then digging a little deeper...well, Elamina has been in a high-profile role recently. She hasn't been to Glastonbury in months as far as I could track her movements."

"Who then?" Marjie asked.

"I suspect that it was one of Elamina's parents," said Juniper. "Or her rather quiet brother, Derse...or perhaps her aunt Sabrina was involved."

"I didn't even know she had a brother," said Delia. "I don't know anything much about the family at all!"

"What did the deleted records relate to?" Marjie asked.

"They all relate to your grandmother," Juniper said, giving Delia a pointed look. "In fact, there's hardly any trace of Etty anywhere. The harder I looked, the more suspicious I became that the family must have been involved in your grandmother's death."

Delia took a shuddery breath in, but another part of her relaxed as she realised her earlier suspicions weren't so warranted. "Elamina can't be old enough to have anything to do with Etty's death. I was a child. Whoever this is...they must be quite old."

"I'd say Sabrina Bracewell was in her twenties at the time when you yourself were only a child," said Juniper. "But witches, especially powerful ones, can live for a rather long time. And that's not all. I took the liberty of going in and doing some other investigating about you."

"About me?" said Delia, feeling suddenly uncomfortable. "What did you dig up on me then?"

"Well, through my networks, I was able to deduce that there's some connection between you and the other crones and a particular secret sisterhood."

"Ah, yes," said Marjie. "Good sleuthing, I suppose. Err... are you accusing us of something?"

"It's not my place to accuse you of anything," said Juniper lightly, folding her arms and smiling. "No, I just felt like there was perhaps a connection, because Sabrina herself also has ties to the sisterhood. In fact, she's been in communication with them rather recently. According to the shadow networks – you see, when people try to use untraceable communica-tions, that's when I become especially intrigued. I can't decipher the nature of her communication with the Sisterhood of the Veil, but given their apparent interest in you lot, I thought you might want to know about it."

"Indeed, I do," said Marjie, "and I'm sure Delia does as well. The plot thickens!"

Delia sighed, finally embracing the sweet, crumbly, aromatic shortbread and downing it with another cup of Marjie's enchanted tea. "Do you think Elamina knows about all this?" she asked. "I really want to trust her. I kind of like her."

"Don't let Rosemary hear you say that," said Marjie, "although I'm inclined to agree with you, especially after the support she gave us recently. That was quite some magic she contributed to rescue you."

"That's right," said Delia. "And why would she want to rescue me if she was involved in some plot against me?"

"I've seen that kind of double dealing before," said Juniper. "They might need you alive for some reason. Of course, Etty was incredibly powerful. She inherited the crone's power of her generation, and she passed it on to you. I believe that perhaps Sabrina and her mother, Lavinia – Etty's sister – may have conspired to try to steal those powers. It's something that's not really advised. Coveting another witch's power is bad enough, let alone trying to siphon it into oneself. I've seen it happen before, usually with disastrous effect, but occasionally people have pulled it off."

"Well, the Order seemed to be keen to get hold of our powers," said Marjie, "and so are the Sisterhood, although they haven't actually tried to separate us from our powers yet, not that we'd give them the chance."

"You're far too powerful for that, of course," said Juniper with a smile.

Marjie preened. "I bet you say that to all the crones."

"Just the good ones," said Juniper. "Now, is there anything else I can help you with in this case?"

"Well, thank you for starters," said Delia. "This is helpful information. I don't know what Elamina knows, or whether she's involved in this plot about taking powers from one side of the family and putting them into the other side...I don't know what to make of all that."

Marjie shook her head. "The Bracewells are notoriously nasty and devious. I can imagine somebody like Lavinia would have been exceptionally jealous to discover her sister was the one who was chosen by the fates to be the Fire Crone. She would not have liked that at all, going by pure reputation alone, and neither would Sabrina."

"I'd take extra care if I were you," Juniper said. "It's possible that the family will try and pick up where they left off."

"And yet they have the grimoire," said Delia. "I need that, otherwise I'm hardly going to be able to wield my power properly. I need to find my dragon."

Juniper blinked at her.

"We probably shouldn't be telling you all this," said Marjie. "Please keep it a secret."

"My lips are sealed," said Juniper.

Delia sighed. "I really need to know how to get hold of

that grimoire. Is there a way of sneaking into the Bracewell mansion where it's held? I'm assuming that's where it is."

"That's what all my research leads me to believe too," said Juniper. "And the Bracewells will have some serious protection, especially if they know that you're after the grimoire. It's not going to be easy. They're hardly going to just hand it over."

"But if they want me," said Delia, "I could hand myself over, and then I could get in—"

"Now, now," said Marjie, "don't be hasty. We want you too – in one piece! And as powerful as you are currently, the Bracewells are all skilled at fire magic, and there would be only one of you, unless you could get us all invited."

"Invited," said Delia. "That's what we need – an invitation. I wonder if Elamina will make good on her attempts to become my friend."

"I wonder that too," said Marjie. "Perhaps we could all come along, though I doubt they'd let us all in."

"Maybe not..." said Delia. "I'd love to be able to talk to Elamina about this, but as you say, Juniper, she's out of town a lot. She gave me her card."

"A lot can be said for initiating a conversation with good intentions," said Juniper. "Magically speaking, it can be very powerful."

"What if my good intentions are to steal the grimoire? I don't think they'd find that particularly good."

Juniper shrugged. "Stealing is quite a loaded term. You merely want to borrow it, perhaps for the rest of your life. It belongs to your family, and in fact, you have more of a right to it than they do. You are the Fire Crone, after all. So your intentions are pure in that. And in reaching out to Elamina, you intend to connect with her and discover whether she's with you or against you, whether she's part of some plot or a friend. Someone as powerful as Elamina will have her own agenda, I'm sure of it. As much as her aunt will demand her respect, Elamina, I imagine, will pay lip service in the way that she was raised. She'll respect her elders, of course, but that doesn't mean that she'll always do exactly what they say, or even be informed of their plots. She is quite distant from her own parents."

Marjie shot Juniper a questioning look. "Sounds like you know her rather well."

Juniper smirked. "I've known her a long time, but we're not close." There was a little tension in the air that came with her words. "It's not relevant to the present conversation, so I won't go into any details. But suffice to say Elamina is her own woman, and an incredibly powerful witch who has a lot of power in Britannia, and with the witching authorities globally. She'd be a good person to have on your side, either way."

"Suppose I could get an invitation to dinner at the mansion..." said Delia. "But would it be like walking into a lion's den or a hornet's nest?"

"I don't imagine it would be the safest situation," said Juniper, "but if you go in with your eyes wide open, you'll at least find out some more information. And sometimes that's just the next stepping stone towards achieving what you need."

Delia took a deep breath. "Well, at least this takes my mind off my other situation."

"Oh yeah, I'm sorry about Gillian," said Juniper.

"Is there anything you don't know?" said Delia, feeling rather cross now to be left out of the loop about her own family.

Juniper smiled. "I do a lot of work with the Burks, and I have encountered Gillian. She's a wonder, isn't she?"

Delia smiled. "She is..."

"It's a hard transition. I've seen it happen before," said Juniper gently, nibbling at another piece of shortbread. "But don't worry, I won't tell anyone."

"Is it a secret?" Delia asked.

"Well, it pays to be cautious about these things," Juniper said evasively, and Delia couldn't help but feel there was something that she hadn't been told yet.

"Is she really doing okay?" Delia asked.

"She's thriving," said Juniper, a subtle note of awe in her voice that made Delia swell with pride. "So many people struggle for years as new vampires, but Gillian is already diving into her work. She's strong. She has so few cravings for human blood, which is almost unheard of so early in the change."

"Well, I suppose that's something to be grateful for," said Delia. "And it makes me feel a little easier about this new information."

"She told me she was going to tell you," Juniper said.

Delia sighed again. "It sounds like you two have become fast friends."

"You might say that," Juniper replied. "I spend a lot of time with vampires – the magic of mages is very closely tied. It is a similar kind of alchemy to vampire magic, only also extremely different."

"I'm glad she has a friend," said Delia, shaking herself out of her own woes of being excluded. "It's probably good for her to know more people in the magical community, not just...vampires."

"The vampires are looking after her very well, rest assured," said Juniper. "They look after their own, the Burk family especially."

"I keep hearing such good things about my bloodthirsty lawyer," said Delia. "Which reminds me, I need to make an appointment, or perhaps I'll just stroll in and see how he's doing. I have a bone to pick with him."

"Gillian didn't want you to know before now," Juniper said gently again. "Everyone was respecting her wishes."

"I see," said Delia. "It's hard not to feel a little betrayed and left out by all that."

"That's natural, dear," said Marjie, "but in times like this, I'm always grateful for my wonderful friends. And I'm so happy to know that your daughter is being well cared for, and we, in turn, will look after you."

Delia smiled with genuine warmth, returning Marjie's expression. "It's a lot to process."

"Indeed," said Marjie.

"And I didn't know about barging in here, really," said Juniper, "except that I felt this latest development was worthy of sharing, and the timing kind of lined up. And I must admit that Gillian also asked me to check in on you."

Tears welled up in Delia's eyes. "She's still looking after me despite everything, even when she needed to keep her distance. She sent through all those case files about my divorce." Delia groaned. "Oh, don't get me started on my divorce."

As the tears cleared, another thought occurred to her. "Do you know," she asked Juniper, "about Gillian's father and the Order of Crimson?"

Juniper nodded subtly. "But Gillian doesn't know about that yet."

Delia took a great shuddering breath and her shoulders relaxed. "I'm glad that I'm not the only one thinking that it's best to withhold that from her for the time being."

"I've been looking into the connection, you see...nobody knows why Gillian was turned," Juniper said, lowering her voice to almost a whisper.

"She told me that..." said Delia. "Is that unusual?"

"Very," said Juniper. "There's usually rather a lot of paper-work with these things. Vampires are awfully bureaucratic, especially since so many of them have been around for a long time. They have so many codes and so many sanctions. And besides, the ritual for creating new vampires is quite a complex one, and is guarded with some secrecy, especially in recent centuries. Only older vampires even know of it, and all the details required."

"Well, that must narrow it down somewhat," said Delia.

Juniper shook her head, scoffing some more shortbread

before elaborating. "You'd think so, but nobody quite knows what happened there. Gillian should never have been turned."

"You don't have to tell me that," said Delia. "I suppose I can be grateful that she'll likely have a long, long life ahead of her, as long as she doesn't get staked or come out in the sunlight. The staking thing is right, isn't it? Or is that a myth too?"

"No, I think that's right. Staked, burned, or exposed to full sunlight, especially for the younger vampires. The older ones get rather hard to kill. Staking might not work for them, but a fire that's hot enough or the full light of the sun would eviscerate even the most ancient among them. Most vampires haven't seen more than a sunrise or a sunset since their mortal life, and that can become quite bleak after a long time."

"That is something to grieve, I suppose," said Delia. She sighed deeply, and Marjie patted her on the shoulder again.

"Well, thank you so much for your visit, Juniper," said Marjie. "I'm really glad you called in."

"Yes," Delia added. "Thanks. I feel more at ease now about the whole situation. It's good to know that Gillian has friends and people looking out for her."

"And so do you," said Juniper. "I'd say focus on Elamina. She's your best chance at getting a look at that grimoire. It won't be easy. She's a tough nut to crack."

"Having met her several times, I believe it," said Delia.

Juniper pushed back the chair and stood up with a flourish. "Thank you for the shortbread, Marjie. It was absolutely delicious."

"Anytime, dear." Marjie beamed.

A moment later, Juniper, with a quick wave goodbye, had disappeared into thin air, leaving Marjie and Delia alone with an empty plate of shortbread crumbs between them.

"What are you going to do now?" Marjie asked.

Delia buried her face in her hands. "I suppose it's time to check in with my lawyer."

6

GWYNETH

The moon shone over the jagged mountains behind the temple as she approached. Gwyneth's heart fluttered against her ribs as she climbed the worn steps. The air carried the scent of thyme and the sweet lingering fragrance of ritual oils.

Inside the temple, elders Breag and Franwen waited like dark sentinels, their robes rustling against the flagstones.

Candlelight flickered across their faces in haunting shadow. Gwyneth's mouth dried as she took her place among them, knowing she must guard every expression, every word.

"We've received new communication from Sabrina Bracewell," Breag announced, satisfaction in her tone. "It seems our old ally may have found another path forward."

Franwen's eyes gleamed. "A way to harness the Crones' power more directly."

Once, Gwyneth would have felt comfortable to question

this. She would have voiced her concerns about ethics and balance. But she had learned the cost of speaking out. Instead, she nodded, forcing her features into a mask of calm interest while her stomach churned.

"Mathilda grows weaker by the day," Breag continued, pacing the stone floor. "The crystal draws too much from her. We need a more sustainable source."

"The Bracewells' fire magic could be instrumental in containing them," Franwen added. "Once they leave Myrtle-wood's protection, of course. That barrier won't last forever."

As they discussed containment circles and binding spells, Gwyneth's thoughts drifted to Mathilda. She had been so vibrant once, her laughter bright as her inspiration. Now she was barely a shadow, her strength feeding the crystal.

The enormous structure had haunted Gwyneth since that very first sighting that had sent Ingrid running from the Clochar. But Gwyneth had persevered. She had believed in the Sisterhood, and when she'd first been inducted as an elder, the sanctity and power of the crystal had seemed such a miracle at first. A beacon of hope for peace. The memory of her own excitement now filled Gwyneth with shame.

Thinking of Mathilda inevitably led to thoughts of Ingrid...who kept surfacing on Gwyneth's mind lately.

Wild, passionate, brave Ingrid, who had seen through the Sisterhood's pretences from the start. They had been young women, so full of passion.

The little hill next to the herb gardens had been their sanctuary, partly sheltered as it was by hedges of elder.

Gwyneth could still smell the crushed camomile under

their bodies as they lay together, watching stars wheel over-head. Ingrid would weave daisy chains and crown Gwyneth like a fairy queen, her touch electric, her kisses tasting of stolen wine and freedom.

Those hidden alcoves in the passageways had been their secret kingdom. How many times had they pressed against the cool stone, stifling their giggles as sisters passed by? Ingrid was always pushing boundaries, sneaking out after curfew, "borrowing" sacred texts, questioning everything. She'd gotten in trouble so often. But to Gwyneth, that rebel-lious spirit had been intoxicating – Ingrid's wild heart had awakened something in her own.

At night, they would often coil together in Gwyneth's narrow bed, sharing whispered plans of escape.

"We could go anywhere," Ingrid would say, tracing patterns on Gwyneth's skin. "Do anything. Be whoever we choose to be."

But Gwyneth had watched Ingrid walk away while her heart shattered into countless pieces. Abandoned.

The years since had been filled with purpose. She'd thrown herself into service, nurturing younger sisters through their trials, teaching them about herbs and healing, maintaining the delicate balance of the Clochar. Her lonely bed had seemed a small price for what she'd believed was a higher calling.

Every day now, her mind circled like a caged bird.

How to free Mathilda?

How to change Breag and Franwen's minds?

How to stop what was coming?

Each night brought fresh regrets, memories of Ingrid's last plea: "Come with me, Gwyneth. This place will destroy you."

It seemed she had been right all along.

"The new moon will be perfect for beginning the preparations," Breag was saying now, and Gwyneth forced herself to focus.

Yet even as she nodded and made appropriate sounds of agreement, something was shifting in her understanding.

She had always believed staying was her destiny – had felt it in her bones even as she watched Ingrid disappear into the dawn.

But what if she'd misunderstood?

The thought struck her with physical force: what if her destiny wasn't to serve the Sisterhood in their obsessive plan for peace, but to fight it? The possibility was as terrifying as it was liberating, though full comprehension remained just beyond her grasp.

Later, in her chambers, Gwyneth's hands shook as she cast the masking spell, feeling the magic settle over her like a cloak of shadows.

They can't know...

She called out to the creature that had always resonated with her spirit.

Come, my friend...I have a message.

The parchment was rough under her fingers as she wrote the words weighted with decades of unspoken truth.

As she finished the note, a soft flutter at her window made her look up. The great horned owl perched there, an embodiment of Gwyneth's secret hopes, the wild spirit that had sung to her own since her earliest days. Those amber eyes held such wisdom, such understanding without judgment.

"Thank you, dear one," Gwyneth whispered, securing the message to the owl's leg. "You know where to go, to find the one who dwells deep within my heart. Please take this to her."

The owl spread her wings, silver moonlight catching each feather as she lifted into the night sky. Mountain winds carried her up and away, a shadow among shadows, bearing words that might change everything.

7

INGRID

A mournful hoot and insistent scratching at the window yanked Ingrid from her dreams. Dawn's first grey light filtered through the warped glass of her bedroom window. She groaned and rolled over in her woven reed bed, its familiar creaks a protest against movement.

The dream clung to her like morning mist – fragments of the Clochar swimming through her consciousness. The herb gardens where she and Gwyneth had first kissed, crushed lavender releasing its essence beneath their bodies. The temple's cool stones against her back as they hid in alcoves, stifling giggles. The mountain paths they'd walked together, picking herbs and sharing secrets. But in her dreams, these memories twisted – the gardens withered and died, the temple's stones crumbled to reveal darkness beneath, the mountains loomed impossibly tall, threatening to swallow the sky.

"Oh, do be quiet," she muttered at the persistent owl, though it had already gone. Her joints creaked as she rose, shrugging on her patchwork robe – each square sewn with different spells, a collage of her life – though most needed mending.

Downstairs, Ingrid waved her hand at the kettle with more flourish than strictly necessary. It floated obligingly to the perpetual fire she'd charmed years ago to burn without smoke or fuel. Another gesture brought her herb basket close, and she selected with care – chamomile for clarity, rosemary for memory, nettle for strength, and just a pinch of mugwort for insight.

The teapot – with the crack she'd mended thirteen times because it made the perfect brew – waited patiently as she arranged the herbs. The whistling kettle poured water from itself in a graceful arc into the pot, sending the herbal aromas into the air.

She was just reaching for the honey – wild, gathered from her own bees who made their home in an ancient oak – when a familiar barking shattered the morning quiet. The earth dragon puppy burst through the door, all wagging tail and muddy paws, her disguise as perfect as ever save for the slight green shimmer of scales when the light hit her just so.

"You impossible creature," Ingrid scolded, even as she bent to scratch behind surprisingly warm ears. "I spelled that door with seven different locks. Seven! And still you let yourself in every morning as if they're mere suggestions."

The dragon-pup yipped, pressing against her legs with

unusual urgency. Her eyes were far too knowing for any normal dog.

"Something's changed, has it?" she asked, more seriously now.

The pup barked once, sharp and clear.

Ingrid sighed, poured her tea to carry with her, and followed the excited creature outside. The forest stretched before them, ancient trees still half-shrouded in dawn mist. She reached out with senses honed by decades of forest-craft, seeking wisdom in the patterns of leaf and root.

Nothing. No signs in the shifting shadows, no messages in the morning breeze. Only two lines crossing in the dirt where deer paths met – a simple intersection that nonetheless made her stomach clench with significance.

The dragon-pup grew increasingly agitated, finally grabbing Ingrid's cloak in gentle, insistent teeth, tugging her toward the back door.

There, wedged beneath it, lay a folded piece of parchment. Beside it, impossibly white against the worn wood, lay a single feather.

Ingrid knelt carefully, her knees protesting. No trace of harmful magic emanated from either object, though both thrummed with a familiar energy that made her heart skip.

She lifted the feather first, turning it in her fingers.

"Owl..." And immediately she was transported back to the nights she'd spent watching a young Gwyneth call to them, their answering cries like welcome home. The owls had recognised something in her, some kindred night-wisdom that matched their own.

With trembling fingers, Ingrid unfolded the note. The handwriting was achingly familiar, though more refined now. More dignified. More cautious despite the bold gesture of sending a secret message.

My dearest Ingrid,

Time has not diminished what we once shared, though I buried it deep beneath duty and devotion. I see now that what I thought was destiny – staying behind while you sought freedom – may have been meant for a different purpose entirely. The Sisterhood is not what it once was, not what I believed it to be. I write to you with the deepest dread and sadness. Mathilda has sacrificed her powers for the sake of the crystal, in the hopes of bringing peace. Her life force is being drained, just as Breag and Franwen plot to draw power from you and the other Crones, and speak of peace while preparing for war.

I know I have no right to seek you out, not after choosing the Clochar over you. But if any ember of trust remains between us, I beg you to help me stop what's coming. If not for the sake of what we were to each other, then for the balance of magic itself.

With regret and hope, and my eternal love for you,
   Gwyneth

. . .

INGRID'S TEA grew cold beside her as she read the words again, feeling the urgency rise up through the painful weight of years and choices.

The dragon-pup pressed against her legs, offering comfort as the feelings churned within her.

Mathilda...Gwyneth...something must be done.

8

DELIA

*D*elia felt a swell of rage as she pushed open the door to Clifford & Burk's building and stormed in.

She'd been going round in circles in her mind about all of this since she first discovered what was really going on with Gillian. Of course there had to be a connection with the lawyer colleague Gillian had recommended to represent Delia in the divorce and all this...and the entire situation, and even though she'd heard bits and pieces of speculation about this from Marjie and even from Juniper, she felt like she was being deliberately kept in the dark by her own daughter and the lawyer who was supposed to be representing her.

Of course, Gillian was the one responsible. By the sounds of it, she did not want to worry her mother, and nothing offends a mother more than not being worried about serious situations with their own child.

After vacillating between rage and sadness and reassurance that Gillian was being well looked after, with a little pride at how well her daughter apparently was managing this whole situation, Delia had left the grandchildren with Kitty. She was ready to find out as much as she possibly could now that she was no longer totally in the dark.

The icy receptionist tried to put her off, but Delia was in no mood to be stopped. She was fiery, after all. She pushed her way through the door to Perseus Burk's office. He looked up from his desk with a calm expression, as if not completely surprised.

"Delia Spark, how may I help you?"

"I think you might know a thing or two about that," said Delia. "I can't believe you didn't tell me about my daughter or about...Don't I have a right to know if I'm being represented by a vampire?"

Mr Burk shook his head. "No. I believe that would violate the rights of the magical creature in question to have their identity revealed, especially as it can be rather a delicate matter. Not everyone takes kindly to vampires." He smiled at her sincerely.

She looked into his beautiful face and wanted to punch it for a moment. She wondered whether her fire powers would surge forth and set the whole place ablaze. But as delightful as that image was in some unhinged part of her mind, she decided having a little chat would be more useful.

"I hear you've been taking good care of Gillian, and I

appreciate that, but you can probably imagine how I might feel upon finding out all of this."

Mr Burk nodded. "It has been on my mind quite a lot, I must admit," he said, the genuine and empathetic tone of his voice making Delia relax just slightly.

"I have a lot of questions," she said.

"About vampires, no doubt," said Burk.

"That's right. Among other things, is it true that Gillian can never be in the sunlight properly again?"

"I'm afraid so. It is not completely unheard of for a vampire to day-walk, but almost all the cases are the thing of ancient legend."

"Almost all the cases," said Delia.

The corner of the lawyer's mouth lifted up. "Almost all the cases, like I said."

"I have so much to learn," Delia said, throwing her hands up in the air. "I don't know about any of this. What do I most need to know? I suppose I can't cook for Gillian," Delia said. "She can't eat human food."

"I'm sure Marjie can explain that, if she hasn't already."

"Oh, she has, she can do blood enchantments, but it's not the same, is it?" Delia asked. "Do you really crave human blood and all you can eat is some sort of processed, fake alternative?"

Mr Burk raised an eyebrow. "To be completely honest with you, there's nothing quite as exquisite as human blood, but it is something modern vampires tend not to consume, myself included."

Delia scrunched up her nose. "Not even from Rosemary? I would imagine she would be some sort of donor to you."

Mr Burk chuckled. "I hardly think that would be the foundation of a healthy relationship, especially as the blood of a magical being can have quite intense effects on vampires. Human blood without the magic infused within it is quite entrancing enough, let alone Rosemary's...powerful magic."

"And what about Gillian?" said Delia. "Her children are magical, and I'm magical, even though we've only just found out about all this. Doesn't she have magic in her blood?"

"That's rather a sensitive issue," said the lawyer, his shoulders tensing. "And that's one reason why my family has been doing our best to protect Gillian and give her as much of a life as we can, given the circumstances. But it's not a safe topic for discussion outside of highly trusted individuals. You understand."

Delia's gut tightened. "Are you saying it could be a risk for her?"

"We don't understand the full nature of the risks. But we're doing our best to ascertain all the contingent factors and triangulate."

"Sounds very strategic," said Delia. "I suppose you get points for that."

"I'll take any points I can get when it comes to a fierce mother protecting her only child," said Mr Burk.

"All right then. I suppose I'll eventually be able to forgive you for holding all this back at Gillian's request, especially if you give me more understanding of what she's going through."

"She's progressing remarkably," said Mr Burk. "And I will provide you with some additional materials that can be quite useful for people encountering vampirism for the first time within themselves or their close circles. Usually we're sworn to secrecy, of course – we can't tell mundane humans, but occasionally vampires already have connections within non-magical communities which can support them. It can be a great help in the transition."

"Can you tell me anything else about the transition?" said Delia.

"I'm afraid much of that is secret, sanctified in ancient codes."

Delia rolled her eyes. "Juniper said you were all highly bureaucratic."

"So you've met our friend Juniper then," said Mr Burk, sounding bemused.

"She's quite a character," said Delia. "I like her, but it's hard not to."

"I agree," he replied. "By the way, I do have an update for you on your case."

Delia rolled her eyes. "Great, just what I need. Let's bring the authoritarian cultist into the mix while we're at it. What's Jerry been up to?"

"He is still totally uncontactable at the moment," said Mr Burk. "All the usual mortal channels have been exhausted. It seems magical channels must be opened to proceed. I assume that's still what you're wanting – to get divorced."

"Goddess yes," said Delia. "It's one of my top priorities. Except that this can't really be a priority right now, can it? Not with all this other mayhem. But personally, aside from the situation with Gillian, I can't wait to get disentangled from that man and to get access to my money again. I assume since he's not who he always pretended to be he will have totally dropped the theatre company. The whole life we built together – all disintegrated into nothing."

Mr Burk raised a finger as if to make a point. "You might be pleased to know that a group has reformed led by your core members – I'm in touch with them, actually, and they would love nothing more than to have you back."

Delia felt a little ache in her heart. She'd cut off ties to everyone following the humiliation of Jerry's betrayal; she didn't want to rehash all of that with anyone other than Kitty, not really. And yet, of course, they cared about her, and perhaps she'd let them down.

"I can't help but feel a little guilty," Delia said. "I haven't talked to any of them at all."

"Well, they've got something new in the mix, but they do miss you. They don't seem to miss Jerry at all, funnily enough."

Delia laughed. "I left my entire life behind! I've hardly thought about it, other than to process my shame and my rage." She sighed. "Why am I telling all this to you? You're not a therapist."

"I am trained in several modalities, but it's not my, shall we say, cup of tea. Speaking of tea?"

"Coffee, please," said Delia dryly.

Mr Burk picked up his phone and ordered a coffee, which arrived moments later, hot and strong, borne on a tray by the icy receptionist with immaculate nails. She plunked it down on the desk, gave a curt bow to the lawyer, and then vanished with preternatural speed.

"She's a friendly one, isn't she?" said Delia.

"I think she enjoys being cold," Burk said, with a hint of amusement. "She's been with me for several hundred years, and those sort of bonds build over time, as you can imagine."

"I can't imagine," said Delia. "And now Gillian's got this potential immortality stretching out before her. I could be really excited about that if I wasn't so terrified."

"It is a lot to contend with," said Mr Burk. "But back to your divorce case."

"Right. What's the development?" Delia asked.

"We've filed for permission to have us move to a magical court, rather than a standard mundane one."

"Why would you want to do that?" Delia asked. "Isn't there already enough magic in the mix. Wouldn't a magical court just make it more chaotic?"

"Potentially, a lot less chaotic," Perseus Burk replied. "There are far more protections. And given Jerry's volatile nature, he will be compelled to attend whether he likes it or not, and the magic in the room will be locked down so that nobody gets hurt. There can still be emotional wounding, of course, in a process like this."

"I like the idea of temporarily stripping him of his power, although I don't even know how magical he really is."

"I assure you he is extremely powerful at the moment,"

said Mr Burk. "And that's one reason why I'm hesitant to pursue this case at all, although it could be a useful challenge. It could wear him down. I gather, from several sources, that there's been a huge power surge in the vicinity of the compound of the Order of Crimson. There's always been a malevolence to that place as far back as I recall, though I'm not sure how old it is or when it really started – perhaps before my time on this earth, or perhaps when I was spending centuries on a different continent. But the dark power has inhabited that land, and it has drawn like minds towards it like flies to an ungainly odour."

"So poetic and disgusting," said Delia, "but it seems very fitting."

"As I said, recently that power has surged," said the lawyer. "And I can't help but think that your ex-husband is involved."

"Well, they do have that giant beast chained up there somewhere, some sort of poor cursed dog, I'm afraid, but it's a terrifying thing."

"Ah, yes, that is the stuff of legends."

"And legends are apparently always a bit true," said Delia, "even if we don't know the full story."

"You seem to have adjusted very well to the magical world," he said. "But I shouldn't be surprised. You have powerful lineage, and your daughter is extremely competent as well."

Delia smiled. "Well, I'm glad you're putting her to work. She really needs that. She needs something to keep her going, to occupy that brilliant mind of hers. And I hear you're taking very good care of her, you and your family, and I will thank you for that, but I'm still furious."

"That is entirely understandable," said Perseus Burk.

Delia sipped her coffee. It was good. "Is there a date for this magical court hearing?"

"It's not too far off. I'll send you all the details once they're finalised. Things are still slightly up in the air, but we like to move things quickly, especially when multiple different magical communities are involved. It can get incredibly messy otherwise."

Delia rolled her eyes. "Great, so now I have a dangerous divorce right in the middle of my series of magical conundrums. Life only gets more interesting."

"Well, you know, the funny thing about boredom," Perseus Burk said, leaning forward at his desk and clasping his hands together, "is it's actually far more painful than pain itself. Boredom is horrendous to the human soul. Research shows that people would rather inflict themselves with pain than sit in a room alone with no stimulation. And as a rather old creature myself, I can verify that we do all that we can to avoid boredom – and mundane humans are no different."

"I suppose I'll count my blessings then," said Delia, "even if I'd rather just set everything on fire."

Mr Burk chuckled. "Well, there's always Plan B."

9

DECLAN

*D*eclan crouched by his small fire in the forest clearing, the pre-dawn air sharp with frost. He'd returned here to give Delia space with the children, though each step away from her cottage had felt heavier than the last.

His fingers moved with practiced precision as he selected herbs from his foraged collection, each one singing a different note of magic as he touched it.

Yarrow for protection, its tiny white flowers still holding moonlight. Nettle for strength, the sting against his skin a welcome reminder of sensation. Rosemary to fortify his depleted magic, its pine-like scent bringing memories of countless forest mornings across centuries. But these weren't enough after recent events. From his leather pouch came three drops of dew collected from spider webs at first light – pure potential, that. A sprinkling of bark from a sacred ancient oak. Three dried purple chicory flowers for their healing energy.

He drew power from the earth beneath him, from the air around him, from the first rays of sun just beginning to pierce the canopy. Each source felt different now, more immediate, more alive since the curse had begun to break.

The enchanted blade Benedict had driven into his chest had changed something fundamental – the scar still ached, a reminder that his immortality was no longer certain. It was what he'd been wanting for a long time, though now, everything had changed.

As steam rose from his cup in complex patterns his mind drifted to the previous night. The warmth of Delia's kitchen, the children's presence, the simple pleasure of doing dishes while feeling part of something larger than himself.

The children's natural magic flowed freely, untaught and raw with imagination. Declan had felt something shift in his ancient heart, watching them play. Their innocence, their instinctive connection to the world's magic, reminded him of things he'd forgotten centuries ago.

He was sure the Order thought him dead, which was an advantage he intended to use. The memory of Benedict's blade piercing his chest on that windswept beach still burned – it should have killed him, would have killed anyone else. But he did not die so easily, though something had shifted, something fundamental had changed. He was no longer the same being who had walked the earth for centuries, numb to everything but his own endless existence.

Whatever it took to protect Delia and those she loved, he

would do it, even if it meant risking his newly uncertain mortality.

The possibility of an ending should have excited him after so long being cursed with endless life. Instead, it made each moment sharper, more precious. He had something to live for now – not only Delia, but this budding sense of hope, vulnerably bursting into bloom in his chest after centuries of apathy.

His thoughts drifted back to the night before. Kitty had taken the children up to bed. He'd climbed the stairs to find Delia. She'd been staring at her window from her position in the bed, moonlight caressing her hair, and when she'd turned to him, her face had been wet with tears. He'd held her while grief and anger poured out of her – about Gillian, about the threats to her family, about everything that had changed so rapidly in her life.

The intimacy of that moment had melted something else in him. He'd held Delia, feeling her mortal heart beat against his ancient one, and old barriers had begun to crack.

Her mortality chilled him now in ways it hadn't before. She burned so bright, so brief – a flame that would inevitably flicker out while he...but would he? Nothing was certain anymore. Yet perhaps that very impermanence made their connection more precious. Nothing in life could last forever, he knew that better than most, and still he found himself opening to this chance at deep connection and meaning.

The healing nature of their connection still bewildered him. Every touch melted another layer of ice around his heart, every shared moment brought him more fully alive.

Her magic called to his, creating something new and unexpected between them. He could feel the bright flame of her presence. He held her in his attention, wondering if she could sense it too – this bridge between them, this understanding that transcended ordinary bonds.

Last night, holding her, he'd felt their magic interweave. Her fire had warmed places in him that had been cold for so long, while his shadows had given her pain somewhere to rest. The sensation had been terrifying and exhilarating.

The curse's grip had loosened, letting in a world of sensation and possibility he'd forgotten existed, leaving him raw and vulnerable, but also more alive. Each moment with Delia stripped away another layer of that protective numbness, revealing something he'd thought long dead – the capacity for hope, for connection, for love.

Declan finished his tea, feeling its magic settle into his bones, fortifying him. The Order would come for them eventually, but there was time to reflect and heal now, and to do some reconnaissance.

The forest stirred around him as he reached out once more with his senses toward Delia's cottage, holding her in his thoughts. Something new was growing from the cracks in his curse, something worth protecting, worth fighting for, worth living – or even dying – for.

10

AGATHA

The Witch's Wort pub's warmth comforted Agatha as she nursed her fourth sherry, the antitoxicity spell tingling pleasantly at the base of her skull. Covvey sat across from her, his weathered face caught in the pub's flickering lamplight, listening intently as she described her latest attempts to communicate with the air dragon.

"It's maddening," she said, her fingers absently tracing the pendant's intricate surface. "The closer I get to relaxing, the more I can sense it there, just on the edge of consciousness. But the moment I start worrying about making contact—"

"It slips away," Covvey finished, his deep voice gentle with understanding. "That's life for you. The harder you grasp, the more things slip through your fingers."

Agatha snorted. "When did you get so philosophical? Must be all those years being a lone wolf turning you poetic."

She pushed herself up from the table, her cane clicking against the worn floorboards. "Another round? Pint for you?"

"Aye, wouldn't say no."

At the bar, Liam was deep in conversation with Sherry and Ferg, the latter's perfectly pressed robes and upright posture in contrast to the pub's comfortable shabbiness.

Agatha ordered Covvey's pint and a peppermint schnapps for herself – something to cut through the sweetness of the sherry.

"—and he swears they're real?" Liam was saying. "Unbelievable."

Sherry nodded. "Says he's seen them with his own eyes."

"Dragons?" Ferg's nasal voice dripped with scepticism, but Agatha's ears pricked up and she began to listen to the mayor more intently – for once. "Surely not. We haven't had a confirmed sighting since—"

"Since medieval times," Agatha cut in.

"I can't believe that," said Liam. "It's the stuff of fairytales."

Agatha silently scoffed. Rather rich of Liam not to believe in dragons, given what he turned into every full moon, but then again, the great beasts had passed into legend long ago. She glared around at the bunch of them. "Who's been talking about dragons?"

Sherry nodded toward a corner table. "New fellow, been here a few nights. Gets in his cups and starts babbling about some secret society. Calls himself Cedric."

Agatha followed her gesture. The stranger sat beside Papa Jack, gesturing wildly as he talked. Even from here, she could sense something off about him – a kind of desperate energy that set her senses tingling.

"The Order of Crimson, he keeps saying," Liam added. "Never heard of it. Load of nonsense if you ask me."

Agatha's pulse quickened. She gripped her cane tighter and made her way toward the stranger's table, bringing the drinks with her. She vaguely recognised the man, though he was far more dishevelled than he'd been when riding with the Order in pursuit of the Crones. She doubted he'd know who she was in his present state. Of course, it could be a trap, but something told her he'd left the Order or been cast out. The boundary that protected Myrtlewood was still intact, after all. This strange drunkard could be useful.

"—and the great beast, chained in darkness!" he cried out as Agatha approached, his words slurring but his eyes fever-bright. "They keep it there, you see, deep beneath the compound, waiting for the right moment to—"

"Evening," Agatha cut in, fixing him with her sharpest stare. Papa Jack, bless him, was already half-asleep in his chair, offering no resistance when she shooed him away with a wave of her hand.

Cedric looked up at her, blinking owlishly. His clothes were travel-worn but of good quality, and something about the way he held himself spoke of formal training. "Who're you then, woman?"

"Name's Agatha," she replied gruffly. "Couldn't help but overhear you talking about dragons." She settled into Papa Jack's vacated chair, ignoring the protest of her joints. "Don't get many people round here who know anything about them."

"Ah, but I do!" Cedric leaned forward, nearly knocking over his half-empty glass. "I've seen one, I have. Great terrible thing it was too, all scales and fury. The Order keeps it—" He caught himself, fear flickering across his face. "Are you a good woman like Sherry over there? Can I trust you?"

"I think you'll find my gender has very little to do with my morality, most days," Agatha said dryly. "The Order of Crimson, you mean?" Agatha kept her voice casual, though her heart was racing. Behind her, she sensed Covvey approaching, drawn by some instinct for trouble developed over their long friendship.

"Shouldn't have said that," Cedric mumbled, shrinking in on himself. "Shouldn't be talking about any of it. They'll find me, you know. They always find their mark."

"Nobody's finding anyone," Covvey rumbled, pulling up a chair. "You're safe enough here."

Agatha shot him a grateful look. Covvey would have heard the entire conversation from across the bar with his sharp hearing. He'd always known exactly when to appear, how to steady a situation with his solid presence. The stranger seemed to relax slightly as Covvey settled in, perhaps sensing the same steadiness Agatha had always relied on, or perhaps the presence of a man was reassuring to someone who'd grown up in perpetual fear of womankind.

"Tell us more about this dragon," she prompted gently. "Must have been quite a sight."

Cedric's hands trembled as he reached for his drink.

"Enormous, it was, with eyes like burning coals..." He hiccupped, face growing pale. "The Shepherd, he means to use the dragons. Says it's the will of the Almighty. He just needs to get hold of them."

Agatha exchanged a quick glance with Covvey. The Shepherd was also known as Benedict, and also known as Jerry, Delia's ex-husband.

Her pendant seemed to grow warmer against her chest. "And where might one find such a creature?" she asked, keeping her tone light despite the urgency building in her chest.

"The Crones," Cedric whispered, leaning close enough that she could smell the brandy on his breath. "The Crones have the power...but the legends say the power is locked deep underground, where the old stones sing with pain. But I've said too much. They'll know. They always know."

"Here now," Covvey said. "Have another drink. Tell us whatever you please. The Order can't get into Myrtlewood. We all know that, here."

It wasn't entirely true. Most of Myrtlewood was oblivious to the Order and the Sisterhood and the work of the Crones.

Cedric was already pulling back, fear replacing the loose-tongued openness of moments before. "No, no. Shouldn't have said anything. They'll find me. They'll—" He started to rise, swaying dangerously.

The pendant at Agatha's throat hummed with energy as Cedric looked between them, clearly torn between fear and the desperate need to trust someone.

She could feel the air dragon stirring, more present than

it had been in weeks, drawn perhaps by talk of its other earthbound kin, and the thought occurred to her that bringing all the dragon stones together could be powerful, even if they didn't know where the fire dragon was hiding just yet...but for now, a more urgent matter awaited.

"You're in no state to go anywhere," Agatha said firmly, her hand shooting out to steady Cedric.

"Covvey," she said sharply. "Our friend here needs a safe place to sleep this off."

Covvey nodded, understanding immediately as he always did. "Got just the spot. Nice quiet room above the stables, where no magic can reach."

11

MARJIE

*M*arjie adjusted her emotional shields the moment she stepped into Ingrid's cottage. The space hummed with overlapping energies – children's joy bubbling like spring water, Delia's maternal concern a deep undercurrent, Ingrid's sharp focus cutting through it all like a blade. Even the animals radiated distinct emotional signatures: Torin's steady canine devotion and the earth dragon-pup's ancient wisdom wrapped in playful disguise.

"For heaven's sake, Ingrid," Agatha was saying as Marjie hung her cloak on the already overcrowded hook. "Would it kill you to dust occasionally?"

"Probably," Ingrid replied from her position by the perpetual fire, not looking up from the kettle she was floating with practiced precision. "I'm quite sure there are several protection spells mixed in with that dust. Better not risk it."

Marjie smiled, making her way to the kitchen area where herbs hung in fragrant bundles from every available surface.

Merryn and Keyne were chasing the earth dragon-pup through the cottage's back rooms, their laughter punctuated by Torin's occasional excited bark.

"Children!" Delia called out, her voice stern but her emotional signature warm with affection. "Try not to knock over any of Ingrid's things."

"Bold of you to assume I'd leave dangerous objects where pesky children could reach them," Ingrid sniffed, but Marjie felt the underlying tenderness in her energy. She had gone soft on these children, though she'd never admit it.

"The way this place is organised, I'm not sure you know where anything is," Agatha muttered, using her cane to push aside a stack of books and make room to sit.

The kettle whistled – leaves flew from the bundles and the tea began preparing itself.

Marjie could feel tension building under the banter, concerns about the Order and a certain vampire daughter and missing grimoires all wanting to burst forth at once.

"Right then," she said as the floating cups of tea made their way to each of the Crones. "Shall we begin with Gillian's situation, or would you rather start with our unexpected guest at Covvey's?"

Delia's emotion flickered like a flame at the mention of Gillian, but she kept her voice steady. "Juniper's been keeping an eye on her. She's doing remarkably well, apparently. The Burks have taken her under their wing."

"Perseus Burk," Ingrid mused, adding a splash of something mysterious from a twisted bottle to her tea. "Now there's an old power. Been practicing law since before any of us were born. Killer instincts."

Marjie felt Delia's spike of maternal worry and instinctively sent a wave of calm toward her friend. "The vampire community is quite structured," she offered. "They'll make sure she's properly supported."

The earth dragon-pup bounded into the room, Torin close behind, both of them narrowly missing Agatha's cane. Merryn and Keyne followed, their energy bright with innocence and possibility. Marjie strengthened her shields slightly – children's uncontrolled magic could be overwhelming.

"Speaking of structure," Agatha said, eyeing the chaos with resigned amusement, "our friend Cedric had quite a lot to say about the Order's hierarchy before he passed out."

"Ah yes, your drunken informant." Ingrid's energy crackled with interest despite her dry tone. "What exactly did he reveal between hiccups?"

"Something about dragons," Agatha replied. "And their leader – the Shepherd, he called him, but I assume that's your ex, Delia – has changed somehow. Become more powerful, more dangerous."

Marjie felt Delia's fear spike as she said, "An Order member here in Myrtlewood...are we certain the barrier—"

"The barrier," Ingrid cut in firmly, "is absolutely secure. I'd know the instant it was threatened. If he's here, he's no longer bound to that silly cult."

"Unless that's what they want us to think," Delia said.

The children paused their play, perhaps sensing the tension in the room.

"No, he'd have never made it through, love," Marjie reassured her.

"Still, I bet he's dangerous," said Delia.

"Well, he's not going anywhere while Covvey's watching him," Agatha said. "And once he's sobered up, I intend to find out exactly what he knows about dragons."

Torin padded over to Delia, resting his head on her knee. Marjie felt the beagle's steady presence help settle his witch's turbulent emotions. The earth dragon-pup, not to be outdone, flopped dramatically at Ingrid's feet.

"Dragons seem to be the theme of the day," Marjie said, seeing an opening. "Delia, tell everyone what Juniper discovered about the Bracewells and your grimoire."

"Apparently Sabrina's been tampering with records." Delia's energy sharpened with focus. "Deleting passages about my grandmother, Etty. And she's been in contact with the Sisterhood of the Veil."

"The Sisterhood?" Ingrid's aura flashed with recognition. "Now that's interesting. I received a message just the other day from an old...friend there."

Marjie felt the weight of old love and pain in Ingrid's energy, carefully masked behind her casual tone. She adjusted her shields accordingly, giving her friend privacy in her emotions.

"What did she want?" Agatha asked, while Merryn crawled into her lap, seemingly drawn to the pendant around the older witch's neck.

"To warn us," Ingrid said. "Something's wrong in the Sisterhood. She didn't give details, but—"

A crash from the kitchen interrupted her, followed by Keyne's worried "Oops!"

"Not the purple jar!" Ingrid called out. Keyne flinched, looking back at her, but she was already smiling. "Actually, that one needed breaking. Been meaning to do it for weeks."

Marjie felt the boy's relief wash through the room, followed by a surge of magic that made all the herbs hanging from the ceiling dance.

"Those children need training," Agatha muttered.

"The Bracewells have the family grimoire, of course they do..." Delia said, returning to the matter at hand. Her determination radiated outward like heat. "And I need it to find my dragon. None of that is new, but their deviousness seems to run deeper than I imagined."

Marjie felt the moment crystallise with possibility. She took a deep breath, aware of how her next suggestion might shift the energy in the room. "Perhaps...perhaps we should try something. Together."

"What did you have in mind?" Ingrid asked, one eyebrow raised.

"Our stones. Has anyone tried bringing them all together?"

The room's energy changed immediately – curiosity, apprehension, and excitement swirling together until Marjie had to reinforce her shields. Even the children grew quiet, sensing something important about to happen.

"Well?" Agatha straightened in her chair. "It's worth a try, isn't it?"

"I don't have mine," Delia said. "Of course…"

"Worth a try though," Agatha said, removing her pendant which hummed with air magic. Marjie placed her water dragon's crystal on the table, feeling its cool energy pulse. Ingrid was last, producing her earth stone from one of her many mysterious pockets.

As the three stones came together, Marjie felt power build in the room like pressure before a storm. The stones began to vibrate, creating a harmony just below hearing.

Torin's ears pricked up, and the earth dragon-pup lifted her head with sudden interest.

But nothing more happened. The power remained potential, unrealised – like a word caught on the tip of the tongue, a spell waiting to be spoken. Marjie could feel it, though: something gathering, building, waiting for the right moment to emerge.

"Well, that was thoroughly anticlimactic," Ingrid said dryly, but Marjie felt her underlying excitement.

"It's not ready," Merryn said suddenly, her small face serious. "The dragons are sleeping still."

Marjie caught the flash of surprised recognition in the other Crones' energies. Sometimes children saw things more clearly than any of them.

12

MEPHISTOS

*M*ephistos stretched luxuriously as he entered the cabin; he loved to make an entrance, ensuring his tail swept dangerously close to the Crone's teacups.

"Mephistos," Ingrid said dryly. "How kind of you to grace us with your presence."

"Your timing is impeccable as always," Marjie said, and blast it if he didn't feel a flicker of warmth at her tone. She'd always been kind to him, even when he didn't deserve it.

"Yes, well." He began grooming one paw with elaborate attention. "I happened to notice your little dragon-stone attempt. Charming, really. Though you might want to know what's happening at the Order's compound before you go waking ancient powers."

Agatha's eyes narrowed. "What have you discovered?"

"Oh, nothing much." He examined his claws in the fire-light. "Just a complete coup, the Elders in chains, and your friend the Shepherd channelling powers that make my fur stand on end. But please, do continue with your stones."

The Crones exchanged glances. His demon nature stirred again, recognising patterns in the magic that his conscious mind couldn't quite grasp.

"Tell us everything," Delia demanded.

Mephistos sighed dramatically. "Must I do *all* the work around here? Very well. But first—" He eyed Marjie's cream-laden scone with obvious intent.

Marjie obligingly pushed her scone towards him, an obvious bribe, but he was willing. The cream was divine – one advantage of this feline form was how exquisitely it experienced pleasure. His demon nature might crave grander, more dangerous, indulgences, but there was something to be said for simple satisfactions.

"The Shepherd," he said between delicate laps, "has gone quite magnificently mad with power. Claims he's channelling the Almighty – their image of God." His whiskers twitched. "The magic feels...familiar somehow. Old. Like something I encountered before this blasted curse."

"Familiar how?" Agatha pressed, ever the historian.

Mephistos flicked his tail in annoyance. "If I could remember properly, I'd tell you. Being cursed into a cat plays havoc with one's memory." He stretched again, this time managing to scatter several stones and leaves the children had carefully arranged on the table. He could hear them outside with those blasted dog creatures and he intended to skedaddle as soon as they returned. "But I can tell you this – whatever power the Shepherd's tapped into, it's the same force that shattered everything the first time. The same darkness that—"

He stopped, surprised by a sudden flash of ancient memory: the witch's tears as she cast the curse, saying it was the only way to preserve...something. Something about balance, about powers that needed to sleep until the right moment.

"Well?" Delia prompted.

"Well what? A cat needs dramatic pauses. Adds to the mystery." He began grooming his tail with excessive attention. "The point is, your Shepherd friend is meddling with forces that broke the world once before. Though I suppose that's what you get when religious zealots start playing with ancient magic. No sense of style at all."

The dragon stones' vibration intensified, making his fur bristle. Blast these physical responses – a demon should be above such obvious tells. But something in their resonance called to his oldest memories, from before the curse, before Von Cassel's summoning.

"You know," he said, affecting casual disinterest while repositioning himself directly between the stones, "it's quite fascinating how history repeats itself. One moment you're a perfectly respectable demon being summoned for a lover's quarrel, the next you're watching religious fanatics tear everything apart. Again."

"A lover's quarrel?" Marjie's voice was gentle, coaxing. Damnably intuitive woman.

"Von Cassel was the one who summoned me. Don't you recall the ancient legend?"

"Oh yes," said Marjie. "The dark mage who betrayed the powerful witch."

"What was her name?" Delia asked.

"I believe it was Demelza," Mephistos purred. "I heard the name as he screamed at her..." Her voice chanting, magic wrapping around him like chains made of starlight.

"She loved him, you see," said Marjie. "Right up until she discovered what he planned to do with her power."

"And what was that?" Delia asked.

Agatha leaned forward, historian's curiosity bright in her eyes. "Something diabolical, no doubt. Von Cassel was renowned for trying to rally the magical community to take over the known world. He wanted to be in charge. Then he disappeared in a blast of magic and rumour which faded to legend. What else do you know, demon?"

Mephistos examined his claws. "That's the irritating part. I can't quite remember. The curse..." He paused, whiskers twitching. "She said it was necessary. That someone had to watch, had to wait. Though being turned into a cat seems a rather extreme way to ensure one's attention."

He looked around at the crones and for a moment he caught a glimpse of something vast – ancient powers sleeping, waiting, the pattern that connected everything: Order, Sisterhood, Crones, dragons, himself. But it slipped away like smoke through claws.

"The Shepherd's tampering with the same forces," he said instead. "Breaking all the old bindings. The magic he's channelling...it feels like Von Cassel's did, at the end. Right before the curse—" He stopped, startled by the emotion in his voice. Cats shouldn't sound so raw. Demons certainly shouldn't.

"I'm not sure you're giving us any new information," Agatha said.

"No, it's useful to think about all this," Delia insisted. "I remember you told me the legend about the witch who was betrayed centuries ago. I didn't know how it connected, but now things are starting to fall into place – like the rift of their magic led to the Order and the Sisterhood, and maybe somehow to the Crones coming into power and the dragons...well, that's where I get lost."

"Well, this is interesting." He stood, circling the dragon stones with careful precision. His tail brushed each one in turn, sending ripples of magic through his form that made his demon nature stir. "You're closer than you think, though not in the way you imagine."

"Stop being cryptic and get to the point," Ingrid said sharply.

"My dear witch, cryptic is what I do best." But the magic was building, pushing at his memories, at the edges of his curse. "The Shepherd isn't just channelling power – breaking through protections that keep certain forces dormant. The kind Demelza died protecting."

His voice caught on her name. Strange, how after all these centuries, it could still affect him so. Suddenly he could smell her magic again – sage and starlight and sacrifice. His memory was reawakening, but it was all in flux, not trustworthy. Nothing was in order.

"We need to wake the dragons up," said Delia. "Of course I have to find the fire dragon first, but isn't it obvious that their power was hidden here in order to help us at a time like this?"

"The dragons aren't sleeping," he said, the revelation surprising even him. "They're waiting. Just like I've been waiting, though I didn't know it. Cursed to watch and remember and..." He trailed off as another piece clicked into place.

The magic pulsed through him like a living thing, awakening memories buried beneath centuries of feline naps and careful indifference. His demon nature surged against its bonds, recognising something in this moment that his cursed form had forgotten.

"Oh, *clever* witch," he purred, the admiration genuine beneath his sardonic tone. "She didn't just bind me to watch. She bound me to *this*. To you. To this precise time." His tail swished through the stones' rising energy. "Though she might have mentioned it would take several centuries. I would have napped more."

A flicker of movement caught his eye – one of Ingrid's hanging herbs swaying without breeze, casting shadows that reminded him of dragon wings.

"The Shepherd is breaking bindings in his seeking of power," he continued, picking his way between the stones with deliberate grace. "But some bindings aren't chains. They're..." He paused, searching for words to describe what he suddenly understood. "They're more like roots. Break them, and everything falls."

The stones' harmony shifted again, and this time he recognised the pattern. Not just magic, but memory. Protection. Purpose. All the things Demelza had tried to preserve when she discovered Von Cassel's true intentions. All the things she'd woven into his curse, waiting for the moment when they'd be needed again.

He could picture her now...remember her in all her power and glory. A singularly powerful magical being, seduced by someone with no care for anyone but power. As a demon, he should have identified with Von Cassel, but no... that was boring. Power could only get you so far.

His whiskers tingled as he settled himself precisely in the stones' centre. "Well then," he said, letting his usual sarcasm mask the weight of understanding.

"The Shepherd's coup isn't just about power," he said, returning to more immediate concerns. "The Order's Elders are in chains, their precious compound transformed into something else entirely. Even the stones sing differently there." He paused to groom one paw, mostly to annoy Agatha. "Of course, I couldn't get too close. Their barriers are..." He sniffed. "Inelegant, but effective."

"And what exactly were you doing prowling around the Order's compound?" Ingrid asked.

"Gathering intelligence, obviously." He switched paws. "Someone has to do the real work while you all sit around making tea and playing with rocks. But the wider situation is interesting..." But the jibe felt hollow – the magic in the room was making his fur stand on end, reminding him of older obligations he'd rather ignore.

"If you say 'interesting' one more time without explaining yourself," Agatha growled, "I'll turn you into a throw cushion."

Mephistos yawned, showing every one of his sharp teeth. "Empty threats from empty heads."

Children's laughter filtered in from outside, followed by excited barking. The earth dragon-pup's disguise was slipping – he could smell ancient magic bleeding through its puppy facade.

"The Shepherd thinks he's channelling some divine power," Mephistos said, "but it's not that. It's poisoned..." He flicked his tail in annoyance as the memory slipped away again. "Well, let's just say it didn't end well for anyone involved. Particularly me."

"Is that why you're suddenly being so helpful?" Delia asked. "Worried history might repeat itself?"

"My dear Crone, I'm helping because I'm cursed to. Though I do appreciate having front row seats to all this delicious chaos." His demon nature stirred at the half-truth. The real reason was more complex, tied to Demelza's final spell, to the schism that had birthed both Order and Sisterhood, to promises he couldn't quite remember making.

"The Shepherd's managed something rather unprecedented," Mephistos said, delicately licking cream from his whiskers. "The magic there tastes wrong." His nose wrinkled. "Like burnt honey and madness."

"You got close enough to taste it?" Agatha's scepticism could have curdled milk.

"Please. I'm an ancient demon. I have *standards*. But even from the shadows, I could sense his power growing."

The dragon stones' vibration gentled, settling into a quiet hum that made his fur tingle. Marjie's expression softened with understanding – blast her empathic powers – and he quickly turned away to groom his tail.

"If you're quite finished playing with rocks," he said, "you might want to know that the Order's planning something. Something big. I heard the guards talking about a beast they're preparing to wake." He paused for dramatic effect. "Though personally, I think they should stick to their book club. Much safer."

Mephistos wasn't sure about what the Order was doing, truth be told, but then again, he was a demon. He enjoyed the dramatic effect. They were certainly up to something, and his memories were reawakening, disconcertingly. He was starting to *feel* things. Sympathy? Empathy? All kinds of nauseating sensations that no respectable demon should ever have to contend with, but that was part of it – the curse that powerful witch had placed upon him, lying dormant, like the dragons until the right time.

The Crones exchanged heavy glances.

Mephistos stretched and stood, having delivered his questionable information with what he considered admirable restraint. Besides, the earth dragon-pup's barking was getting closer, and he had no intention of being cornered by that enthusiastic menace.

"Well, this has been delightful, but I have some very important napping to attend to. Do try not to get yourselves killed. It would be terribly inconvenient for my curse-breaking plans."

He padded toward the window, and he slipped into the night, leaving them to ponder his warnings. Being cryptic was exhausting work, but someone had to do it with style.

13

DELIA

*D*elia glanced out the window as a very expensive-looking Rolls Royce pulled up in front of her cottage. She peered out, wondering whether a fancy diplomat or celebrity might be visiting the neighbourhood.

"*She's* here," said Keyne.

"Who?" Delia asked.

"The woman from the card!" He pointed at the small rectangular card on the table, the one that Elamina had provided, with her contact details.

Delia had fished it out of the kitchen junk drawer earlier that day, deposited it on the table, and looked at it for a few minutes.

She had contemplated calling her cousin but was yet to make the effort to actually do so, considering she wasn't entirely sure what to say that might warrant getting her an invite to the Bracewell mansion where the grimoire was most likely kept.

Delia had rather been avoiding dinner parties for much of her career, finding them generally rather tiresome, with few exceptions, but it seemed like a good way to get into the house if she could somehow wrangle it.

She didn't know quite how request an invite without it seeming suspicious.

Keyne knew, somehow. His intuition was clearly off the charts. Something to watch, lest it get out of control, but in this situation it could be useful.

"Why do you think she's here?" Delia asked, looking at her grandson's cherubic face.

"You'll see," he said, with an angelic smile.

Delia peered out at the Rolls Royce, looking for Elamina's form, but the car seemed empty apart from a driver.

It wasn't Elamina with her icy white hair and austere demeanour. Perhaps Keyne was wrong. Instead, the driver, with hair greying around his temples, posture military straight in his old-fashioned-looking uniform, marched promptly up the path and knocked on the door.

Delia cleared her throat before opening the door to him.

"Hello?" she said, with a definitive question in her tone.

"Ms Spark," the man said in a dry and formal tone with no room for questions.

"I suppose that's me. Yes," said Delia.

He produced, as if from thin air, a purple envelope adorned with silver.

"You are invited by the grace of Madame Elamina

Bracewell to attend dinner at the Bracewell residence this Thursday evening," he announced.

Delia shot a look at Keyne. It turned out he was right after all.

The child winked at her, although not properly knowing how to, it was more a cheeky blink, followed by a giggle.

Delia turned back to the driver.

"Delightful," she said, before wondering if she sounded too enthusiastic. "May I bring a friend?"

"The details are all contained within this envelope," he replied, passing it across. "I'm not at liberty to discuss them, nor do I have any additional information."

The expensive paper caught Delia's attention as she took the envelope from the man who bowed and promptly retreated down the path before she could ask any more questions.

"Wasn't he a bit strange?" she said to Keyne with a light chuckle, hoping not to let her anxieties crowd in. "How did you know it was from our cousin?"

"Cousin?" Keyne said, eyes widening. "I didn't know we had any more cousins."

Delia grinned at him, reaching down to give him a cuddle and kiss. "But you're so clever – you knew it was related to the card on the table. How did that happen?"

"I don't know," Keyne said with an exaggerated shrug. "It's just the same feeling."

"That was rather cryptic," Kitty said, sidling in as Keyne trotted off to find his sister, who was busy gathering leaves in the back garden to make a spell.

"Yes, these children are quite something," Delia said.

Kitty threw back her head and cackled. She was still clad in her dressing gown. "Little marvels," Kitty agreed. "Extremely magical, you know?"

"I really do. It makes me wonder if some of our magic will affect Gillian too. Apparently she's adjusting amazingly well for a new..." Delia's voice trailed off as if not quite being prepared to speak the next word.

Kitty patted her on the shoulder. "It's a lot to adjust to."

"Yes. My lawyer said it's unusual...and perhaps I shouldn't speak about Gillian's transformation and her witch heritage outside of trusted confidants."

Kitty cocked an eyebrow. "Oh really...more secrets! I love some good intrigue. What do you think that's about?"

Delia shrugged. "Who knows? But let's focus on the bright side. Gilly is doing well, considering. I could do with a bit of optimism right now. Besides, I just got invited to my cousin's house!"

"Oh, that snooty-tooty one who you're angling to get to know better?" Kitty asked.

"That's right," said Delia.

"Well, put on your glad rags, lady. You've got some schmoozing to do."

Delia sighed. "I'm afraid you might be right, but I ran out of patience for schmoozing a long, long time ago."

"Can I come?" Kitty asked. "I'm dreadfully nosy."

Delia shook her head. "I'd better take someone like Marjie."

Kitty's shoulders tightened. "Someone with powers, you mean? Not pathetic mundane old me?"

"Oh, darling," said Delia. "You know that's not what I mean."

But the conversation would not be dropped.

"It's dreadfully unfair," said Kitty, as she and Delia tidied up the kitchen that evening. The children were asleep in their beds, or at least they were supposed to be by now having had plenty of stories and having all requests for cuddles met.

"What's unfair?" Delia asked, though she thought she already knew.

"Oh, you know," said Kitty with a dismissive wave, "you're taking a woman you've only met a couple of months ago as your 'plus-one' to this family dinner party, while I stay back here with the children."

"I thought you hated dinner parties," said Delia.

"No, darling, you're the one who hates dinner parties," Kitty said with a wicked grin. "I love an opportunity to rub people the wrong way."

"Well, that's definitely a reason why you should stay here," said Delia.

"Oh, come on," said Kitty. "You know I can be diplomatic when I have to be, Delia."

Delia shook her head. "I know you feel left out but it might be dangerous, and besides, I can't have you, my dearest most wonderful friend, offend my long-lost magical family and ruin my chances of getting the grimoire. You know I love you to bits, but you're not the most tactful person in the world."

Kitty smacked her with the dishcloth. "That's what you think, sweetie. I'm actually rather good at getting my way."

"I can't argue with that," said Delia. "And what are you even doing while you're here? Don't you need a distraction to keep things interesting?"

"What am I even doing? That is the million-dollar question," said Kitty. "Your coven friends tell me it's not safe for me to leave town. I was even thinking of getting back in touch with Roger."

Delia threw up her arms in mock horror. "And receive more plastic flowers and cheap bubbly for your efforts? Heaven forbid."

Kitty shrugged. "It's been a dry season, slim pickings in Myrtlewood."

Delia shook her head. "Well, you did have fun with him. I don't see the harm in sending him a message if that's what you want."

Kitty crinkled her nose. "After your revelation with Jerry I hardly think it's advisable. He might be one of those red-cloaked chappies. I'd better err on the side of caution."

Delia chuckled as she put away the cutlery. "Cautious? You?! Anyway, I think he's in the clear on that count. Marjie did some scrying to check if any other Order members had infiltrated our personal lives and he came up clear. Just don't expect him to find Myrtlewood. It's not an easy place to get to unless you know what you're doing."

Kitty sighed. "I suppose there's no harm in a few dirty

messages exchanged here and there. I might have to put my foot down on gifts though. I am a bit worried I'll overstay my welcome with you and I don't have many friends in town."

"Impossible. You're always welcome to stay with me – as long as you like," said Delia, "and if you really want to come to dinner, we can make it happen."

"Oh really?" Kitty asked.

"Sure," said Delia. She'd been mulling it over in her mind. She'd wanted to bring Marjie. The invitation didn't specify that she could bring anyone else with her, but it didn't prohibit it either, and what were the Bracewells going to do if she showed up with extra people? It was rude, sure, but it hardly felt safe showing up alone and asking ahead might mean she'd be denied the opportunity. "Let's do it," she said to Kitty. "We'll find a babysitter or something. Maybe the kids can go and stay with Una and Ashwyn, have a sleep-over with their adorable little ones."

Kitty shrugged. "As long as you decide I'm worth the risk."

"Of course, you are, darling," said Delia, "but on one condition."

"What's that?" Kitty asked, flicking the tea towel over in another devious gesture.

"Well, if on the off chance we need you to create the most dramatic distraction of your life, you have to put your all into it. There'll be a signal."

"I like the sound of this," said Kitty with a grin.

"However, other than that, you will be on your extremely best behaviour, as if you're meeting with royalty."

Kitty scoffed. "Oh pish, you know I don't give a toss about royalty."

"Consider them dangerous royalty then, because they are. And we'll be walking into their stronghold. It's rather perilous, and as you know that's another reason I'd prefer for you to stay here. But you're a grown-up, and you seem to have a way of getting yourself both in and out of trouble without too much bother."

"I'm glad you think so highly of me," said Kitty, smiling like the cat who got the cream. "Now for the big question, what on earth are we going to wear?"

14

GWYNETH

*T*he novice's knock came at dawn, urgent and sharp against Gwyneth's chamber door. "Sister Gwyneth! The Elders require your presence in the chamber of visions immediately."

Gwyneth had been awake already, troubled thoughts of Ingrid and her unanswered message keeping sleep at bay.

Light streamed through the chamber's high windows as she approached. Her heart quickened – being summoned here was never trivial.

The familiar scents washed over her as she entered: the smoke of frankincense, beeswax candles, and the peculiar sharp-sweet tang that accompanied prophecy. Today that last scent was especially strong, making the fine hairs on her neck rise.

Oracle Maeve sat in her carved chair, white hair flowing loose over her shoulders, her unseeing eyes reflecting candlelight. Breag and Franwen flanked her like anxious attendants, their usual composure fractured by barely contained excitement. Oracles could never give perfect predictions, but as probability shifted between possible futures, some things became clearer. This was how the Sisterhood stayed one step ahead. Unfortunately, the Order of Crimson had access to similar magic.

"Sister Gwyneth," Breag said, her voice tight with urgency. "The Oracle has received a significant vision."

The Maeve's face turned toward Gwyneth, though her milky eyes focused somewhere far beyond the chamber walls. When she spoke, her voice emerged like smoke, ancient and new at once:

"Fire rises from earth's heart, where stone bleeds and mountains breathe. The dragon stirs in her molten cradle, waiting. When earth splits and stone flows like water, she will wake."

"A volcano!" Franwen's voice trembled with excitement. "The fire dragon will emerge from a volcano!"

Breag began pacing, her boots clicking against worn flag-stones. "But that's impossible. There are no volcanoes in Cornwall. None in the entirety of Britannia! How can we possibly—"

"Perhaps it's metaphorical?" Franwen suggested, though her face showed doubt. "The dragon's power manifesting as volcanic energy?"

"Or—" Breag stopped abruptly. "We'll have to go abroad." She spoke the last word as if it tasted bitter.

"Abroad?" Franwen wrinkled her nose. "The Sisterhood

hasn't left this soil in centuries. Surely there must be another interpretation."

As her fellow Elders debated, Gwyneth studied Oracle Maeve's serene face. The old woman's lips curved in that knowing smile that always suggested she saw far more than she revealed.

"Sister Gwyneth," the Oracle said suddenly, her voice cutting through Breag and Franwen's discussion. "You're very quiet."

"I'm considering the implications," Gwyneth said carefully. The truth was, her mind raced with possibilities – and with the urgent need to share this information with Ingrid. Her note had gone unanswered, but that wasn't unexpected. Ingrid had always been cautious, strategic in her responses, even before...

"The fire dragon's power could be ours," Breag was saying, her eyes bright with ambition. "If we can only determine the location—"

"The signs will become clear," Oracle Maeve interrupted. "When the time is right."

Gwyneth's heart ached at the familiar way Breag and Franwen exchanged glances, their shared excitement about capturing another's power.

Once, she would have joined their planning without question. Now, each passing day brought more doubts, more memories of Ingrid's warnings about the Sisterhood's growing hunger for control.

"I should consult my scrying bowl," she said, rising. "Perhaps I can divine more details about the vision's location."

She approached the Oracle with the traditional offering – a honeyed fig on a silver plate. As the old woman took it, her fingers brushed Gwyneth's wrist. "The past has ways of circling back to us," she murmured, too soft for the others to hear.

Gwyneth's steps echoed through the Clochar's corridors as she made her way back to her chambers. Behind her, she could still hear Breag and Franwen's voices rising and falling in heated debate.

Her own pulse quickened with each step, urgency building in her chest.

The Oracle's words about the past circling back struck too close to her heart. These past weeks, as her faith in the Sisterhood crumbled, memories of Ingrid had begun surfacing with increasing frequency – her wild laugh, her fearless questioning of authority, the way Ingrid had felt like home in a way nothing else ever had.

In her chamber, Gwyneth lit fresh candles and drew her heavy curtains against the afternoon light. Her hands trembled slightly as she began the motions of preparing for scrying, though she had no intention of looking for volcanoes. Instead, she reached out with her magic, feeling for the familiar presence of owls in the surrounding woods.

One responded immediately – she could feel its wings cutting through air, its keen eyes already turned toward her window. But she needed more than just a messenger. Settling cross-legged on her meditation cushion, Gwyneth closed her eyes and stretched her magical senses further, across the landscape toward Myrtlewood.

Towards Ingrid.

The connection between them had once been so strong she could find Ingrid anywhere, their souls resonating like perfectly tuned strings. Now, after decades of silence, reaching out felt like pressing on an old bruise – painful, but with an underlying sweetness she couldn't ignore.

The Sisterhood and the Order both had access to oracles, yet the Crones did not, which meant that even if the steps Ingrid and her friends took were leading towards the potential future Gwyneth had just learned of, they were at a disadvantage. Gwyneth could not tolerate it anymore.

All her years of loyalty to the Sisterhood, of believing in their higher purpose, had unravelled like a poorly wound spell. She thought of Mathilda, growing weaker each day, of the crystal's hungry light, of the Oracle's prophecy about the fire dragon.

Power calling to power, but at what cost?

15

CEDRIC

*C*edric's head pounded with roosters crowing somewhere far too close. Straw poked through his shirt, the scent of hay and horses overwhelming his already queasy stomach. For one terrifying moment, he thought he was back in the Order's stables, but no – the light was wrong, filtering through wooden slats in unfamiliar patterns.

Memory came in fragments: the pub's warmth, Sherry's kind smile as she poured his drinks, the old woman with the dragon pendant asking questions. Then talking, too much talking. About dragons and darkness and things he should have kept buried. His stomach lurched at the thought of what he might have revealed.

Heavy boots on wooden boards announced company. A tall, scarred man appeared – somehow familiar from the night before – carrying a steaming mug that smelled of herbs and whiskey.

"Hair of the dog," the man said gruffly, handing the mug over along with a hard bread bun. "You'll need it."

Cedric struggled to sit up, straw falling from his clothes.

The man – Covvey, that was his name – had the look of someone who understood being an outsider. Not like the Order, and not whatever passed for normal in this strange town. Someone who'd carved his own path.

"Why am I..." Cedric began, then winced at the sound of his own voice.

"Because you know too much about dragons," Covvey said simply. "And about the Order of Crimson. And you needed somewhere safe to sleep it off."

Cedric shivered, wondering what details he had already revealed.

The herbal-whiskey concoction burned Cedric's throat, but the warmth spread through him, easing both hangover and the constant tremor of fear he'd lived with since fleeing the Order. He tore into the bread – fresh-baked, still warm, nothing like the bland loaves of the compound.

"The Order will be looking for me," he said, though whether as warning or confession, he wasn't sure.

Covvey settled on an upturned bucket, his presence solid but undemanding. "They won't find you here. Myrtlewood has its protections."

Cedric laughed, a harsh sound that made his head throb. "Protections. Right. Everyone wants to protect something, usually while they're stealing power from someone else."

Images flashed through his mind: Benedict's rage, that

poor cursed beast in the depths...His fingers tightened around the mug.

"Sherry asked after you," Covvey said casually. "Wanted to make sure you were safe."

Something warm that had nothing to do with whiskey bloomed in Cedric's chest.

He remembered her smile, the way she'd listened without judgment as he'd rambled about dragons. But then his mind imagined other possibilities of those who'd use his words against him.

"Nothing's safe," he muttered. "Not really. Not anymore. The Shepherd's changing everything...And the Crones..." He stopped, suddenly uncertain how much he'd revealed last night.

"The Crones what?" Covvey's voice remained neutral, but something in his stance suggested personal interest.

Cedric took another sip of the healing brew, buying time. His head was clearing now, bringing with it sharper memories of his own conflicted loyalties.

"Everyone wants the dragons," he said finally. "Order, Sisterhood, Crones. They all think they know best how to use that power. But they don't understand what they're dealing with. I've seen it, down in the depths of the compound. The beast they keep chained...that was created by the dragons...it's horrible." He shuddered, remembering its cries echoing through stone corridors.

"Seen a lot, have you?" Covvey asked.

"Too much. Not enough." Cedric's laugh held no humour. "Everyone's choosing sides, making grand plans, and nobody sees how it's all..." He gestured vaguely, frustrated by his inability to articulate the wrongness he sensed.

The morning light brightened, dust motes dancing through hay-scented air. Something about this place, about Covvey's steady presence, made Cedric want to trust. But trust had betrayed him before.

"Sherry mentioned you're good with horses," Covvey said, changing tack. "Could use help here in the stables, if you're planning to stay."

The offer caught Cedric off guard. Simple work, honest work – when was the last time he'd done anything that didn't involve secrets and schemes?

"I...I shouldn't stay," he said, though the words felt hollow. "It's not safe..." He paused, trying to piece together his drunken revelations. "How much did I tell you?"

"Enough about dragons and betrayal to interest us," Covvey said. "Not enough to be especially useful."

Relief and anxiety warred in Cedric's gut.

"This town," he said, gesturing at the sunlit stable doors. "It feels...different. Like something real. Something true." He shook his head, immediately regretting the movement.

A horse nickered from a nearby stall reminding Cedric of the time he'd spent as a stable hand for the Order, growing up, before the glamour of books and parchment scrolls drew him away.

"The Shepherd's breaking everything," he found himself saying. "Not just rules or bindings but...reality itself. And the Sisterhood thinks they can control it, and the Crones..." He stopped, remembering the old woman's dragon pendant, the way it had hummed with power he recognised.

Cedric's mouth snapped shut, clarity cutting through his hangover haze. He was doing it again – talking too much, revealing too much. The healing brew had loosened his tongue just like the whiskey had. He stared into the mug, shoulders tensing.

"Anyway," he said stiffly, "it doesn't matter now."

Covvey seemed to sense the shift, adjusting his own stance to something less direct. "Must have been different, growing up in the Order. Always having people around."

"Always having purpose," Cedric corrected, on safer ground now. "Every day mapped out. Prayers, studies, training. Everyone working toward the same goal." He paused, remembering morning prayers to the Almighty, echoing through stone halls, the comfort of ritual. "Never alone, yet somehow always lonely."

"Belonging's not nothing," Covvey said quietly. "Pack life's similar in some ways. Knowing your place, having others you can rely on." His voice roughened. "In a good pack, anyway."

Something in his tone made Cedric look up. The big man was staring out the stable door, his expression distant.

"My mother took my sisters when I was young," Covvey continued, surprising them both perhaps. "Left me with my father and his...problems. Always wondered what was wrong with me, why I couldn't go too."

The words hung in the air between them, heavy with unspoken pain. Cedric recognised the tone – the same one he'd heard in his own voice when speaking of betrayal.

"Sometimes belonging's a trap," he said carefully. "Sometimes it's real. Hard to tell the difference until it's too late."

Covvey shifted uncomfortably on his bucket seat. "Don't know why I'm telling you this," he said gruffly. "Not something I usually talk about."

Cedric nodded, understanding the need for silence around old wounds. But Covvey continued, words coming slow and careful like approaching a spooked horse.

"Father got mixed up with a rough pack after she left. Lost touch with our culture, our ways. Everything became about power, dominance." He paused, jaw working. "Wasn't much of a childhood after that."

The morning light caught the scars on Covvey's face, telling their own story. Cedric thought of the Order's hierarchy, of Benedict's growing madness for control. Some patterns repeated everywhere.

"Ran away when I was sixteen," Covvey added. "Found work with a blacksmith who didn't ask questions. Learned to rely on myself." He stood abruptly, as if surprised by his own openness.

A sound at the door made Cedric tense – the distinct tap of cane on wood. His headache surged back.

"Well," Covvey said, gathering the empty mug. "It seems that we have a visitor..."

16

AGATHA

*A*gatha's cane pressed into damp earth as she made her way along the path to Covvey's farm, her steps lighter than usual despite the morning chill. The air dragon had finally spoken to her in her dreams – cryptic as ever, but present, real. Its voice still echoed in her mind like wind through ancient stones.

The morning dew caught early light, turning everyday fields into something magical. Rather like her friendship with Covvey, she mused. What had begun as mere acquaintance had deepened into something precious since the Order's threats had drawn them all closer. Strange, how crisis could forge such bonds.

She'd never been interested in romance of any sort, and still wasn't, but this easy companionship that had grown between them was welcome. No expectations, no complications, just the comfort of someone who understood.

She inhaled the scents of his farm: wood smoke, fresh bread, straw and horses, and underneath it all, that particular wild magic that clung to shapeshifters. Her pendant hummed softly, responding to the layered energies.

Covvey would have scented her coming, of course. Would have heard her steps, recognised her particular gait with those keen wolf senses of his. Which was why she felt no compunction about pausing when she heard voices from the stables.

The stranger – Cedric – sounded rough with hangover, but it was Covvey's voice that made her stop, her historian's heart quickening.

Standing motionless in the early morning light, Agatha strained to catch every word. In all their years of friendship, she'd hardly ever heard Covvey speak of his past like this. He'd told her little bits about his troubled past, and it explained so much about the man she'd known for decades. His fierce independence, his occasional awkwardness, the way he'd throw himself into protecting others while maintaining careful distance.

Her mind swam with possibilities as she thought of his long-lost mother, his sisters.

The town records went back centuries; surely there would be mention of his family.

The researcher in her couldn't resist a mystery, especially one that might help her friend understand his own story better.

Something in Covvey's voice spoke of wounds never properly healed. All these years, she'd respected his privacy, never pushing when he deflected personal questions. Now, hearing the pain still raw beneath his gruff exterior, she wondered if she should have pushed harder, sooner.

She waited until their conversation wound down before tapping her cane deliberately against the door. No point pretending she hadn't heard—Covvey would know exactly how long she'd been standing there.

"Morning," she called out, keeping her voice light despite the weight of revelation pressing against her chest. The stable's interior smelled of hay and horses and Covvey's healing brew – her recipe, she noted with satisfaction, though he'd added something of his own. Probably that bitter root he favoured.

Covvey met her eyes across the space. She saw the warning there, clear as daylight. Cedric was vulnerable. Unstable.

Cedric's harsh laugh cut through their moment of understanding like a blade. "Should have known," he spat from his hay bale, face twisted with bitterness. "Crones, always prying into everything. Think you have the right, don't you? With your magic and your self-righteous—"

"Now see here," Agatha started, her morning's good mood evaporating.

"No, you see here." Cedric struggled to his feet, swaying slightly. "I've seen what happens when women start poking around in things that don't concern them. Sisterhood, Crones – all the same. Manipulating, controlling, using magic to—"

"Enough." Covvey's voice cut through Cedric's rant. The air in the stables shifted.

But Agatha had already heard enough. The man was clearly still half-drunk, trauma-addled, and nowhere near ready for reasonable conversation. She'd learned long ago to pick her battles, and this one would have to wait.

"Right then," she said crisply, drawing herself up to her full height. "I'll leave you to your nursing duties, Covvey. But this conversation isn't over."

He nodded curtly.

As she turned to leave, her pendant hummed with renewed energy. The air dragon's presence brushed against her awareness, reminding her that some mysteries revealed themselves in their own time. Others needed a little help.

17

DELIA

The town hall was filled exuberant energy. After weeks of read-throughs, character work, and Ferg's incredibly detailed scheduling charts (colour-coded by scene, season, and relative magical intensity), they were finally bringing Ash's vision to life.

"Places for the Midwinter confrontation scene," Delia called, her director's voice settling into place like coming home. Ash, playing the Spring Maiden, stood centre stage, her whole being alight with the dual energy of writer and performer.

This was their story, their magic, and it showed in every gesture.

"Remember," Delia said, watching Sid take her position as the Cailleach, "this is where the balance begins to shift. Sam, your chorus represents the sleeping earth – subtle but essential." Sam nodded, clearly more comfortable being part of the ensemble than having all eyes on them.

Ferg adjusted his elaborate red and gold brocade coat, his ceremonial chains jingling importantly. "According to my research," he began, producing a thick folder from somewhere in his robes, "the traditional midwinter ceremony requires exactly seventeen ritual gestures—"

"Thank you," Delia said, trying not to roll her eyes.

"I've prepared extensive notes on the historical accuracy of each gesture," he began, producing a thick folder.

"Thank you, Ferg," Delia cut in smoothly. "Let's save those notes for after rehearsal. We have quite a lot to be getting on with for now. Sherry, are you ready for the opening invocation?"

As everyone took their places, Delia felt that familiar thrill of watching a production coalesce.

Delia had stepped into Cerridwen's role after much urging. Now, as the scene began, she felt real power stirring.

Their makeshift stage area – really just the cleared space between the hall's pillars – filled with focused energy as everyone took position.

"Within the depths of winter's reign," Ash began, her voice carrying both strength and vulnerability, "I feel the stirring of fire."

She moved with natural grace, each gesture embodying the awakening of spring. The connection between writer and character gave her performance an authenticity that made Delia's director's heart soar.

Sid stalked forward, her firefighter's presence lending

natural authority to Cailleach's power. "You are nothing but a dream of warmth," she challenged, frost seeming to form in the air around her. "Winter's grip cannot be broken."

The chorus, led by Sam with surprising resonance, began their low chant about cycles and seasons. Ferg's Herald role marked each pivotal moment with elaborate (if occasionally over-choreographed) ceremonial gestures.

Delia felt the power building as she stepped forward into Cerridwen's role. "The cauldron holds all wisdom," she intoned, feeling real fire magic stir beneath her skin. "Even winter's deepest secrets."

The air in the town hall shifted. When Ash confronted Sid's winter goddess, actual cold pressed against warm air, creating swirling patterns visible in the late afternoon light. As the Spring Maiden's defiance grew, tiny flowers seemed to bloom in impossible places – between floorboards, along windowsills, even in the folds of Ferg's elaborate robes.

"The land remembers," Ash declared, the words they'd written now charged with genuine power. "Beyond ice, beyond frost, beyond the longest night – the land remembers spring!"

Real magic surged through the performance, taking even Delia by surprise. As Cerridwen, she felt fire answering fire – her own power recognising something ancient in Ash's words, something that transcended mere theatre.

The chorus's voices rose, Sam finding confidence in the shelter of harmony. Frost patterns spiralled across windows as Sid's Cailleach raged against the changing season. But it was Ash who held the scene's centre, her Spring Maiden embodying both fragility and adamantine strength.

"The price of wisdom," Delia spoke Cerridwen's lines, feeling them resonate with truth, "is transformation."

"And I am ready to pay," Ash responded, her voice carrying all the authority of author and actor combined.

Green light emanated from her skin, while actual leaves stirred in a wind that couldn't exist inside the town hall.

Even Ferg forgot his precise choreography, caught up in the moment's power. His Herald became truly otherworldly.

The magic peaked as spring confronted winter. Sid's Cailleach thundered defiance while Ash's Spring Maiden stood unwavering, the chorus weaving harmony through their clash. For a moment, reality itself seemed to blur – winter and spring, theatre and magic, performance and truth all merging into something transcendent.

There came three, sharp claps from the doorway.

The spell broke. Magic settled back into mundane reality. Everyone turned toward the sound.

A figure leaned against the doorframe, one leg crossed elegantly over the other. The violet suit was perfection, the copper-framed cat-eye glasses pure theatre, and that knowing smile—

"Marcus?" Delia's voice cracked with surprise.

"Darling," he drawled, unfolding himself from his pose.

"What are you doing here?"

"What am I doing?" Marcus asked, as Delia rushed forward to hug her friend and former colleague. "I came to see what it is you're doing in this charming little..."

"You're here," said Delia, narrowing her eyes. Only magical beings seemed to be able to find Myrtlewood...

His umber skin seemed to glow in a way Delia had never noticed before, his deep brown eyes holding impossible depths. How had she worked with him for fifteen years and never seen the glamour? The distinctly otherworldly grace?

"I am," Marcus replied. "And what are you doing?"

"We're rehearsing," Delia said, suddenly defensive of her makeshift company. "This is Ash's play about—"

"About seasonal goddesses, yes, I heard." He waved an elegant hand dismissively, and Delia was glad the others were now out of earshot. "Derivative of course, but you managed to make it..." His perfect eyebrows rose. "Interesting."

The others were busy mulling around, debriefing on the remnants of their magical performance. Ferg appeared speechless, eyeing Marcus's suit with obvious envy from across the hall.

"Perhaps," Marcus said, "a drink or three is in order?"

THE PUB WAS quiet for a Thursday evening. Sherry, having rushed ahead after rehearsal, had a bottle of red breathing on their table – the good stuff she kept for special occasions. Marcus examined the glass with perfectly arched eyebrows before taking a surprisingly appreciative sip.

"Well," he said, "at least your exile has decent wine."

"It's not exile," Delia replied, though the word stung. "I chose to come here...at least I think I did."

"Darling." He leaned forward, those impossible eyes catching lamplight like scattered stars. "You ran away. Understandable, given Jerry's absolutely *criminal* behaviour, but really. Community theatre?" He paused delicately. "The West End misses you terribly, darling. And really, you can do so much better than..." He gestured around.

Delia looked closer at her friend. There was definitely something different about Marcus – something she should have noticed during all those years of choreographing West End shows together. The way light bent around him, the subtle shimmer in the air...

"You're fae," she said, the realisation clicking into place. She'd had very little experience with the fae, yet somehow this seemed obvious.

"And you're a witch." His smile widened. "How delicious. Though really, darling, you could be doing so much more with it. Your performance tonight – that was real power. Imagine what you could do on a proper stage, with proper backing. I've never seen you act before, other than pretending to enjoy Jerry's company of course!"

"Marcus..."

"The Midnight Court would adore you. That's what we're calling ourselves now. We could mount a production that would make your little seasonal pageant look like a primary school nativity."

"The Midnight Court?" Delia took a long sip of wine. "That sounds very fae."

"You sound surprised."

Delia shook her head. "I'm still new to all this. Though I suppose...your magic explains all those impossibly perfect productions you choreographed. The ones where audiences left feeling like they'd dreamed the whole thing."

"Because they had, darling." He preened slightly. "Though your little show today...there was something rather raw about it. Unpolished, of course, but that moment when spring confronted winter..." He shivered theatrically. "The magic was quite real."

"It's Ash's writing," Delia said firmly. "And Sid's presence, and Sam's growing confidence, and even Ferg's...ridiculous ceremonial gestures. They're creating something honest."

"Honest?" Marcus laughed, the sound like silver bells. "Oh my dear, when has theatre ever been about honesty? It's about transformation, about glamour, about making people believe the impossible." He leaned forward, dropping his voice. "Which is exactly what you could do with us. Imagine it – productions that literally transport audiences to other realms. Magic and theatre becoming one."

The offer tugged at something in Delia's heart. She thought of many vibrant opening nights, of standing ovations and critical acclaim. But then she remembered today's rehearsal – the genuine wonder in Sam's eyes, the way Ash's words had called to something ancient and true, the real magic that had nothing to do with pomposity.

"I'm not ready," she said softly. "Maybe I'll never be ready for that kind of theatre again. Here, I'm..."

"Darling," Marcus sighed, swirling his wine with perfect

theatrical timing. "You're wasting your fire on village hall acoustics and people who think brocade is suitable for *any* occasion."

Delia snorted into her glass. "Says the man wearing a violet suit that probably cost more than my monthly rent."

"The difference, my dear, is that *I* can pull it off." His grin was infectious. "Though I must admit, watching those ceremonial gestures was rather like seeing a peacock attempt synchronised swimming."

"Stop it!" But she was laughing now, remembering countless backstage moments just like this, Marcus's cutting observations always laced with just enough warmth to take the sting out.

He reached across the table, catching her hand. The glamour around him softened slightly, showing something ancient and knowing in his eyes.

"Maybe you're not ready," he conceded. "But you will be one day. You're a firecracker, Delia, and you need to light up the whole sky."

"Is that right?" Delia said, humouring him.

"I've known that as long as I've known you," Marcus continued. "You've poured all that talent into other people, but one day, you're going to be ready and brave enough to shine again. It's going to be absolutely fabulous."

The words settled around her like a well-made stage costume. She squeezed his hand. "And when that day comes, you'll what – whisk me away to dance with the fae?"

"Darling," he drawled, his perfect eyebrows arching again, "you know I'm always down for a good dance party."

18

MARJIE

*R*ose petals and lavender lay scattered across Thorn Manor's kitchen table as Marjie worked, the dragon stone gleaming stubbornly silent before her. Evening light filtered through herb-hung windows, catching dust motes and magical residue from her latest failed attempts at connection.

She'd tried everything – water scrying, emotional resonance spells, even singing the old songs of the sea her grandmother had taught her. The stone remained beautiful but inert, its blue depths holding secrets she couldn't quite reach.

With a sigh, she reached for her basket of magical supplies. Her fingers found the spool of enchanted twine she used for binding spells – deep blue, almost the same shade as the stone. Working by feel as much as sight, she began weaving an intricate pattern around the stone's edges.

Over, under, through – the familiar movements soothed her frustration. She hummed quietly as she worked, letting her empathy flow into the weaving. The kitchen filled with the scent of her magic – sea salt and rose petals, comfort and healing. By the time she finished, the stone hung from a net of delicate knotwork that somehow enhanced its natural beauty.

Slipping it over her head, she felt the stone settle against her heart. Something about it felt right, as if it had been waiting for this. Still, connecting with its power remained elusive, and her attempts had left her drained.

"Bath time," she muttered to herself. "Everything looks better after a good soak."

The old claw-foot tub in Thorn Manor's main bathroom was one of Marjie's favourite places. She'd added her own touches over time – shelves of bath salts and oils, crystals arranged on the windowsill to catch moonlight. Tonight she chose her special rose bath salts.

Steam rose in lazy spirals as she sank into the hot water, the stone still hanging around her neck. The bathroom filled with the scent of roses and salt air, ocean depths...possibilities. She closed her eyes, letting the warmth seep into tired muscles, feeling her empathic shields soften in the safety of solitude.

The first hint that something was different came as a subtle shift in the water's movement. Then a presence brushed against her magical awareness – ancient, vast, wise beyond imagining. Marjie's eyes flew open.

The water dragon filled the tub, its form somehow both there and not there, like seafoam caught in moonlight. Its long body curved through water that had become deeper than physically possible, scales shimmering with every colour she'd ever seen in the ocean. Eyes of impossible blue – the same blue as her stone – met hers with gentle amusement.

"Oh!" Marjie managed, her heart racing. "I didn't expect —I mean, I've been trying to—"

Sometimes, a voice like waves on distant shores whispered in her mind, *the deepest connections come when we stop trying so hard.*

The dragon's presence filled the room with something beyond magic – a deep knowing that reminded Marjie of sitting by the ocean, feeling all of life's emotions flow like tides. Its form shifted constantly, now like morning mist over water.

You feel everything, the dragon observed, its voice carrying currents of understanding. *Like water, you reflect what flows through you. Like water, you can learn to float in it, rather than drowning. Let it flow through you. Allow.*

"Sometimes it's overwhelming," Marjie admitted, her empathic nature resonating with the dragon's energy. "All their feelings, their hopes, their pain..."

Yet you stay open. The dragon's form rippled with approval. *Like the ocean that remains vast enough to hold every storm and still find calm beneath.*

Joy bubbled up in Marjie's chest. This was nothing like

she'd imagined – it was better, deeper, as if she'd found a teacher who understood parts of herself she'd never been able to explain to anyone.

"I've been trying so hard to reach you through the stone," she said, touching the pendant that now pulsed with gentle light. "But that's not right, is it? Water needs to flow."

The dragon's laugh felt like summer rain. *Clever one. Yes. Connection need not mean trying so hard. Water finds its own level, its own way.*

Steam curled around them like sea mist as the dragon's form shifted again, becoming something like moonlight on waves. Marjie felt her natural empathy expanding, touching emotions deeper than human feeling – the ancient patience of coral reefs, the wild joy of dolphins, the vast knowing of whales singing in the deep.

Your gift is rare, the dragon observed. *You flow like water.*

"Not always gracefully," Marjie laughed softly. "Sometimes I feel like I'm drowning in everyone else's feelings."

The ocean fights those who fight it, came the response. *But cradles those who learn to float. Watch how water moves – it does not waste energy breaking rocks, but smooths them over time. It does not fight the moon's pull, but dances with it.*

The bathroom had become something impossible – both the familiar space she knew and somewhere else entirely. Through the window, she could have sworn she saw bioluminescent creatures drifting in dark water instead of the manor's garden.

"I could create an amulet to hold the stone," Marjie

mused, her mind flowing with possibilities. "With moon-blessed water and shells that have known the tide's song. Something that echoes the ocean's rhythms...allow you to access your magic that way."

Yes. The dragon's approval felt like warm currents. *A dwelling that remembers freedom. A space between spaces, like the shore itself – neither fully water nor fully land.*

As they spoke, Marjie noticed the water never grew cold, somehow maintaining perfect warmth despite the bathroom's usual tendency to chill quickly. The dragon's form continued its mesmerising shifts, now like deep sea currents, now like morning mist, never quite the same twice.

Your friends carry much pain, the dragon observed suddenly. *The fire one especially burns with it, though she hides it well.*

"Delia." Marjie nodded. "Yes, and her daughter..." She paused, something occurring to her. "You can sense them all, can't you? Through the water in their bodies, their tears, their blood..."

The dragon's presence rippled with something like amusement, but also ancient concern. *All things flow together in time. The changes coming to Myrtlewood...some currents run deeper than others.*

Marjie sat up straighter, sending small waves against the tub's sides. "What do you mean?"

But the dragon was already fading, its form becoming indistinguishable from the bath water. *Create your amulet,* its voice came like the whisper of distant surf. *We will speak again when the tide is right.*

The bathroom returned to normal – or almost normal. The water held a peculiar luminescence, and Marjie could have sworn she smelled sea. Her mind raced with plans for the amulet, but also with questions about the dragon's cryptic words.

19

DELIA

*M*arjie's tea shop smelled of lavender shortbread and possibility. Delia sat with Kitty at her favourite corner table, grateful for a few moments of peace since Una and Ashwyn had taken the children to the park. After the morning's chaos – Merryn accidentally turning all the toast blue, Keyne having an argument with Torin about proper beagle etiquette – the quiet felt luxurious.

"The pamphlet says Gillian should avoid any sunlight for at least the first century," Delia said, frowning at the glossy brochure titled 'So Your Loved One Is Undead: A Family Guide to Vampiric Transition.' "Though apparently some vampires develop resistance to indirect light over time. There's a whole section on sunscreen options."

Kitty stirred her coffee. "At least she won't have to worry

about aging. Though I suppose that's covered in the part on 'Eternal Youth: Blessing or Curse?'"

Kitty had been enthralled by the pamphlet earlier in the day, crowing with laughter over the subheadings.

"Right after 'Blood Types: A Nutritional Guide' and before 'Dating Tips for the Recently Deceased.'" Delia reached for a scone. "I can't believe there's actual vampire bureaucracy for this sort of—"

The bell at the back of the tea shop chimed. A figure in a startlingly bright cornflower blue suit entered from what appeared to be a storeroom, carrying what appeared to be...

"Are those plastic peonies?" Delia whispered, her director's eye automatically cataloguing everything wrong with his outfit. The suit looked like something from a community production where the costume budget had run out halfway through.

"Roger!" Kitty brightened. "You found us!"

"As if I could stay away, doll." His accent was pure 1950s cinema. He presented the artificial flowers with a flourish. "Permanent beauty for a timeless dame."

Delia blinked at him, noting his slicked back Elvis-styled hair. "Why did you come in from the back? And how exactly did you find Myrtlewood?" she asked, unable to keep suspicion from her voice. She'd been here long enough to know that ordinary people didn't just stumble upon this place.

"Oh, I told him good luck finding us," Kitty said, eyeing the peonies warily. "Didn't think he actually would."

Roger smoothed back his brilliantined hair. Everything about him screamed mid-century modern, from his wing-tipped shoes to his carefully maintained quiff. He even smelled vintage – like pomade and old movie theatres.

"A real cool cat always finds his kitten," he said, sliding into the chair beside Kitty. "Always thought this town was a real gas."

Delia caught Marjie watching from behind the counter. As if on cue, she approached their table with a fresh pot of Earl Grey and a knowing look.

"Are you going to tell them?" Marjie asked Roger directly.

"I...I don't know what you mean," he said, suddenly fascinated by the tea shop's decorative doilies.

Marjie simply stood there, radiating that particular quiet authority that made even the most difficult customers confess to stealing spoons.

"Oh, man," Roger sighed, running a hand through his perfect hair. "The jig is up, kitten. I'm...well, I'm not exactly current, if you catch my drift."

"You're..." Delia began.

"A vampire," Roger admitted, fiddling with his period-perfect cufflinks. "As of 1959. Got turned at a mod do. Quite the scene, I tell you what."

Delia's fingers tightened around her teacup. Another vampire. Just when she'd started getting her head around Gillian's transformation, here was this walking anachronism with his plastic flowers and dated slang, pursuing her best friend.

"The plastic flowers," he rushed to explain, seeing their expressions. "They were all the rage back then – permanent beauty..." He grinned, showing just a hint of fang. "Plastic's immortal, baby. Just like my feelings for your friend here."

"Smooth talker," Kitty said, but she was smiling.

Trust Kitty to take a vampire suitor in stride.

Delia shook her head and pulled out her pamphlet again. "It says here that vampires often fixate on the era of their turning. Though usually it can fade after the first few hundred years."

"Some of us are just naturally retro." Roger winked. "Say, kitten, I've been meaning to ask – you must be some kind of witch, right? No ordinary dame finds her way to a magical hotspot like this."

"Oh, I'm perfectly ordinary." Kitty laughed.

"Not buying it, sweetheart. You're far too amazing to be mundane."

"Well, I am fabulous," Kitty conceded. "But I don't think that makes me magical. That's all Delia."

"Is there a test for that sort of thing?" Delia asked Marjie.

Marjie tilted her head, considering. "Of course there is, though I never thought to check...actually." She disappeared behind the counter and returned with a polished silver bowl of water. "May I?"

The tea shop was quiet except for the gentle bubbling of kettles and the distant chime of wind bells. Even Roger sat still, his usual fidgeting with decade-appropriate accessories momentarily forgotten.

"Well, this is dramatic," Kitty said, but Delia caught the slight tremor in her voice.

Marjie added three drops of something that smelled like

roses and liquorice. The surface rippled without being touched.

"Oh!" she exclaimed softly. "Oh my."

Delia leaned forward, protective instincts flaring. The pamphlet about vampire family members crinkled in her pocket, reminding her how quickly the magical world could complicate ordinary lives. Not that Kitty had ever been ordinary – she'd taken both theatre disasters and magical revelations with equal aplomb.

"What do you see?" Roger asked, his dated accent slipping slightly with genuine concern.

"Druid lines," Marjie murmured, "and something older. Mage blood, definitely, but there's something else...something not quite..." She squinted at the water. "It's like looking at a collage."

"Wonder of wonders," Kitty said softly. "And yet here I am without enough magic to float a teaspoon."

Marjie shook her head. "Some people never learn to use magic actively," she said gently. "Like our wonderful Detective Neve – from here and with so much strength. She has the heritage for it, but it just never came through."

"Maybe I'm a dud," Kitty said, nonchalant.

Delia looked at her oldest friend as if through new eyes. "You've always been magical to me." How many times had Kitty simply *known* things? How often had her practical solutions bordered on magical? "Maybe that's why we were drawn to each other," she said.

Kitty giggled. "That and our amazing senses of humour."

Roger began whispering in Kitty's ear exactly how magical he thought she was.

Delia tried not to listen. Instead, she flipped through the pamphlet, for distraction.

The section on 'Integrating Into Magical Communities: A Guide for the Recently Transformed' seemed less relevant now that apparently everyone she knew had some connection to magic.

"I could try to teach you some basics," Marjie said to Kitty, moments later as she returned with a tray of freshly baked scones. "Though I'm not sure what tradition would suit you best. There's something mercurial about your magical signature."

"Let's not get ahead of ourselves," Kitty said practically. "I have plenty to be getting on with!"

"I'll keep you busy," Roger said quickly, standing with that peculiar grace that Delia now recognised as vampiric. His blue suit caught the afternoon light oddly, as if it existed slightly out of time with everything around it.

"Those flowers really are something," Delia muttered, but she caught the genuine warmth in Kitty's smile as she tucked them into her bag.

"She'll be fine," Marjie said, reading Delia's concern. "Some people take to magic like..." She paused.

"Like vampires to plastic peonies?" They both laughed, but Delia's eyes strayed to the scrying bowl, where the water still moved in strange patterns.

"You're something special, Kitty Hatton," said Roger, and Delia had to agree.

"Absolutely fabulous, not mundane at all," Kitty agreed. "Though I always thought that was just my sparkling personality."

Delia pointed to the pamphlet. "So you got stuck in your turning era like it says here. Explains the James Dean routine."

"Hey now, daddy-o," Roger protested, straightening his already knife-creased trousers. "Dean was a square compared to yours truly. I was more of a..." He caught their expressions and deflated slightly. "Okay, maybe I do overdo the fifties bit. But you try staying current for seventy years. Fashion's exhausting."

"Unlike plastic flowers, which are eternal," Delia said dryly. Still, something about Roger's too-perfect period performance set her theatre-trained instincts tingling.

Marjie had glanced back at the scrying bowl. "There's definitely some Irish blood here," she mused. "Old magic. And something else...something that almost looks like..." She trailed off, frowning.

"Like what?" Kitty asked.

"I'm not sure. It's like the magic itself is playing hide and seek."

Delia thought about her own journey of magical discovery, about Gillian's transformation, about how many secrets Myrtlewood seemed to harbour.

20

DECLAN

*L*ong shadows stretched through the forest as Declan foraged for wild food. He thought of how he'd explained his foraging techniques to Delia's grandchildren. His awareness of her remained constant – a warm pulse in his consciousness that somehow made his life feel more like gift than curse.

A twig snapped deliberately. Declan's magic surged, centuries of survival instinct rising, but the wolf that emerged from the shadows carried a familiar signature. Its fur held hints of silver that matched the human form's scars. Moments later, Covvey stood there, looking ruffled.

"Need your counsel," Covvey said. "Got a situation."

"Most people start with hello," came a drawling voice from above. Both men looked up to see a sleek black cat draped across a branch, tail swishing with obvious amusement.

"Demon," Declan acknowledged, recognising ancient power when he saw it. The cat's eyes held centuries of secrets.

"What gave it away? The devastating charm? The excellent posture?" The cat stretched languorously. "Though I must say, it's refreshing to be understood by someone other than those delightful crones. Perhaps you gentlemen are honorary members? The testosterone division, as it were? Mephistos is the name, by the way."

"Is the cat always like this?" Declan asked Covvey.

"Unfortunately," Covvey growled. "Agatha complains about him. But we've got bigger problems."

Damp earth and pine needles cushioned their steps as they followed Covvey through the darkening forest.

Mephistos kept pace above them, leaping from branch to branch with supernatural grace while maintaining a running commentary on their "charming but provincial" surroundings.

The herbs in Declan's pouch released their scents with each step – wild chives, thyme, and something older that only grew in magical soil for which he'd long forgotten the name.

His awareness of Delia flickered warmly at the edge of his consciousness, like a hearth fire in a distant window.

"We have a new friend. He's from the Order."

Declan's posture stiffened. "How is he here? Have the protections fallen?"

"He's left them, according to him. Was drunk down at the pub raving about dragons," Covvey said, ducking under a low branch. "Started with mundane complaints about his hangover, then shifted to darker stuff. Order conditioning running deep."

"Deeper than he knows," Mephistos added. "I've seen it before. The Order does love their mental manipulation. Almost as much as they love those dreary red robes. Absolutely no sense of style."

"Papa Jack's with him now," Covvey continued. "Something about the man's presence seemed to help."

THEY EMERGED from the treeline to see Covvey's farm. Even from here, they could hear Cedric's voice raised in desperate protest: "They'll corrupt everything! Women and their magic, twisting the natural order—"

"Charming," Mephistos drawled. "I do so love a man with opinions."

The door creaked open to reveal Papa Jack seated on an upturned bucket, whittling a piece of pine. "Brought the cavalry, did you?"

Cedric thrashed in the hay, sweat darkening his shirt despite the evening chill. "The Shepherd knows! The Shepherd sees all! We can't trust them, can't trust any of them—"

"Yes, yes," Mephistos said, settling onto a roof beam. "Women are terrifying with their opinions and their magic. I'm sure the Shepherd has a lovely manifesto about it all. Probably written in blood with terrible punctuation."

"You!" Cedric said, pointing at Declan. "Tracker!"

Declan nodded but didn't speak. He'd only ever known the man as the Cleric of the Order of Crimson, but now he was different. Declan studied Cedric's energy field, recognising the magical residue of long-term conditioning that was slowly being broken. Similar to curse magic, but more insidious.

"Here." Papa Jack produced a large thermos. "Hot chocolate. My recipe."

"Chocolate won't fix all our problems," Covvey muttered, but accepted a steaming cup.

"No," Papa Jack agreed, "but it might help us think clearer. Even you, cat. There's cream in it."

Declan watched Cedric's struggles subside slightly as Papa Jack approached with a cup. The old man's gentle presence seemed to cut through the panic, though whether that was natural empathy or something magical, Declan couldn't quite tell.

"The women," Cedric muttered, but with less venom. "They'll take everything, change everything..."

"Change comes anyway, son," Papa Jack said softly. "Fighting it's like fighting the tide. Here, drink this. Chocolate is good for a troubled soul."

Covvey's eyebrows rose, but he said nothing, just watched Cedric's trembling hands wrap around the cup.

"You can't trust what you've been taught," Declan said slowly. "The Order has had so much control over your mind, but that kind of power thrives on isolation, on making you think you're alone with their truth. But here we are – a cursed immortal, a lone wolf, an old man who knows too much, and a..."

"Devastatingly handsome demon cat," Mephistos supplied.

"...all outside their control, and we can help you."

Cedric's eyes cleared slightly. "But the Almighty was everything – I've lost everything. Shepherd says—"

"It sounds to me like the Shepherd says a lot of things," Papa Jack cut in, his voice gentle but firm. "Most of them nonsense. More chocolate?"

21

DELIA

The Bracewell mansion seemed to burst from the twilight like something out of Delia's more ambitious theatrical productions – soaring gothic towers and windows that caught the light. Her modest car looked decidedly out of place.

Carved stone dragons wound around massive pillars, their eyes following visitors with unsettling attention to detail. The whole place radiated old money and older magic, the kind that had been accumulating since well before indoor plumbing was available.

"Well," Kitty whispered, "this isn't terrifying at all. Rather like that experimental production of Macbeth where the castle was actually trying to eat people."

"At least that was just special effects," Delia muttered.

"It's certainly impressive," Marjie said. "I knew the

Bracewells were powerful. The magical signatures here are fascinating. The protection spells alone must be—"

"Not helping," said Delia, reaching up towards the large brass handle that looked like a goblin.

The door swung open before she could reach for the knocker, revealing a butler who might as well have been storing disapproval since the Victorian era. He looked down his nose at them with the air of someone discovering mould in the wine cellar.

"Ms Spark." He managed to make her name sound like a personal insult. His gaze swept over Marjie and Kitty with magnificent disdain. "And...guests."

The entry hall beyond him soared up three stories, crowned by a crystal chandelier that scattered light across marble floors. Gilt-framed portraits of stern-faced ancestors stared down at them, probably judging their lack of proper magical breeding. The air smelled of inherited wealth, with an underlying crackle of old magic that made Delia's powers spark in response.

Elamina appeared, descending the sweeping staircase, resplendent in a silver gown that matched her hair.

"How lovely of you to come at such short notice," Elamina said, each word precisely placed.

"Thank you for having us," said Delia as they moved through to the drawing room. "I hope your new year is off to a good start." A sharp sound drew Delia's attention.

Sabrina Bracewell sat in a high-backed chair that could have doubled as a throne, her silver hair arranged in perfect waves, her aged face set in lines of careful politeness that didn't reach her eyes.

"Aunt Sabrina prefers the old ways," Elamina said smoothly. "The traditional calendar marks the year's end at Samhain, of course, right through to the solstice. By this time the year is well and truly underway."

"Of course," Delia replied, catching Marjie's warning glance. The tension in the room crackled.

The butler announced the entrance of Ada and Warkworth Bracewell who emerged from a side door like winter personified – all sharp edges and perfect posture.

"Mamma, Pappa," Elamina said, offering them polite air kisses.

"So," Ada said, her voice carrying the weight of carefully curated breeding, "this is our...cousin."

The way she paused before "cousin" suggested both "questionable" and "regrettable" without actually voicing either.

Delia felt Marjie and Kitty step closer, a united front against the waves of calculated superiority rolling off the Bracewells.

This wasn't just a family dinner. This was a performance, and everyone had their carefully rehearsed parts.

She just wished she knew what play they were actually in.

"Dinner is ready to be served," the butler announced.

Delia, Kitty, and Marjie followed the Bracewells into an enormous dining room that could have fit her entire cottage inside it.

"The table settings are rather lovely," Marjie said brightly, examining the elaborate array of silverware with what appeared to be genuine interest. "Is that the original Winterwood pattern? I've only ever seen it in books."

Ada's perfect eyebrows rose fractionally. "You know your magical silverware."

"Among other things." Marjie smiled, taking her seat with comfortable ease that made Delia envious. Marjie had history with the Bracewells. Her mother worked for them at one point and had been treated badly, but she'd set her reservations aside in order to appear friendly. They either needed to convince this family to hand over the grimoire or find a way to steal it from them. Either way, lowering their guard would be helpful.

Kitty, settled between two particularly judgmental-looking portraits, leaned close to whisper, "I don't suppose you brought a flask? I'm feeling the need for something stronger than wine."

Delia shook her head. "I told you it wouldn't be any fun," she whispered back.

Sabrina sat at the head of the table like a queen holding court, her aged hands arranged just so on the perfectly starched tablecloth. There was something unsettling about her carefully pleasant expression – like watching an actor hit all the right marks while completely missing the emotional truth of the scene.

"You know," she said, fixing Delia with sharp eyes that belied her years, "you do remind me of dear aunt Etty. Something about the way you hold yourself. Though she had rather more...experience with her magic, of course."

The temperature in the room plummeted. Elamina's hand paused fractionally as she reached for her wine glass.

"Did you know her well?" Delia asked, watching the ripples of reaction around the table.

"Oh yes." Sabrina's smile didn't waver. "Such a tragedy, that fire. I was quite young at the time, but one doesn't forget such things."

Marjie's foot found Delia's under the table – a warning or reassurance, she wasn't sure which.

The first course arrived, carried by servants who moved with suspicious synchronisation.

"Mother always said Etty was careless with her power," Ada commented, examining her soup with practiced disinterest. "Though of course, that's what happens when natural talent isn't properly trained."

"I'm going to need more wine," Kitty muttered. A footman obliged.

Delia felt her own magic spark in response to the implied insult.

The leek and walnut soup was over-wrought and expensive tasting, like everything else about the Bracewells. Too much cream. Not enough acidity to cut through the richness.

"Your grandmother," Sabrina continued, watching Delia over the rim of her second glass of wine, "never did understand the responsibilities that came with her power. Such a waste, really. All that raw talent, no refinement."

"I've heard Etty was one of the most powerful fire witches of her generation," Delia said defensively.

"Power without proper training and direction is meaningless." Sabrina's aged face settled into lines of practiced disappointment. "The fire crone magic should have gone to someone who understood its true worth. Someone with the right...ambitions."

"Someone like you?" The words came out sharper than Delia intended.

"I was rather young at the time," Sabrina said, something flickering behind her careful smile. "Only in my twenties... But yes, the power should have stayed with those who knew how to use it properly."

A servant appeared with a crystal decanter. The wine inside caught the light strangely, shimmering with colours.

"Our special reserve," Sabrina said. "Perfect for...family reconciliation."

Marjie's foot found Delia's under the table – a clear warning. But Delia hardly noticed. Something in Sabrina's tone, that casual dismissal of her grandmother's worth, had ignited a fury that had been building all evening.

"Is that why you've been deleting records?" Delia asked, having given up all attempts at playing nice. "Trying to hide what really happened that night?"

The floral table centrepiece burst into sudden flames, reflecting Delia's fury. Around it, roses wilted and fine linen smouldered.

"Really?!" Sabrina extinguished the fire with a dismissive

wave. "Such a childish display. This is exactly why the power should never have gone to your line. No control, no finesse."

Sabrina's laugh was unexpected – a sound like breaking crystal. "Oh, you foolish girl. You think I killed your grandmother?"

Delia stood up from the table, hands trembling as she pointed at Sabrina. "The evidence—"

"I deleted those records to protect my mother's memory," Sabrina said, setting down her wine glass with careful precision. "Poor, brilliant Thero Bracewell was so much more talented than her silly sister, Etty. She couldn't bear it, you see – watching her sister's magic flourish while she had to make do without the legacy of the Crone's power. She always knew her line should have inherited that power."

The room went absolutely still. Marjie cleared her throat loudly, trying to catch Delia's eye.

"It was all Mother's idea," Sabrina continued, something like pride mixing with the bitterness in her voice. "The herbs, the ritual, the careful planning."

"So the family did kill Etty!" Delia said.

Sabrina shook her head. "Nothing so dramatic. We weren't trying to kill her, you must understand. Just subdue her, alter the magical bloodlines. But Etty..." She laughed again, shorter this time. "That stubborn witch burst into flames as if to spite us. All that power, lost to pure defiance."

Delia pushed herself up from her chair, furious and ready to protest.

"Do sit down," Ada said icily. "You're making a scene."

"Oh, I'll show you a scene." Kitty waved her wine glass in the air. "I know how to make a scene."

Delia reached for her own wine glass, hands shaking with rage, but Marjie knocked it violently aside. The crystal shattered on the marble floor, liquid spreading in unnaturally iridescent patterns.

"Poison!" Marjie's voice rang through the dining room.

Delia glared daggers at Sabrina. "You were really going to do it again!"

"You absolute monsters." Kitty stood, throwing her napkin down. "Killing your own sister, and now trying to murder your cousin at dinner? Were you planning to set Delia on fire too, or was that just a bonus last time?"

"None of you are leaving," Sabrina announced. "Not until we resolve this...unfortunate situation. The fire crone magic will finally go where it belongs."

"I don't think so," Marjie said quietly. She raised her hands, and suddenly every liquid in the room – wine in glasses, water in pitchers, soup in bowls, even the condensation on the windows – began to rise. The droplets caught the chandelier light, suspended in the air.

"What are you—" Sabrina started.

Marjie flicked her wrists. The liquid exploded into steam, filling the enormous dining room with a hot, disorienting mist. The fine silverware rattled as Bracewell magic clashed with Marjie's power.

Through the chaos, Delia caught glimpses of the family – Sabrina's face contorted with rage, Ada's perfect composure finally cracking, Elamina watching with that same unreadable expression.

Through the swirling steam, Marjie was already digging in her handbag – the sensible one that always contained exactly what they needed in a crisis. She pulled out what looked like a small silver disk engraved with spiralling patterns.

"Cover your eyes!" she called, hurling it at the nearest wall. The disk hit the window and exploded in a blast of blue-white light. When the glare faded, an arched doorway appeared in place of the windows.

"Now!" Marjie grabbed Delia's arm. Steam billowed around them as they ran, their feet sliding on the marble floor. Behind them, Sabrina's voice rose in fury, but her words were lost in the chaos.

As they burst through the magical doorway, into crisp night air, stairs descended down to the perfectly manicured Bracewell gardens which stretched before them, lit by elaborate magical lanterns that cast strange shadows across topiary dragons and enchanted roses.

The three women sprinted across wet grass, evening gowns hiked up, feet slipping on dew-soaked earth. Steam still poured from the mansion's windows, but angry voices and running feet were getting closer.

"I can't believe," Kitty panted as they ran, "they tried to poison you! At dinner! How monumentally rude!"

"Less commentary," Marjie suggested, "more running!"

They didn't stop running until they reached Delia's car.

They piled in, Kitty practically climbing over the seats in her haste.

"Go, go, go!" she urged, though Delia's foot was already on the accelerator.

They roared away from the mansion, its gothic towers looming behind them like accusations. For several minutes, no one spoke.

Finally, when the Bracewell estate had faded into darkness behind them, Kitty started laughing. It was the slightly hysterical laugh of someone who'd just escaped death by dinner party.

"Did you see their faces?" she gasped between giggles. "When Marjie turned everything to steam? Priceless! Worth getting poisoned for...Almost."

"I wasn't actually poisoned," Delia reminded her, though she was fighting back her own slightly manic laughter.

"Thanks to me," Marjie said primly, but her eyes sparkled with leftover adrenaline. "Though I must say, that was some of the finest steam-work I've ever done. The timing on the condensation alone..."

They were all giddy with escape, terror transmuting into exhilaration. But underneath their laughter lay darker currents – the truth about Etty's death, the knowledge that Sabrina wouldn't stop trying to claim what she saw as her birthright.

"Well," Kitty said finally, smoothing her steam-dampened dress, "I suppose that's one way to end a family dinner."

"Next time," Delia suggested as they turned onto the road home, "let's just order takeaway."

22

INGRID

*I*ngrid's cottage smelled of earth magic and evening shadows, herbs hanging in practiced disorder from every beam. She sat in her favourite chair by the perpetual fire, turning Gwyneth's message over in her hands. The owl feather lay on the table beside her tea, bright white against dark wood.

Memory rose like mist – young love in herb gardens, stolen kisses in hidden alcoves, promises whispered under stars. Then later: that sense of betrayal. Gwyneth had chosen the Clochar over her.

"Stop that," Ingrid told herself sharply. "You're too old for wallowing."

The earth dragon-pup whined softly, sensing her turmoil. Ingrid stroked her ears.

The feelings persisted, complex as tree roots. She'd spent decades building walls against this particular pain, crafting sharp wit and sharper boundaries. But now, with Gwyneth reaching out after so long, with talk of crystals and corruption...and Mathilda.

The fire crackled, sending shadows dancing. Ingrid watched them, remembering what the earth had taught her about cycles and seasons. Everything returned to soil eventually. Every death fed new life. Even pain could be composted into wisdom, if you weren't afraid to get your hands dirty in the process.

"Nothing grows without breaking down first," she muttered, earning an agreeing yip from the pup. "Old leaves must rot to feed new saplings. Old pain needs the same treatment."

"Well, this is thoroughly inconvenient," Ingrid announced to her cottage at large. "Here I was, perfectly settled into my comfortable animosity, and now I have to be *mature* about it."

The earth dragon-pup wagged her tail.

"Don't look so pleased," Ingrid scolded. "Some of us prefer our grudges well-aged, like fine wine. Or cheese."

But wisdom, like roots, grew deeper than comfort. The earth itself had taught her that transformation required both death and rebirth, that nothing new could grow from ground that hadn't been broken. She'd spent years teaching others this truth while carefully avoiding its application to her own heart.

"Suppose I can't very well lecture other witches about facing their fears if I won't face my own," she grumbled, gathering her cloak. "Though I'd like it noted that I'm doing this under protest."

The forest path to the sacred pool lay thick with autumn leaves. Each step released scents of decay and renewal – nature's endless cycle of letting go and becoming. The earth dragon-pup bounded ahead, occasionally startling squirrels who clearly knew better than to believe its innocent disguise.

"At least someone's enjoying this," Ingrid muttered.

The pool lay in the forest's heart, where earth's wisdom ran deep.

"Of course she'd choose now to reach out," Ingrid muttered, watching ice melt from bare branches outside her window. "End of winter, when everything's mud and mess and uncertain weather...after all these years. Very symbolic. Very *Gwyneth*."

The forest path squished unpleasantly underfoot. Bare branches dripped overhead, catching the evening light like scattered jewels.

The earth dragon-pup bounded ahead, crashing through icy mud with glee.

"Show-off," Ingrid muttered, picking her way around a particularly treacherous puddle.

The journey itself was teaching her something, as the earth always did. Everything was in transition – ice becoming water, dead leaves revealing new growth beneath, last season's certainties giving way to possibility.

"Like my heart isn't muddy enough without all these metaphors," she told a nearby oak. The tree, having known her for decades, simply dropped another load of melting snow near her feet. "Oh, very helpful. Thank you for that wisdom."

The sacred pool lay ahead, partially iced over but with clear dark water at its centre.

The earth dragon-pup circled the edges, sniffing at places where the ice was thinnest, where transformation was already happening.

Ingrid settled on a relatively dry stone, drawing out Gwyneth's feather. "Right then," she said to no one in particular. "Let's see what kind of mess we're really dealing with."

The owl feather trembled between Ingrid's fingers, still holding traces of Gwyneth's magic—that particular blend of discipline and wild possibility that had always characterised her former lover's power.

The pool's surface began to shift.

Through the water's dark mirror, images swirled: the Clochar's herb gardens, frost-bitten but showing hints of green; stone corridors that hadn't changed in centuries; Gwyneth hurrying through them, her face lined with worry but still beautiful, still *her.*

Ingrid's chest ached.

"Ingrid..." Gwyneth had reached her chamber mirror, their eyes met. For a moment, neither spoke. What could you say to someone who had been both salvation and heartbreak?

Gwyneth's voice sounded ethereal through the water. "I wasn't sure you'd..."

"Well, I didn't have anything better to do," Ingrid said tartly. "Just a perfectly good evening by the fire to waste. Though I suppose impending magical catastrophe waits for no one's comfort."

A ghost of a smile touched Gwyneth's lips. "You haven't changed."

"Oh, I have. Just not in any way that makes me more pleasant."

"The crystal," Gwyneth said, her reflection wavering like guilt in water. "It's all getting worse."

"Of course it is," said Ingrid. "I told you it was bad."

Gwyneth shook her head. "No. It's worse than you could imagine. This is about Mathilda."

Ingrid drew back. "My sister?" Ice crackled around the pool's edges. "What has the Sisterhood done to her?"

"She's powering it. Willingly. She says it's her calling, her chance to serve."

"Of course she does." Ingrid's voice cracked. "Mathilda's always been the perfect believer. Even when we were children, she loved their rules, their certainties." The earth dragon-pup pressed closer, sharing warmth as Ingrid's rage built. "But to use her like this..."

"She volunteered," Gwyneth said softly.

"Volunteered?" Winter itself seemed to speak through Ingrid's fury. "The way everyone 'volunteers' when the Sisterhood speaks of duty and sacrifice? My sister would throw herself into a fire if they told her it would bring peace."

"That's why I had to tell you. The crystal...it's draining her. More than they understand...and it's influencing the Clochar, subduing people. It's awful..."

"How bad is it for Mathilda?" Ingrid demanded, decades of complicated feelings about her sister's blind devotion warring with protective instinct.

The earth dragon-pup whined softly, picking up on undercurrents of emotion that ran deep as tree roots. Mathilda had always been the good sister, the one who found comfort in the Sisterhood's rigid certainties while Ingrid questioned everything.

"She's growing weaker." Gwyneth's reflection rippled with concern. "But she wouldn't listen to reason. Says the crystal's work is too important, that true peace requires sacrifice."

"Sacrifice." Ingrid spat the word like poison. "The Sisterhood's favourite excuse for everything."

Silence stretched between them, broken only by the steady drip of melting ice into the pool. In the gathering darkness, Gwyneth's face showed signs of strain Ingrid hadn't seen before.

"So this is where your precious sisterhood gets you," Ingrid grumbled. "And now you've betrayed them to me. Explain that."

"That's just it," Gwyneth said finally. "Things I once believed without question...The other elders speak of harmony and balance, but their methods..." She paused, choosing words carefully. "The crystal's power feels wrong. Like something twisted out of true."

"Wrong how?" Ingrid pressed, even as the earth dragon-pup's growl confirmed her own sense of something askew in the magic. "What aren't you telling me about this crystal?"

Gwyneth's image wavered, uncertainty crossing her face. "Something about its resonance...speaks of darker magics. Manipulation. Not what the Sisterhood claims to stand for at all."

"And my sister sits at its heart, feeding it with her life." Frost crackled across the pool's surface, matching the ice in Ingrid's voice. "Tell me, does she still quote the old texts about necessary sacrifice? Still believe every pretty lie they wrap in ceremony?"

"Ingrid—"

"No. I don't want to hear about her choice or her calling or whatever nonsense they've filled her head with this time." The words came sharp as icicles, but underneath them lay decades of helpless watching, of losing her sister to zealotry one doctrine at a time.

The earth dragon-pup pressed against her leg, offering warmth against memories as cold as midwinter. Something in its touch reminded her of deeper wisdom – earth's patience, its way of holding both death and life in the same soil.

"I need to speak with the other Crones," she said finally. "This isn't just about Mathilda anymore, is it?"

Gwyneth's silence was answer enough.

23

ELAMINA

"Not again," said Kitty as Merryn screamed and began to wail.

The children had had a tempestuous morning.

"There must be something in the air," said Delia. She had just finished patching up Keyne's bruised knee, and she and Kitty rushed outside to see that Merryn was lying on the ground with her fists thrashing against the damp grass.

"They won't talk to me! They won't talk to me!" Merryn shouted.

"Who won't talk to you, love?" said Delia, kneeling beside her granddaughter.

"The fairies – they're so mean, they won't talk to me!"

Kitty and Delia looked at each other, unsure whether this was a game or there were indeed real fairies, because who knew what existed in the world at this point? After vampires and dragons, fairies in the garden talking to the children seemed entirely possible.

"Fae are a thing, aren't they?" Kitty said. "Una is part fae. She's told me her father was some kind of dark fae lord. Sounds sexy, but I didn't tell her that!"

"I don't know anymore," said Delia. "It's all so much to deal with. I'm not sure I can handle wayward fairies, after all of this."

Rain pattered against the windows as they ushered the children inside.

"Nanna...Will you have a tea party with me instead?" Merryn asked, her tears already drying on her cheeks.

"Of course, my love," Delia said, just glad to have an opportunity for some even footing with the children. Earlier they'd been fighting about which of them was most powerful, which had led to several rounds of tears. Kitty had helped separate them, taking Merryn aside until she calmed down.

In the last few days, the children had been more emotional. Perhaps they were missing Gillian, or perhaps it was something in the weather or some other magic in the air.

Just as she'd managed to sit Merryn up and prepare for a tea party, the doorbell rang. She and Kitty eyed each other, tension crackling between them.

"Are you expecting anyone?" Delia asked.

"No, are you?"

"Roger said he might pop by later. This is far too early for him. We're still in daylight."

Delia frowned. "If this isn't good news, I'm not prepared to receive it at all."

"Fair enough," said Kitty. "You've got enough going on with that mad, murderous family of yours and not being able to get your own damn grimoire—"

"Exactly," said Delia. She opened the door to see a woman standing there – none other than Elamina Bracewell.

Delia was taken aback. She'd figured the Bracewells wouldn't be showing up at her door after that fateful dinner party where everything went awry. Perhaps they'd come in the night to abduct her or magically whisk her away somewhere to steal her powers, but a house call?

She'd been trying to figure out other ways that she could get into the stronghold to get a glimpse of the grimoire, but it seemed impossible. Here Elamina was standing on her doorstep, her icy hair pulled back in a tight bun, wearing a silver suit, neatly tailored and embroidered, and holding an enormous book.

"Is that..." Delia asked, eyes widening as she took in the ancient tome.

Elamina nodded.

The book seemed to pulse with its own energy, ancient leather binding worn smooth by generations of hands. Rain beaded and dispersed on Elamina's perfectly pressed suit which failed to diminish her aristocratic bearing.

"What are you doing here?" Delia asked.

"I've come to bring this to you," said Elamina. "It's what you need, isn't it?"

"What?"

"I'm serious," Elamina said. "This is for you, the family

grimoire. You're part of the family. You're in line for it." She handed over the book.

Delia took it with trembling hands. The grimoire felt warm despite the cold day, its magic responding to her touch. It tingled a little in her fingertips, as though recognising her, and a thrill of satisfaction passed through her, but her mind whirred with confusion.

"Why are you doing this?" Delia asked.

"It's the right thing to do," said Elamina. "And while my family and I may not always do what other people consider to be right, I'm not without my own code of conduct. This is something you need and from all the research I've done, this is the best place for it to be right now. Something bigger is coming. The powers of the Myrtlewood Crones were bestowed for a reason, whether my aunt likes it or not. She's not the one who gets to decide everything."

"So you've stolen this."

Elamina shrugged slightly. It was a casual gesture for her. "I prefer to say I've borrowed it from the family estate to lend to a family member."

"But Sabrina doesn't know," said Delia. It wasn't a question.

"Of course not," said Elamina. "She'll find out, and she'll come after you – that's a risk you might want to take at this point. I don't pretend to understand her agenda in all this, but Sabrina always has an agenda, as do my parents."

"As do you," said Delia, with a pointed look.

Elamina shrugged. "I suppose we all have our agendas, don't we? But I have nothing to gain from this situation, other than not causing any additional chaos. My work is tricky enough at the moment with the witching parliament. The last thing we need is somebody in my family upsetting the balance of power around here, and these ancient things can take a huge toll on the world if they go awry. I believe that's why the protections were put in place in the first place."

"Tea's ready!" A clatter of toy teacups drew their attention to where Merryn had set up an elaborate tea party on her small wooden table. Stuffed animals sat in careful arrangement around tea cups, and wooden blocks had been stacked into precarious towers meant to represent cakes and sandwiches.

"Would you like to join us?" Merryn asked Elamina, her earlier tears forgotten in the excitement of a new guest.

To Delia's surprise, Elamina's severe expression softened. "I would be honoured," she said, folding her tall frame into one of the tiny chairs with remarkable grace.

"This is where the fairy queen sits," Merryn explained, handing Elamina a chipped pink teacup. "And Mr Bear always takes three sugars."

"How appropriate," Elamina said, accepting the cup with perfect seriousness. She pretended to sip, her pinky extended just so, as Merryn went around the table serving her stuffed animals.

"Do you know anything about why?" Delia asked, settling into another small chair. "I mean, about what actually happened with the Crone magic...originally?"

"From everything I can gather," said Elamina, pausing to accept a wooden block "cupcake" from Merryn, "a great injustice caused a tremendous imbalance centuries ago – somewhere around the middle ages as far as I can gather. The rift from this was potentially devastating to all of Myrtlewood and the land beyond. The fae and dragons, who were still immersed in this world at the time, and the witches and the other magical beings all got together. The dragons had been in a migratory process, leaving this realm – it was no longer safe for them, as magic was being stripped from the world through a spell."

"A spell?" Delia asked, pretending to eat the wooden block that Merryn had given her.

"More tea?" Merryn interrupted, hovering with her empty teapot.

"Thank you, dear," Elamina said. "You know, in the fae courts, tea parties are very important."

Merryn's eyes widened. "Really?"

"Oh yes. Sometimes the fate of entire kingdoms has been decided over cucumber sandwiches." She gestured to a wooden block. "Speaking of which, this looks delicious."

"What kind of spell strips the magic out of the world?" Delia asked, watching this unexpected side of her cousin emerge.

"Of course you don't know any of this," said Elamina, balancing her teacup as Merryn rearranged the stuffed animals. "When human beings scientifically discovered that they weren't the centre of the universe, there was a huge loss of faith and magic and a huge focus on the rigidity of the scientific method. The scientific method is not a bad thing, of course – we use a similar process in our own magical discoveries – but the mundane approach did not take into account that a method of science and knowing facts from fiction can only go so far in helping us understand what to believe in a richer, deeper broader sense. We need magic and mystery. We need faith in something. We need to feel empowered. The world has gone awry in its focus on this great spell where everything is reduced to nothing, everything is reduced just to matter and method."

"I can understand that," said Delia, watching Merryn serve another round of imaginary tea. "I can see how magic has been stripped from people's understanding over the last few hundred years, and I actually thought that was a good thing up until recently."

Elamina shrugged, careful not to disturb her teacup. "It's a good thing sometimes. Magic can be awfully deceptive to mundane people. They're always getting caught up in the delusions of marketing mages and politicians, being swept away in some Neptunian current or other."

"You are far wiser than I gave you credit for," Delia admitted.

"I've gotten awfully philosophical lately," said Elamina.

"The fairies like philosophy," Merryn announced, arranging a napkin for her favourite bear. "They're nodding right now. They want to know more about the dragons."

"Are they?" Elamina asked with perfect seriousness. "Well then, they might be interested in what happened next. You see," she continued, accepting another wooden block cake, "at the time, there was so much fear of what was happening that some mythical creatures like the dragons had chosen to return to their own realm. It was no longer safe here, yet everyone knew the power of the dragons might still be needed someday. The magical community united to save the world from the crisis. The dragons had to leave, but as part of the resolution, the elemental dragons offered to stay, to rest dormant in their elements, as dragons can do for millennia. They were bound to four powerful witching families of Myrtlewood at that time who could pass this wisdom down through the generations, so that if it ever happened again, there would be four wise women among us who could rise to the challenge and restore balance to the world."

Merryn listened intently, her eyes wide as she poured more invisible tea. Even her stuffed animals seemed to lean forward, caught up in the tale.

"What does that mean about the Order and the Sisterhood?" Delia asked, noting how naturally Elamina had woven this serious discussion into the children's tea party.

"They are remnants of that time, as far as I understand it," said Elamina. "Formed from the magical rift. Apparently, women who believed that the great power released by the tragedy should be able to create peace in the world began to flock to that location and built their Clochar. And there was the cult that followed Baron von Castle, who wanted dominion over the world. They wanted to strip power from women. And those groups coalesced around the remaining power that had been released from the tragedy. Secretly, they built themselves up over the centuries feeding on the ancient power imbedded in their land."

"The fairies don't like them," Merryn declared firmly, rearranging her bear's bow tie.

"Very wise fairies," Elamina agreed. "More cake?"

"And your aunt has something to do with the Sisterhood," said Delia.

Elamina raised an eyebrow. "She's your aunt too, you know."

"That's harder to digest at this point," Delia said, setting down her block of wood cupcake.

"Yes," said Elamina. "I don't know exactly of her involvement, but with Sabrina, there's always something deeper going on beneath the surface."

The tea party had somehow made this intense conversation easier to bear, as if the presence of stuffed animals and invisible fairies helped soften the weight of ancient secrets and family betrayals.

"Thank you so much for the grimoire," said Delia. "But how safe am I? Will Sabrina come after it?"

"I've cast a protection over your house which your friend Marjie can reinforce. That kind of magic is hard to break through because the energy of houses is so innately connected to those who dwell in them. That escape magic you performed the other night was brilliant, by the way. It exploited a weakness in the mansion's energetic field."

"Marjie did well," Delia acknowledged.

"As for the book," Elamina continued, "I've done my best to disguise it. It looks as though the grimoire is still there in its case. Sabrina won't notice it's missing until she goes in and tries to read it herself. But I put some additional protections in there too to try and buy some time for you."

"Thank you so much," said Delia. "I don't know what else I'd have done. Nobody has ever helped me quite this much. Well, nobody who could just as easily have been my enemy."

"I don't have any interest in being your enemy," said Elamina curtly.

"I think I can trust that now," Delia said. "Unless this book explodes."

"I assure you it will not," Elamina said with a chuckle that sounded almost warm. "Thank you so much for the tea," she said graciously to Merryn. "Your hospitality rivals that of the highest fae courts."

She rose from her tiny chair with remarkable dignity, bid Merryn farewell, and nodded to Delia before leaving promptly into the rainy afternoon.

Through the window, Delia watched her cousin's silver suit disappear into the mist, while behind her, Merryn explained to her stuffed animals that they had just hosted a real magical princess for tea.

24

AGATHA

Myrtlewood's municipal buildings loomed grey against the winter sky as Agatha approached, her cane finding sure purchase on icy steps. The building's magic hummed against her senses. Usually she preferred her own library, built up over decades of careful collection, but some records only existed in official archives.

Ferg's desk dominated the entrance hall, positioned for maximum bureaucratic impact. Today he wore a violet waist-coat embroidered with silver threading that actually sparkled with magic worked into its fabric. He looked up as she entered, his face lighting with that particular combination of officiousness and alarm she'd come to expect from this strange man with many jobs, including now being the mayor.

"Agatha! What a pleasure. I've just reorganised the municipal access forms. Did you know we now have separate categories for historical research versus genealogical inquiry? And a fascinating new subsection about magical artifact provenance—"

"Not today, Ferg." She moved past him with practiced determination.

He scrambled to his feet, waistcoat twinkling frantically. "But the procedures! We've implemented a new colour-coding system for different levels of archival access. The purple forms are for—"

"Still not interested." She was already halfway to the basement door.

"Paperwork exists for a reason!" His voice rose in pitch. "There's a proper procedure for accessing records!"

"Which I've memorised by now," she called back, her cane tap-tap-tapping down the stairs. A casual flick of her fingers sent a soundproofing charm sealing the door behind her. Let him have his bureaucratic tantrum in silence.

The archives spread out before her, rows of shelves disappearing into shadowed corners. Preservation spells lay thick as dust, their magic mixing with the scent of old paper and forgotten secrets. Her own footsteps echoed against worn stone floors as she made her way to the family records section, confidence born of countless hours spent in these stacks.

The Bracewell files practically preened with their own importance, bound in expensive leather and gleaming with protective magic. Of course they did – everything about that family demanded attention, commanded respect. Even their paper felt superior.

Agatha settled into her favourite reading nook, a worn armchair she'd smuggled down here years ago despite Ferg's protests about "inappropriate furniture in municipal spaces." He wasn't the mayor back then, so she'd succeeded without much trouble. The reading light she conjured cast a warm globe around her as she began sifting through the Bracewell records.

Page after immaculate page documented their achievements. Sabrina Bracewell's contributions to magical education filled an entire shelf: founding three schools for young witches, establishing scholarship funds for "disadvantaged magical youth," creating innovative teaching methods that had been adopted across Britannia. Each accomplishment read like a carefully crafted press release, designed to project maximum benevolence while accumulating influence.

"Nobody's this perfect without hiding something," Agatha muttered, noting how each charitable act seemed to expand the Bracewells' power base. Even the scholarship recipients ended up mysteriously loyal to the family, taking positions that enhanced Bracewell influence in key magical institutions.

Elamina's father's retirement from Bermuda appeared equally calculated – a graceful exit from power that somehow left all his connections intact. The records spoke of "well-earned rest" and "focusing on family matters," but mentioned nothing about why such a powerful magical politician would step down at the height of his influence.

Frustrated by the Bracewells' immaculate facade, Agatha turned to her other curiosity. Covvey's family records were much harder to track down. Eventually she found something, lurking in a neglected corner of the local pack histories, their folders thick with dust that no preservation spell had bothered to address. His father's name appeared first – articles about pack politics, territory disputes, growing isolation from traditional ways. The man had become increasingly erratic after his wife left, rejecting his cultural heritage in favour of a more aggressive, territorial approach to wolf magic.

Then she saw it. A small note, easily missed if you weren't looking carefully. Two names that made her blood run cold.

Covvey had sisters...

He'd never told her anything about his family, not really. He'd forbidden her to dig into his past too. A wave of guilt almost knocked her over, but Agatha wasn't about to be bullied by troublesome emotions. She had more important things to worry about. Covvey might be happy to hide from the past, but it was time he faced the music. Her hands trembled slightly as she pulled more records. Did he even remember them?

"You poor wolf," she whispered to the silent archives.

The implications spiralled out like ripples in a pond. If she was right about the connections...if these names meant what she thought they meant...

A sound from upstairs interrupted her thoughts – probably Ferg attempting to magically bypass his own soundproofing charm. That man never could leave well enough alone. But for once, Agatha was grateful for the interruption.

Some discoveries needed time to process, needed careful consideration before action.

As she climbed the stairs, her mind was already cataloguing connections, plotting research paths, considering implications. Behind her, the archives settled back into silence, holding their secrets until the next time someone thought to look beyond the obvious.

25

COVVEY

The scent hit Covvey first – lavender, sherry and old books, determination and carefully contained excitement.

Agatha.

His wolf senses picked up her distinctive gait long before she appeared: the tap of her cane against earth, that slight hesitation in her left step that spoke of an old injury, the rustle of papers she perpetually carried. She had never visited his home before recent events, and now here she was again, heartbeat carrying a tension that suggested this wasn't a casual social call.

His hut stood apart from the village, his land straddling wilderness and civilisation much like himself. Rough-hewn beams supported a roof he'd thatched himself. Inside, pelts draped over hand-carved furniture – much of it built by his own hands.

His nose twitched at the medicinal scents drifting from the stable where Cedric slept fitfully, the ex-cleric's dreams still haunted by Order's conditioning.

Through the window, caught sight of the workshop where he did his metalwork. Tools lay at the ready. His territory, hard-won and carefully maintained.

And now Agatha approached, carrying the scent of something that made his hackles rise.

Her boots scuffed against the worn path.

"Don't bother with the door," he called gruffly. "It's open."

Agatha entered, bringing with her the smell of dust and preservation spells and secrets too long buried. She had been rustling though history that was none of her business.

"Whatever you found," he said, turning to pour tea into mugs, "I don't want to know."

"It's about your sisters."

The mug he was holding cracked in his grip.

Sisters.

A word he'd buried so deep even his wolf couldn't track its scent. Images flashed unbidden – small hands braiding flowers into his fur, giggles in darkness, the sound of a door closing in the night.

He hadn't let himself think of them in decades. His mother had left, and that was torture enough...but she'd taken the girls. They were young, the youngest barely a toddler.

Pain stung at his heart.

"Don't," he growled, but the memories came anyway. His

father's rages growing worse. The way his mother's face had grown more haunted with each passing week.

"Do you even remember their names?"

"I don't want to remember," Covvey said. "It was beaten out of me. Even my mother's name…"

"Greta," Agatha said.

Covvey shook his head. "I knew her as Mother. That's painful enough."

"I can't let this go, Covvey," Agatha said. "You have sisters. They're still alive."

His heart clenched in agony.

"Nothing good comes of digging up the past," Covvey grumbled.

"You and I both know that isn't true," Agatha insisted, matching his gruffness with her own brittle stubborn nature. He usually appreciated this quality of hers, but today it was unwelcome. He was outmatched. Like a dog with a bone, she wasn't going to let this go. "At least hear their names."

"Go on then. What are their names, since you insist on disrupting my morning with old ghosts."

"Ingrid and Mathilda—"

Covvey's heart clenched further than he knew it could. He tried to shut it out – shut it all out. But his treacherous mind was already piecing things together. Ingrid's fierce independence…her determination, her strength. Something about her reminded him of his mother, long ago, before she'd been broken. How had he not seen it before? The way they moved, something in their eyes, echoes of his mother's grace. He wasn't familiar with Mathilda. She must have been the younger one.

Sisters.

The concept seemed alien to him now. He'd been alone too long.

"I can't..." Covvey said, wiping back tears as rage built in his torso.

"It must have ripped you apart," Agatha said. "She left you behind and took them."

Covvey shook his head as the tears continued to pour out.

"Your mother took them to protect them," Agatha pressed on, immune to his growing anger.

"Couldn't you leave it buried?" His voice came rough as bark. "What good does digging up old bones do?"

"You deserve to know the truth."

"Truth?" He laughed, a sound closer to a snarl. "Truth is, she left me. Truth is, I wasn't worth taking. Truth is—" He stopped, scenting Cedric's approach before the man appeared in the doorway, drawn by the raised voices.

The long-supressed memories flooded back now. His mother's face in moonlight, tears tracking silver. His father's increasing violence, the pack's growing savagery. They'd gone too far, rejecting anything that didn't fit their narrow view of strength. Women were for breeding, magic was weakness, and his sisters weren't wolves...His sisters had shown signs of power that terrified them.

"You should talk to Ingrid," Agatha said softly, pulling him back to the present.

"Like hell." The words came automatically, even as something in him ached at the name. His sister.

Gods, how had he not known? Looking back now, he could see it. He growled, cutting off the thought.

"I don't need anyone. Least of all—"

"Family?" Agatha's voice carried centuries of archived wisdom. "Or is it the old feelings of rejection you're afraid of?"

The growl built in his chest, wolf and man united in denial. But underneath lay that pup he'd once been, watching his mother choose his sisters over him. The worthlessness that followed, the knowledge that he hadn't been enough. Couldn't protect her, couldn't save any of them.

"They've built lives without you," Agatha continued, her words cutting deep. "Ingrid's stronger than you know."

"Get out." His voice held winter's edge.

For once, Agatha listened. But at the door she paused, heavy with sympathy he couldn't bear. "We can't change the past, but we can learn to live with it."

The silence after her departure pressed like storm clouds. Cedric shuffled fully into the room, pouring tea with hands that shook only slightly. The ex-cleric's scent carried understanding – he knew something about betrayal.

They sat in silence broken only by the fire's crack and pop, two broken men nursing wounds too deep for healing.

In Cedric's eyes, Covvey saw his own betrayal mirrored – the Order's false family as cruel as his own had been. The kettle swung gently, marking time like a pendulum between past and present.

His wolf paced beneath his skin, agitated by memories he'd been supressing for decades.

"Talk if you like," said Cedric. "Or not. I don't mind, either way..."

"You know what's funny?" Covvey said, surprising himself. "I've spent decades building this place, making everything just right. And now I find out my sister – my bloody sister – has been living in the forest just down the road this whole time."

"It's a lot to take in," Cedric acknowledged. "And that woman who keeps coming here, Agatha, she didn't let it rest when you told her to. She insisted on dragging you through the mud. Women can't be trusted, after all."

Covvey shook his head. "It's not that. I know Agatha. I know she means well but I..."

"Your mother left you," Cedric said. "Don't defend her."

"She had to leave," Covvey said, finally. "I wasn't strong enough to protect her. I was a liability. So she left me. She didn't have any better choice to make." He laughed, the sound as hollow as his chest felt. "Doesn't stop it feeling like having your heart ripped out through your ribs, though."

"Parents," Cedric said, reaching for the Covvey's bottle of whiskey. "They mess you up. Your mum ran away, I was born into a cult to no fault of my own. Makes you wonder how any of us survive."

"By building very sturdy walls," Covvey replied, accepting a generous pour. "And developing a healthy appreciation for solitude."

But even as he said it, he knew something had shifted.

Knowledge, once gained, couldn't be unlearned. His sisters were out there – not lost to time and distance as he'd believed, but real, alive, living their own lives.

The fire burned low as the men sat, neither speaking, both understanding that some pains went beyond words. Some betrayals carved too deep for healing. But maybe, just maybe, there was something to be said for sharing the darkness rather than drowning in it alone.

26

MARJIE

*M*arjie balanced her laden picnic basket as she approached Ingrid's hut, through the forest. The air held that particular quality of changing seasons – winter's bite giving way to spring's promises. Her senses tingled with the forest's awakening.

Ahead, Ingrid's hut looked like something from a fairy tale. Smoke curled from the chimney in spirals, the gardens hummed, mystical and fragrant.

As she approached the back garden, and the earth dragon-pup bounded past her, shimmering in the sun, Merryn and Keyne ran after her, followed by Delia's beagle familiar, Torin.

"Don't eat anything the children give you!" Delia called out. "They've been experimenting with Ingrid's herbs."

"Too late," Ingrid said dryly from the back doorway.

"Though I'm sure whatever potion they've concocted won't affect anyone with a decent constitution."

Marjie spread her picnic blanket and set up the afternoon tea beneath the ancient elder tree. She'd brought freshly baked herby bread, scones, pasties, and tiny elderflower cakes which drew the children in briefly from their play.

Agatha arrived last, her emotions unusually muted. Marjie frowned slightly – her grumpy historian friend typically radiated curiosity and determination, but today her feelings were locked down tight as a sealed archive.

"You've outdone yourself," Delia said, reaching for another scone just as a crash came from the garden shed followed by gleeful giggling.

"If they've broken another cauldron..." Ingrid began.

"The dragon will sort them out," Agatha said quietly – her first words since arriving. Something in her tone made Marjie look closer, but Agatha's emotions remained frustratingly opaque.

"Show us this grimoire then," Ingrid said, brushing crumbs from her hands.

Delia produced the massive tome from a large carry bag. Magic radiated from its worn leather binding, making Marjie's skin tingle. The grimoire seemed to pulse with its own fiery heartbeat as Delia opened it.

"Elamina just appeared on my doorstep with it," Delia explained, recounting the surprising visit. "Right in the middle of Merryn's tea party, if you can believe it. And there she was, playing along, pretending to sip tea with teddy bears while explaining ancient magical catastrophes."

"The Bracewells aren't known for their whimsy," Agatha murmured, but her usual sharp interest in historical matters felt dulled, replaced by something heavier that Marjie couldn't quite read. "Suspicious if you ask me. But this looks to be the real deal."

As they pored over the grimoire's pages, Marjie divided her attention between the ancient text and the swirling emotions around her. Delia's excitement tinged with anxiety about Sabrina's eventual reaction. Ingrid's focused intently with only slight shifts when certain passages caught her interest. And Agatha...Agatha's feelings remained locked away, like a door bolted from the inside.

"Here," Ingrid said suddenly, pointing to a passage. "This connects with what Gwyneth's message said about—" She stopped, a flush colouring her cheeks.

Marjie caught the surge of complex emotions at Gwyneth's name – longing, pain, hope, fear, all tangled together like threads. Interesting. Very interesting. But she knew better than to pry – Ingrid was formidable for a reason.

"What did Gwyneth say exactly?" Delia asked.

"Just that Mathilda..." Ingrid's voice hardened. "That she's given her power to their crystal. She's being drained by it. Voluntarily...supposedly. Always the perfect believer, my sister."

The bitterness in her voice carried deeper currents. Marjie sensed old hurts, childhood patterns playing out again.

Sister.

The word seemed to echo strangely in the air.

A sob broke the tension. They turned to find Agatha with tears streaming down her face.

Marjie blinked.

Agatha was...crying!

"Sister," Agatha choked out. "Oh goddess, I can't keep this in anymore. Ingrid, there's something you need to know about sisters...and brothers."

"What are you talking about?" Ingrid's emotions spiked with alarm, making Marjie wince at their intensity.

"I've been researching," Agatha said, wiping her eyes. "Old pack records, family histories. Your mother was a woman named Greta, is that right?"

"So?" Ingrid said sternly.

"So, you may not remember this but Greta had another child. A boy. Older than you and Mathilda."

Ingrid shook her head. "I can't remember much about life before the Clochar. There was darkness. Violence. I suppose my mother had to leave the boy behind. He wouldn't have made it into the Clochar at all, and even if he could get in he'd never have been allowed to stay. Mother made...questionable choices. But what's done is done," she said, gazing out towards the forest as if the trees could steady her. "He's probably long gone now, whoever the boy was."

"Well, that's the thing," Agatha said, her voice cracking further. "It was Covvey...Covvey is your brother. Yours and Mathilda's."

"Impossible!" Ingrid cried.

"That's what I thought at first too," Agatha admitted. "Covvey looks so much younger than you – no offence."

Ingrid narrowed her eyes. "Now's the time you want to start avoiding offending me, is it?" She shook her head. "Age isn't the problem. We all know that shifters age slowly when they're in animal form. I just can't believe it."

Marjie felt Ingrid's certainty waver as if hidden memories stirred beneath her fierce denial like fish beneath ice.

"I couldn't believe it at first either," Agatha said. "I thought I knew the history of the magical families in this town, but there were so few records of yours...or his. He's forbidden me from digging into his past before, but I couldn't help myself." She shook her head sadly. "I only hope he forgives me for this."

From the garden came shrieks of laughter as the dragon-pup chased the children through Ingrid's herb beds. The simple joy of their play contrasted with the heavy emotions swirling under the elder tree.

"I still can't believe it," said Ingrid. "Where's your proof? The records might have been mixed up."

"Show them," Agatha said to Marjie. "You can scry it, can't you? Show her the truth."

Marjie hesitated. "Recovering buried memories...it's delicate work."

"Do it," Ingrid commanded, but Marjie sensed fear beneath her brusque tone. "I need to see real evidence."

Marjie produced her scrying bowl from her basket – she'd felt she might need it today, though she hadn't known why. The water within caught the winter sunlight as she added three drops of her special sight-enhancing tincture.

"I remember so little," Ingrid admitted, her usual formidable presence softening. "Arriving at the Sisterhood with Mother. Running through the night. There was...there was fear. So much fear."

The water began to swirl, images forming in its depths. They leaned forward to watch as the past unfolded before them:

A SMALL COTTAGE, *moonlight streaming through windows. A woman with Ingrid's bearing but hunched over with terror in her eyes hurriedly packing bags. Two little girls clutching each other's hands – one wild-haired and defiant, the other quiet and watchful.*

"They're coming," Ingrid whispered. "The pack's getting restless. Father's been drinking."

"We must go now," Greta said to the girls. "But first, I must say goodbye."

She went into the room where a boy slept, barely into his teens but strong and vital. "Covvey," she whispered, "my brave boy. I can't...I can't take you with us. They'd never stop hunting us. A male shifter child..." Her voice broke. "It's safer this way," she whispered, kissing his forehead. "He won't let me take you. The pack would sooner kill us all..."

THE VISION FADED. Marjie felt the shock ripple through the group. Beside her, Ingrid's hands trembled.

"I remember now," she whispered. "My wolf brother... How could I have forgotten?"

"The Sisterhood," Agatha said gently. "They're rather good at helping people forget inconvenient truths, it seems."

"Memory magic," Ingrid spat, her emotions roiling so strongly that Marjie had to strengthen her shields. "They took those memories from me. From Mathilda too, I'd wager. I'd forgotten entirely about life before. Not that it was entirely bad to forget all that fear and pain..."

She let out a small sob, leaving everyone startled.

"But if it's buried deep, it festers...It can't be processed," Marjie said gently. "Now you can heal."

"I don't have anything to heal!" Ingrid protested, sending a tremor through the foliage around the house.

Marjie wasn't so sure about that, but she decided not to press it.

The dragon-pup paused in its play, sensing the surge of magical energy. In the garden, Merryn and Keyne continued mixing potions from stolen herbs, blissfully unaware of the emotional storm under the elder tree.

"He was protecting us even then," Ingrid said softly. "He would try to protect us from father's wrath, even if it got him hurt...And we left him. Mother left him."

"Covvey can't bear to think of it either. His memory was buried too, though perhaps just through his own grief."

Marjie quickly began bottling the scrying water, sensing its importance. "For Covvey," she explained when Agatha raised an eyebrow. "Though something tells me that stubborn wolf won't be easily convinced to look."

"He won't," Agatha agreed, relief evident in her aura now that she'd shared her burden. "He's...not taking the news well."

"When did you tell him?" Delia asked.

"This morning. It went about as well as a cat in a rain shower." Agatha's attempt at humour couldn't mask her distress. "He practically threw me out of his hut."

Marjie felt Ingrid's emotions spiral – shock, anger, grief, and underneath it all, a deep longing she was trying to suppress. The elder tree's branches swayed without wind, responding to the powerful feelings beneath them.

"We need to focus on the immediate threat," Ingrid said finally, her voice harsh. "The crystal, the Sisterhood, this business about volcanoes and fire dragons. Family drama can wait."

But Marjie noticed how Ingrid's hands shook as she turned the grimoire's pages, how her eyes kept straying toward the forest. Some wounds ran too deep for simple healing. And some families needed more than magical intervention to make them whole again.

27

CEDRIC

*C*edric shivered as wind howled through bare winter branches outside the hut. He sat close to the hearth, leaning into the fire's warmth.

Cedric rocked slowly back and forth. The motion soothed him, like the endless repetition of prayers once had. But those prayers rang hollow now, tainted by memories of the Shepherd's madness, of chains and darkness and that poor beast they kept below.

Covvey had left at dawn to check his traplines, more withdrawn than usual. His shoulders had been tight, his few words clipped and harsh. Cedric had heard everything through the hut's thin walls – Agatha's revelations about Covvey's sisters, about the Sisterhood's manipulation of memory and truth. The historian's words had landed like physical blows, each one driving his new friend deeper into despair.

The fire crackled, sending a shower of sparks up the chimney. Cedric watched them dance, remembering how the Order's ritual fires had seemed holy once. He'd been so certain then, so sure of his path.

The compound's rigid routines had given structure to his days – prayers at dawn, study in the archives. Even the Shepherd's growing darkness had been easier to bear than this new uncertainty.

But here, in this small hut on the forest's edge, he'd found something real. Something true. Covvey didn't demand prayers or submission, didn't wrap control in scripture and ceremony. He simply existed – hunting, gathering herbs, preparing food and sharing drink.

The wolf-shifter understood silence, understood pain.

The wind's pitch changed, rattling the windows. He added another log to the fire, watching flames lick across bark still silvered with frost.

His rocking intensified as thoughts turned darker.

Covvey's own mother and sisters had abandoned him and fled to the Sisterhood of the Veil – of course they would be involved. Another group claiming wisdom while wielding power like a blade. They'd taken Covvey's family from him, twisted their memories. Just like the Order had taken young men's faith and forged it into chains.

And the Crones, with their dragons and prophecies, making everything more complicated than it needed to be. Stirring up ancient powers...The rocking grew faster, his fingers digging into his knees as certainty crystallised like ice in his chest.

Covvey's distance had been painful. Just when it felt like Cedric had a new friend, he'd retreated into old pain at that woman's revelation.

"We were happy," he whispered to the flames. "Before she told him. Just us here." The fire popped in response, and he nodded as if it understood. "Could be simple again."

The Order had to fall – Cedric had known that since fleeing their compound, since seeing the darkness in Benedict's eyes and in the Almighty's power that had driven him to the brink of madness. The god he'd once dedicated his life to serving had been a lie. A demonic power, rather than a divine light.

But now he saw the fuller truth. The Sisterhood had to go, too. As did the Crones with their meddling magic. All of them blighted the earth with unnatural power.

It all had to end.

Then maybe Covvey would stop looking so haunted. Maybe they could return to quiet evenings by the fire, sharing silence and understanding.

Yes, he could do this for Covvey. A gift for his first true friend. He would tear it all down – Order, Sisterhood, Crones. Burn away the complications until only simple truths remained: hunting in the dawn, bread baking in the coals, two broken men finding peace in silence.

Covvey couldn't know, of course, but in time, he would understand.

The fire flickered as his rocking continued, plans taking shape in his mind. He knew the Order's weaknesses. The Sisterhood would be vulnerable during certain rituals – he remembered reading about them in the compound's archives. And the Crones, for all their power, were just women playing with forces they couldn't truly control.

That Agatha was a problem, but soon she wouldn't matter. None of them would. Soon everything would be simple again.

His laughter joined the fire's crackle as he rocked, dreams of destruction warming him more than any flame could.

The crunch of boots snapped Cedric from his reverie. Covvey's familiar tread approached, heavy with more than just the day's hunting. The door opened on a blast of frigid air, bringing the wolf-shifter's bulk and the sharp scent of fresh blood. Two hares hung from his belt.

Covvey barely glanced at Cedric as he moved to the preparation table, his movements precise with contained violence. The knife came down harder than necessary as he began his preparations, each stroke speaking of buried rage.

"How was the hunt?" Cedric asked.

Covvey grunted, the sound more wolf than human. "Good enough."

The silence stretched between them, broken only by the fire's pop and the wet sounds of Covvey's work. Cedric's rocking slowed but didn't stop, his mind spinning with possibilities. He could help. He could fix this. Just had to remove all the complications, all the people who kept making things harder than they needed to be.

"You don't have to talk about it," he offered finally. "What Agatha said—"

The knife slammed into the wooden table, quivering. "Don't." Covvey's voice held winter's edge.

"Right. Of course." Cedric nodded, rocking faster. "Doesn't matter anyway. Won't matter soon."

Covvey turned, eyes narrowing. "What's that supposed to mean?"

But Cedric just smiled. Everything would be simple again soon. He'd make sure of it. They could just live here in peace, hunting and talking and drinking, without all these complications.

"Nothing," Cedric said. "Just thinking..."

Covvey studied him for a long moment, something shifting in his expression. But he turned back to his work without comment, and Cedric returned to his plans.

The rabbits simmered in a pot over the fire, filling the hut with savoury aromas that couldn't quite mask the tension. Covvey had barely spoken since his return, each movement precise and controlled in a way that reminded Cedric of caged things at the Order's compound. The wolf-shifter's shoulders remained tight as bowstrings as he methodically sharpened his hunting knife, the rhythmic scrape of stone on steel matching Cedric's rocking.

"Remember when we first met?" Cedric asked suddenly, his voice dreamy. "Me half-dead from Order wine, babbling about dragons, and you just...helped. Didn't ask questions. Didn't want anything." His rocking intensified. "Simple. Right."

Covvey's hands stilled on the whetstone. "Nothing simple about it."

"Could be though. Could be so simple." Cedric's eyes reflected firelight as his mind whirred with plots and plans.

28

INGRID

The wind rattled against Ingrid's cottage windows. Inside, firelight caught on bundles of dried herbs. The earth dragon-pup had spent the last hour systematically destroying her careful arrangements and generally making a nuisance of herself.

"If you're quite finished," Ingrid said as the dragon puppy dragged another cushion across the floor, "I do have actual work to do."

The pup wagged her tail. She had been acting strangely since Ingrid had learned about Covvey, as if sensing her inner turmoil.

Brother.

The word still caught in her throat like a thorn. She pushed the thought aside, focusing instead on her preparations.

The mushrooms had been harvested at exactly the right

moment – when the full moon touched autumn soil and earth's magic ran strong and deep. She'd dried them with particular care, wrapping them in leaves and singing the old songs her mother had taught her. Not that she'd tell the others about the singing. She had a reputation to maintain, after all.

A knock at the door interrupted her thoughts. Marjie entered in a swirl of emotional sensitivity.

"I can feel everyone's anxiety from across town," she said, unwinding her scarf. "It's like a storm about to break."

"Then it's good we've got the wards up." Ingrid gestured to the protective symbols she'd spent hours crafting. Earth magic lay thick in the air, grounding and containing whatever might emerge during their ceremony.

Marjie immediately began fussing with the tea settings – four earthenware cups, each painted with symbols of the elements. "What if someone drops one? Should we—"

"Stop," Ingrid said firmly. "The cups are fine. You're just picking up everyone's nerves."

"I know." Marjie sighed. "But it's not just that. There's something else building. I can feel it in the water magic, like pressure before a storm."

"All the more reason to do this properly." Ingrid checked her fire, adding another log with precise movements. "We need answers, not just about the fire dragon. The Order's getting stronger, the Sisterhood's crystal is draining Mathilda, and—" She stopped, swallowing hard.

"I'm not used to you being so emotional, Ingrid. Has this Covvey situation got you worried?" Marjie asked gently.

"I'm worried about everything," Ingrid grumbled. "And I usually do my best not to worry at all as it's not helpful. Now make yourself useful and help me finish setting up."

They worked in comfortable silence until Delia arrived, looking harried.

"More bad news?" Marjie asked.

Delia sighed. "I'm afraid so. The divorce is coming up in the courts in just a few days! Can you believe it?"

The earth dragon-pup abandoned its cushion-arranging to press against Delia's leg, offering comfort in its own way. Ingrid watched her friend's hands shake as she tried to unbutton her coat.

Before she could respond, Agatha burst in without knocking, her cane striking the wooden floor with unusual force. "That stubborn, thick-headed, absolutely impossible —" She stopped, noticing everyone staring. "What?"

"Let me guess," Ingrid said dryly. "Covvey's still not speaking to you?"

"Won't even open his door! I tried to explain about the importance of acknowledging the past, but he just growls. Actually growls! Like being a wolf means he doesn't have to deal with emotional complexity."

"Give him time," said Marjie. "You've just shocked his system. He needs to process."

"He's not the only one," Ingrid muttered.

"When is the hearing?" Marjie asked Delia, perhaps sensing a change of subject was in order.

"Three days," Delia replied, hanging her cloak on Ingrid's overcrowded hook. "Three days until I face Jerry in magical court and I still haven't told Gillian the truth about him. About who he really is, what he's done. How do you even begin that conversation with your daughter? 'Oh by the way, your father isn't just the man who abandoned us – he's actually the leader of a murderous magical cult who's been lying to us for decades.'"

"Sit," Ingrid commanded, pointing to a cushion. "Tea first, crisis later."

"But Perseus says this hearing will make everything public record in the magical community. She'll find out one way or another. And after everything she's going through with the vampire transition..." Delia's hands shook as she tried to unbutton her coat.

"One thing at a time," Ingrid said firmly. "That's why we're doing this tonight. We need clarity – about the fire dragon, about the Order's plans, about all of it. We have some complications to work out."

"Speaking of complications," Delia said, "I've been studying my family grimoire. Some of those Bracewell ancestors were..." She shuddered. "Well, let's just say power-hungry doesn't begin to cover it. There are spells in there that make the Order look positively benevolent."

"Any mention of the fire dragon?" Agatha asked.

"Nothing direct. But there's this recurring reference to 'the heart of earth's fire' and something about 'when stone flows like water.' It feels significant, but—"

"But we're all too caught up in our worries to see clearly," Ingrid finished. "Which is exactly why we're doing this tonight." She gestured to the perfectly arranged tea setting.

"The mushrooms will show us what we need to see, not what we want to see."

"Like last time?" Delia asked wryly. "When I had no idea what I was drinking?"

"This time you're choosing to walk through the door," Ingrid said. She paused, studying her friends' faces in the firelight. "You're all sure about this?"

The others simply nodded.

"Right then." Ingrid began measuring the precious mushroom-laced tea into each ceremonial cup. "We are going to use Delia's grimoire as a magical signature to follow into this inner journey – it should help us to get more information on the fire dragon." She gestured to the grimoire set on the table between them. "But first, ground rules. Whatever we see, whatever comes up – no running away. No hiding. No pretending it didn't happen tomorrow."

"Like you're doing with Covvey?" Agatha muttered.

Ingrid's hands stilled on the kettle. "I'll make you a deal," she said finally. "I'll talk to my long lost brother if you all promise to face whatever truths the tea shows us. Deal?"

A weighted silence fell, broken only by the fire's crack and pop.

"Deal," said Agatha sternly. "Suppose I can't very well lecture Covvey about facing the past if I'm not willing to face a few magical visions."

Ingrid nodded, satisfied. The thought of starting a conversation with Covvey now was as unpalatable as an old leather boot for afternoon tea, but she knew she was tough enough to weather it, even if it meant being growled at.

The earth dragon-pup circled their seated forms once before settling by the hearth.

The tea's steam carried scents of earth and moss, of secrets buried deep and truth rising like sap in spring.

"This is a healing brew. The visions will be different for each of us," Ingrid explained, her voice taking on the tone she used for teaching young witches. "But they'll show us what we need to see, not necessarily what we want to see. Don't fight them. Don't try to direct them. Just...let them come."

"And if what we need to see is horrible?" Delia asked quietly.

"Then we face it together," Marjie said firmly. "That's what we do, isn't it? Face the horrible things together?"

Ingrid raised her cup. "To facing horrible things together, then."

"And to finding that bloody fire dragon," Agatha added, lifting her own cup.

"And to family," Marjie said softly, her eyes on Ingrid. "Lost and found."

They drank as one. Then, they sat in silence until, gradually, the fire's flames began to dance in unusual patterns. Shadows deepened, colours intensified, and the space between thoughts grew fluid and strange.

"Oh," Marjie breathed, her empathic defences softening as the tea opened her mind. "Oh, I can feel...everything..."

Ingrid watched her friends' faces transform as the visions took hold. The fire cast strange shadows, and beneath her palms the wooden floor seemed to pulse with earth's slow heartbeat.

Marjie spoke first, her voice distant and dreamy. "Oh...the water shows me such patterns. Everything connected, flowing together. The crystal..." She gasped, hands flying to her mouth. "It's trying to sing out in sorrow...to cry all the tears of the world...to unite people despite their suffering." Tears streamed down her face, though Ingrid couldn't tell if they were her own or borrowed from someone else's pain.

"I see a dragonfly...over the ocean. It's leading me to an island...a chamber," Delia murmured, swaying slightly as she stared into the fire. "Deep under the earth where stone turns to fire. The fire dragon...it's waiting, but..." Her hands reached toward the flames. "I can't see where."

"Volcano!" Agatha's eyes flew open. "It's in a volcano – of course it is! The air currents show me...ripples spreading outward from an ancient breaking. Like cracks in glass, but in reality itself."

Ingrid felt earth's wisdom rising through her like sap through roots, showing her truths buried deeper than bone. Her mother's face in moonlight, heavy with secrets. Tiny Mathilda practicing her first spells while their brother kept watch, his wolf-form alert for danger. Gwyneth in the Sisterhood's halls, torn between duty and truth. Each memory pierced her heart.

"The earth remembers everything," she heard herself say. "Everything we've lost, everything we've forgotten...it's all still here, in the soil, in the stones, in our bones."

Their separate visions began to weave together. Through

Marjie's overwhelmed whispers, Agatha's sharp insights, and Delia's fire-touched murmurings, Ingrid saw the pattern emerging. A great magical sundering centuries ago. Powers split that should have remained whole. Dragons bound as guardians until balance could be restored.

"The Order seeks dominion," Delia was saying, her voice strange with fire's knowledge. "The Sisterhood seeks peace through mind control. But neither understands..."

Marjie cut in, trembling. "The crystal drinks Mathilda's power because she carries fragments of the original magic. In her blood. In all your blood, Ingrid. That's why they took you in, why they made you forget..."

"The Order wants to gather all those fragments now," Agatha added, air magic swirling visibly around her. "But if either side succeeds..."

The earth dragon-pup howled, ancient knowing filling the room. Through their combined sight, filtered through earth's deep wisdom, Ingrid saw truth unfolding like roots spreading through soil: the fire dragon's resting place, the Order's plans, the Sisterhood's desperate gambit, all converging toward a point of no return. A great magical sundering centuries ago. Powers split that should have remained whole. Dragons bound as guardians...

29

BENEDICT

*F*ather Benedict, the Crimson Shepherd – *Chosen of the Almighty* – stood in his strategy room, dark satisfaction coursing through him as he surveyed his domain.

Maps and charts lined the pristine walls in perfect patterns, their edges so precisely aligned that even a millimetre's deviation would have offended his sense of divine order.

Artifacts of power sat on polished shelves, each positioned according to sacred geometry – ancient daggers pointing true north, crystals arranged by resonance frequency, scrolls arranged by both age and potency.

The air crackled with barely contained energy. Power thrummed through him constantly now, dark and delicious, demanding release.

But control was everything.

Control separated the truly powerful from mere chaos merchants like those insufferable Crones.

A hesitant knock interrupted his contemplation of a particularly promising tactical diagram showing Myrtle-wood's theoretical weak points.

"Enter," he commanded, not deigning to turn from his study. The door creaked – he'd have to have someone oil those hinges – and soft footsteps approached, accompanied by the rustle of robes and the distinctive sound of nervous swallowing.

"Cleric Mateas." Benedict could smell the fear on him. The new cleric's upper lip would be beaded with sweat by now, his watery blue eyes darting about like a trapped animal's. A poor replacement for the traitor, but he served his purpose.

"Shepherd...there's been a development." Mateas's voice quavered slightly.

Benedict felt a flicker of irritation disturb his careful composure. "Speak."

"It's about...your divorce proceedings, Shepherd."

The word hit Benedict like a physical blow. His shoulders tensed beneath his robes as the Almighty's power stirred, responding to his displeasure.

"That mundane nonsense is beneath our notice," he said, his voice dropping to a dangerous whisper. "The marriage was merely a tactical position, long since abandoned. A necessary evil to maintain our cover while we gathered strength."

"Yes, Shepherd, but..." The sound of hands being wrung

together. "The case has been transferred to the magical courts. You are...required to appear."

The Almighty's power surged through Benedict before he could contain it. Several perfectly arranged artifacts tumbled from their shelves, their crashes echoing through the chamber.

"Required?" The word emerged as a snarl.

"The summons is magically binding," Mateas explained, shrinking back as the power continued to pulse through the room. "If you don't appear voluntarily, the court's power will...compel your presence."

Dark energy crackled visibly around Benedict's form as the Almighty's might responded to his growing rage. His perfectly ordered domain – built through years of careful control – threatened to descend into chaos.

But then a thought struck him, and the power's angry surges transformed into something darker, almost gleeful. "The Crones," he breathed, a slow smile spreading across his face. "They'll be there. Outside Myrtlewood's protection..."

"Yes, Shepherd. They will likely attend to support...her." Mateas shifted uncomfortably, his robes rustling against the stone floor. "However, there is something else you should know. The witching court prohibits the use of power within its walls. All magic is neutralised during proceedings."

The rage that exploded from Benedict this time was unprecedented. The Almighty's power swept through the room like a dark tsunami, sending papers flying in a whirl-wind and knocking Mateas sprawling to the floor. Maps tore from walls, artifacts crashed from shelves, and the perfect order of the chamber descended into utter chaos.

"Neutralised?" Benedict's voice shook the very foundations of the compound. "The Almighty's power cannot be contained by mere courts and procedures!"

Mateas struggled to his feet, robes askew and face pale with terror. "The-the restrictions are absolute, Shepherd. Every participant's power is bound for the duration. But..." He licked his lips nervously. "The protections end once the court adjourns."

Benedict went very still, the Almighty's power settling around him like a dark cloak. Objects stopped falling, suspended in the sudden silence. "After the proceedings..."

"Yes, Shepherd. They'll have to leave the court's protection eventually."

A plan began crystallising in Benedict's mind, bringing with it a calm more terrifying than his rage.

"Prepare tracking spells," he commanded. "The most powerful you can create. Every variant. I want them traced the moment they step outside those doors." His eyes gleamed with fanatical light.

"Of course, Shepherd." Mateas bowed deeply, relief evident in his posture. "But what of the actual case? The mundane lawyer was...dismissed some time ago."

Benedict's lip curled in contempt. "Prepare documentation showing why I deserve to retain all assets. The theatre company, the accounts – everything. I will not lose to her. I will destroy her. Make it clear her abandonment of duties and pursuit of magical corruption justify complete forfeiture." He began pacing, each step precise despite the debris littering the floor. "Detail every missed performance, every breach of contract when she fled. Paint her as an unstable element, corrupted by forces beyond her comprehension."

"And if she brings evidence of your...true activities?"

His smile grew cruel. "They have no jurisdiction over the Order's internal matters. Focus on her failures as a wife and business partner. Make the case airtight."

"Yes, Shepherd. I'll begin immediately." Mateas backed towards the door, careful not to turn his back.

"Go." Benedict's attention returned to his ruined tactical displays, mind spinning with possibilities. The breach in Myrtlewood's defences would come. The dragons would be captured. The real battle would begin the moment they stepped outside those courthouse doors.

The Almighty's power purred within him like a satisfied beast, anticipating the moment when all his enemies would finally be within reach.

30

DELIA

*D*elia sat in her favourite armchair by the fireplace in her cottage, the Bracewell grimoire heavy in her lap. The visions from the mushroom tea still swirled in her head. First, there was a dragonfly.

Marjie had told her the dragonfly was often associated with transformation, adaptability, and spiritual insight, reflecting the creature's graceful ability to dart and hover through its environment with speed and precision. She didn't feel all that graceful, especially in facing something as terrifying as a volcano, but intuition told her that inner transformation was required.

The children were finally asleep after three bedtime stories, two glasses of water, and one lengthy negotiation about whether fairies needed their own pillows.

Their magical abilities seemed to be growing stronger by

the day – this morning, Merryn had accidentally turned all the porridge into butterflies.

"Don't wait up, darling," Kitty called from the hallway, the click of her heels punctuating her words. She appeared in the doorway wearing a remarkably sparkly dress.

"Good lord," said Delia, "you look like you've been attacked by a glitter factory."

"That's rather the point. Roger appreciates a bit of glamour," Kitty said in an ironic tone as she twirled.

"At least he's stopped bringing plastic flowers," Delia observed. "The crystal roses last week were an improvement."

"Oh, hush. Not everyone can have a brooding immortal who brings hand-picked wildflowers and meaningful glances." Kitty adjusted her lipstick in the mirror above the mantle. "Speaking of your mysterious man, where has Declan been lately?"

"Around," Delia said vaguely, though she had been acutely aware of his presence at the edges of her consciousness, like warmth from a distant fire. "He has his own work to pursue. I'm not some lovesick teenager pining away."

"No, you're a powerful witch with excellent taste. Much better." Kitty grabbed her coat, a silver thing almost as sparkly as her dress. "Don't do anything I wouldn't do while I'm gone."

"That leaves my options remarkably open," Delia called after her, but she was smiling as the door closed behind her friend.

Alone now except for the fire's companionship, Delia let out a long breath and turned her attention back to the grimoire. Last night's mushroom tea visions still swirled through her mind like a whirlwind – the volcano, the crystal's hungry light, the sense of ancient breaking that needed to be mended. There had been so much information, yet trying to grasp any specific detail felt like catching smoke.

She ran her fingers over the grimoire's worn leather cover, feeling the magic pulse beneath her touch. The firelight caught strange reflections in its metal clasps, almost like writing that disappeared when she tried to focus on it...

Delia tilted the grimoire toward the fire, trying to catch that elusive glimmer again. There – along the edges of the pages, something flickered just beyond sight. Like words written in light, or perhaps in fire itself. But every time she thought she could make out a letter or symbol, it slipped away like water through her fingers.

"Blast," she muttered, shifting the heavy book in her lap. The tea's insights had shown her so much about the fire dragon, about ancient magics and broken bonds, but here she sat with her family's most powerful magical text and couldn't make heads or tails of its secrets.

She'd been through every page a dozen times since Elamina had delivered it – studying the Bracewell family trees, the carefully documented spells, the margin notes that spoke of power and ambition. Some entries made her skin crawl with their casual cruelty, while others showed glimpses of wisdom and connection to fire's true nature. But nothing that specifically pointed to the dragon she needed to find.

A soft knock at the door interrupted her frustrated musings. Her heart quickened – she knew that knock, knew the presence behind it as surely as she knew her own magic. Still, she took her time rising, setting the grimoire carefully aside. No lovesick teenager indeed.

When she opened the door, Declan filled the frame. His eyes caught firelight from behind her, reflecting gold for just a moment before returning to their usual darkness.

"Hello," she said, aiming for casual and missing by miles.

His smile was slight but warming. "Hello yourself."

Then his arms were around her and she was melting into him, all her carefully maintained composure dissolving like frost in sunlight.

His kiss tasted of winter air and woodsmoke and wild magic, wrapped in hunger she felt echoing in her own blood. Her hands found the cold dampness of his coat, the warm solidity beneath, as the door clicked shut behind them.

"I missed you," she murmured against his mouth, then pulled back with a scowl. "Though I wasn't pining or anything ridiculous like that. I had plenty to keep me busy."

His laugh rumbled through his chest where she pressed against it. "Of course not. You're far too sensible for pining." His fingers traced her cheek, surprisingly gentle for hands that could wield such power. "I missed you too."

They settled by the fire, Declan shrugging off his snow-dusted coat while Delia made tea. The familiar domestic motions helped ground her after the intensity of their reunion. When she returned with the steaming cups, he had claimed her usual chair, leaving her to perch on its broad arm beside him.

"So," she said, passing him a cup, "want to tell me where you've been skulking about?"

"Keeping an eye on our friend Cedric." His arm slipped around her waist, anchoring her. "He's still staying at Covvey's place, but something's not right. His mind is...fracturing. One moment he seems to be healing from the Order's conditioning, the next he's ranting about burning everything down to make it 'simple' again."

Delia shivered despite the fire's warmth. "That sounds ominous."

"It is. Covvey's watching him closely, but..." Declan's jaw tightened. "That's not all. Mephistos has been prowling around, dropping cryptic hints about ancient magic and binding spells. Says he remembers something about the original breaking that caused all this, but can't quite access the memories through his curse."

"That demon cat does love being mysterious." Delia took a sip of tea. "Though speaking of mysterious, wait until you hear about our mushroom tea ceremony last night."

She told him everything – the visions of the volcano, the crystal's hungry light, the sense of time rushing towards some crucial moment. His hand traced absent patterns on her back as she spoke, but she could feel the tension in his fingers.

"The timing concerns me," she said when she finished. "I'm supposed to be facing off against Jerry in court in two days. And I still can't make any more sense of this blasted grimoire." She reached over to where it sat on the side table.

"Look at this – there's something in the firelight, like shimmers that appear, but I can't quite..."

Declan studied the book's edges where they caught the flames' glow. "Have you tried actually using fire on it?"

"Marjie suggested that, actually. Since her tea spill revealed the path to the water dragon. But burning books seems..." She trailed off, frowning. "Though I have been tempted to throw the whole thing in the fire out of pure frustration."

"Delia." His dark eyes held hers, intense and certain. "Do you really think a powerful family of fire witches would let their grimoire burn?"

The question hit her like a brick. Of course they wouldn't.

"I'm doing it." Delia stood, grimoire heavy in her arms, heart pounding.

The fire crackled invitingly, flames dancing as if they knew what was coming. Still, she hesitated.

"This could be an absolutely terrible idea," she said. "What if I'm wrong? What if it does burn? Elamina risked so much to get this to me, and it's an irreplaceable piece of magical history, and—"

Declan's hands settled on her shoulders from behind, steady and grounding. "Trust your instincts. Fire knows its own."

She took a deep breath, remembering all those theatre productions where she'd told actors to trust themselves, to take the leap into their roles. Time to take her own direction.

"Right then," she muttered. "Here goes everything."

She hefted the grimoire and, before she could second-guess herself, tossed it directly into the flames. For one heart-stopping moment, bright red fire engulfed the book entirely. Delia's sharp intake of breath caught in her throat as the magical flames roared higher, filling the entire fireplace with crimson light.

Then, as suddenly as it had flared, the fire died down. The grimoire sat among the coals, glowing a deep, pulsing red like a heart about to beat.

"Well," Delia said dryly, "I don't think that was in the Bracewell family lending policy."

She reached into the fire without thinking, her fingers closing around the book's spine. It was cool to her touch despite its red glow, as if it had absorbed the fire's energy without its heat. When she drew it out, the leather binding shimmered. The metal clasps gleamed like fresh-forged steel.

"Look!" She set it on the table and began turning pages. New text had appeared throughout – notes in the margins written in what looked like liquid fire, diagrams that moved and shifted in the firelight. But most dramatically, an entire section had manifested at the back of the book, pages that definitely hadn't existed before.

"It's a portal spell," she breathed, scanning the text. "One that can only be cast on the new moon, when fire's power peaks and the veil between realms is thinnest. It's meant to open a doorway to...to wherever the fire dragon sleeps! When's the next new moon?"

"Two days," Declan said quietly.

"The same day as my divorce hearing."

They looked at each other in the firelight, understanding passing between them without words. Everything was converging.

"Well," Delia said finally, attempting lightness, "at least I won't worry about trivial things like what to wear."

But Declan didn't smile. His eyes were distant, calculating. "The timing's too perfect. The Order will be watching. The Sisterhood too, probably…"

"Then we'll get ready for them." Delia squared her shoulders, feeling fire stir in her blood. "We're more powerful than any of them know. Besides, I've got an immortal warrior on my side, haven't I?"

"Always," he said, pulling her into another kiss.

31

INGRID

The forest floor dampened Ingrid's footsteps as she approached Covvey's land, fallen leaves releasing their earthy scent with each careful step. She'd walked these paths hundreds of times over the decades, gathering herbs, noting the changing seasons, respecting the unofficial boundary that marked his territory.

Now every step felt weighted with new meaning.

She paused at the edge of his clearing, watching smoke rise from the cabin's chimney. The afternoon light caught on frost still clinging to shadows, making the whole scene look like something from a half-remembered dream.

Brother...

The word still felt foreign in her mind, like a plant she couldn't quite identify. But memories were surfacing now - fragments of childhood spinning through her thoughts like leaves caught in wind.

A boy who let her practice spells while he kept watch.

A wolf who carried her and Mathilda on his back through moonlit forests.

A protector who took their father's rage so she and her sister and mother wouldn't have to.

The wind shifted, carrying her scent toward the cabin. She felt rather than saw Covvey's awareness spike - that particular stillness that comes before recognition. Moments later, a massive grey wolf emerged from the tree line, his movements liquid grace despite his size.

His eyes held decades of loneliness.

"I didn't know," Ingrid said softly, her voice rougher than intended. "They addled my memories. The Sisterhood - they must have..." She stopped... the inadequacy of words....

The wolf - her brother - regarded her steadily. His fur had more silver now, but it was him. The recognition hurt like frost-bite.

"Mother made her choice," Ingrid continued, needing to fill the silence with truth. "She chose to save what she could. But you..." Her voice caught. "You tried to save all of us, didn't you? Even then. Even so young."

Covvey's ears flicked - the tiniest tell. But he remained in wolf form, watching her with eyes that held too much human pain.

Wind stirred the branches overhead. A stray leaf landed on Covvey's nose. He didn't shake it off.

"I remember now," Ingrid said. "How you'd let us braid your fur. How you'd curl around us on cold nights, keeping watch. How you..." She had to stop, unexpected tears threatening. She hadn't cried in decades. She wasn't about to start now.

The wolf took a single step forward, then stopped. The pain of separation hung between them like mist - too thick to see through, too insubstantial to grasp.

Ingrid straightened her spine. "I'm not here to disrupt your life. You've built something here - I respect that." She gestured at the cabin, the carefully tended land. "I just needed you to know that I remember now. That I..." She couldn't quite say the words that sat like stones in her throat.

That I'm sorry. That I miss who we were. That I wish things had been different.

But Covvey's eyes held understanding. Of course they did - he'd had decades of carrying this pain of abandonment. Trying to forget, while she'd been blissfully unaware.

A crow called overhead, breaking the moment. Ingrid took a step back, then another.

"If you ever..." she started, then shook her head. They were both too old, too set in their ways for false promises.

The wolf watched her go, silently. Only when she reached the edge of his territory did she hear it - a single, soft howl that spoke of recognition, of loss, of things too complicated for human words.

The sound followed her home.

32

SABRINA

*T*he first inkling came as Sabrina prepared for bed, a subtle wrongness that prickled at the edges of her magical awareness like a loose thread begging to be pulled. She paused in brushing her silver-streaked hair, the antique ivory brush hovering mid-stroke as she studied her reflection in the vanity mirror.

Something was...off.

She set the brush down with precision. The mansion creaked around her, settling into night's silence, but beneath its familiar sounds lay that persistent sense of disturbance.

"Ridiculous," she told her reflection. But her feet were already carrying her down the dark corridors, following paths worn smooth by generations of Bracewells. The library door recognised her touch, ancient wards humming beneath her fingers as she entered.

Moonlight spilled through the tall windows, catching on leather bindings and gilded spines.

She entered the back room, lined with the most sacred volumes of magical books.

The grimoire's case stood exactly as it always had, centred perfectly on its pedestal of polished obsidian.

The book itself lay within, apparently undisturbed.

Sabrina's shoulders relaxed fractionally. "You see?" she murmured to herself. "Letting paranoia rule at your age? What would Mother say?"

But sleep proved elusive. She tossed in her silk sheets, that nagging sensation returning like a splinter beneath skin. By three in the morning, she could stand it no longer.

This time when she entered the library, she lit every lamp with a gesture, flooding the space with unforgiving light. The grimoire still appeared perfectly normal, Elamina's protection spells shimmering subtly around it.

Sabrina frowned. Since when did Elamina add protective enchantments without consulting her?

When Sabrina reached for the case, the protections sparked violently, throwing her back several feet.

She caught herself against a bookshelf, her dignity suffering more than her person, but rage bloomed hot in her chest. How dare anyone – even family – place wards that would reject her? Her! The Bracewell matriarch, keeper of family traditions, guardian of their legacy!

She straightened her dressing gown, drawing herself up to her full height. Power gathered around her like storm clouds, decades of magical mastery focusing into razor-sharp intent. No mere protection spell would deny her access to her own family's grimoire.

The first counter-spell shattered against Elamina's wards like waves against stone. The second merely made them shimmer mockingly. By the fifth attempt, Sabrina's carefully maintained composure had cracked enough to let a few choice words slip that would have scandalised the magical council for proper conduct.

"Enough games," she snarled, abandoning finesse for raw power. Fire magic – the Bracewell birthright – roared through her veins as she systematically dismantled each layer of protection.

Sweat beaded on her forehead, but she pressed on, methodically stripping away enchantment after enchantment until finally, finally, the case clicked open.

Inside lay a book that, at first glance, appeared to be the grimoire. But as soon as her fingers touched it, the glamour dissolved, revealing a much smaller volume bound in cheap leather. Its title, stamped in peeling gold leaf, read *A Beginner's Guide to Proper Magical Etiquette*.

For a long moment, Sabrina could only stare at this insult masquerading as literature. Then, very carefully, she placed the book back in its case, closed it, and smoothed her silver hair back into perfect order.

The Sisterhood would need to be informed, of course. Their agreement with the Bracewells stretched back generations – they had promised powers beyond imagination, elevation above the petty bureaucracy of the witching parliament, freedom from that insufferable Arch Magistrate's rules and regulations. All in exchange for certain...considerations.

Rage continued to flare as Sabrina paced the library. The room seemed to bear witness to her plight, just as it had for generations of magical knowledge carefully curated by Bracewells who understood their true place in the grand design. Not like Elamina, with her modern notions and political ambitions.

It had to be Elamina. The protections bore her magical signature, and who else would dare such an elaborate deception? Who else would have both the skill and the sheer audacity? The girl clearly didn't understand what was at stake. Their family's destiny, carefully nurtured through centuries of strategic alliances and calculated sacrifices, all of it threatened by one headstrong child's misguided ideas.

The Sisterhood would be...displeased. Sabrina could already imagine Sister Breag's reaction. The crystal's hunger grew stronger daily, they'd told her, its need for power more urgent than ever. The Bracewell grimoire contained secrets that could help satisfy that hunger – secrets that belonged in proper hands, not scattered to the winds by foolish young women who thought they knew better than their elders.

"Our agreement was simple," Sabrina muttered, pausing before the portrait of her great-grandmother. The stern face looked back at her with painted eyes that seemed to hold real judgment. "Keep the Sisterhood informed. Guide events from the shadows. When the time comes, take our rightful place among those who truly understand power."

But where would Elamina have taken it? Her apartment

in London? Her office in Bermuda...? No, she must have... Sabrina's hands clenched as realisation struck.

Delia.

That upstart cousin who'd somehow gained Crone powers while Sabrina, with all her training, had been passed over.

The lamp flames flickered as Sabrina's anger flared, but she forced herself to breathe slowly, deliberately. Rage was a commoner's indulgence. Revenge required patience, precision, and above all, proper timing.

She moved to her writing desk, selecting a piece of cream-coloured stationery embossed with the family crest. Her quill scratched softly as she composed the letter.

"The best revenge," she murmured, sealing the letters with deep green wax, "is served at precisely the right temperature." A small smile curved her lips as she pressed her signet ring into the cooling wax. "And I've always preferred my revenge chilled."

Dawn was breaking by the time she finished her preparations. She stood at the library window, watching light creep across the estate's frost-covered grounds. Let Elamina think she'd won this round. Let Delia believe she was safe with her stolen power and borrowed book. Soon enough, they would learn what happened to those who got in her way.

33

DELIA

*D*elia's hand trailed along the damp wall as she descended ancient stone steps wound down into Glastonbury's magical courthouse, wondering about the centuries of spells layered into the very stone. The walls here were obviously thick with protection magic.

"Whoever decided to put magical court in an actual dungeon clearly had a flair for the dramatic," she muttered, carefully navigating the slippery steps in her sensible shoes, glad she hadn't opted for heels.

"Actually, the location was chosen specifically for its natural properties," Agatha offered from behind. "The ley lines cross here in a way that—"

"Not now, Agatha," Ingrid cut in. "Some of us are trying not to break our necks."

"At least we know the Order can't use magic either,"

Marjie said softly from beside Delia, clearly sensing her anxiety about the coming confrontation.

Delia nodded, though her mind was already racing ahead to what would come after. The portal to find the fire dragon needed to be opened tonight as close to the new moon as possible.

"One thing at a time," Marjie murmured, squeezing her arm. Sometimes her friend's empathic abilities were a blessing.

The corridor at the bottom was lit by floating orbs. The stone walls pressed close, the ceiling low and vaulted. It felt appropriately medieval for what they were about to face.

Delia was about to comment on the atmosphere when she saw a familiar figure waiting outside the heavy wooden courtroom doors. Her heart stopped.

"Gilly?"

Gillian stood perfectly still in that unnaturally graceful way that Delia had begun to recognise: only vampires seemed to manage it. Her skin was paler than ever in the dungeon's low lighting, making her eyes seem darker, deeper.

"Mum," Gillian said, and then they were holding each other tightly. Despite her daughter's cold skin, the embrace felt like coming home.

"You shouldn't be here," Delia whispered, even as she clutched Gillian closer. "I didn't want you to have to face him...he's..."

Gillian pulled back slightly. There was something new in her expression – a hardness, a predatory gleam that hadn't been there before. "I know, Mum. I read the case files," she said. "All of them."

"Oh, darling." Delia reached to smooth her daughter's hair, an old gesture from childhood comfort. "I wanted to tell you myself, but with everything you've been going through..."

"I understand why you didn't," Gillian said. "I suppose 'your father is a leader in a secret magical cult' seemed like it was a bit much news on top of everything. But he betrayed us both, didn't he? All those years, everything was just...manipulation. Part of his grand plan for his precious Order." The darkness in her eyes when she spoke about her father sent a chill down Delia's spine.

Before she could respond, the corridor filled with echoing footsteps and rustling robes. Order members arrived like a wave of crimson, Jerry—at their centre. His eyes swept over them all before fixing on Gillian with genuine surprise.

The hiss that escaped Gillian's lips was purely inhuman. Her fangs flashed briefly before Perseus Burk smoothly stepped between them, his own vampiric nature evident in the fluid grace of his movement.

"I believe the proceedings are about to begin," he said pleasantly, as if he weren't standing between a vampire and the father who had betrayed her. "Shall we?"

The courtroom itself was larger than Delia expected, its high ceiling lost in shadow above floating magical lights. Ancient wooden benches creaked as the Order members filed in, taking up far more space than seemed necessary. Their red robes made the room look like it was bleeding.

"Subtle," Ingrid muttered as they took their seats. "About as subtle as a brick through a window."

"Speaking of subtle," Marjie whispered, nodding towards where Jerry sat with his legal representative. "Someone's not enjoying being magically constrained."

Delia watched Jerry's fingers twitch and clench, his jaw tight with barely contained fury. The magical protections of the courtroom seemed to physically pain him, as if he'd grown too dependent on whatever dark power he now apparently channelled. She felt a grim satisfaction.

The judge entered – a severe-looking witch with steel-grey hair pulled back in an elegant knot. Her robes of office rippled with subtle enchantments even the dampening field couldn't fully suppress. "All rise," called the bailiff, his voice echoing off stone walls.

The court proceedings began, though with distinctly magical touches. The oath was sworn on a crystal that glowed with truth-telling enchantments.

The Order's representative rose first – a thin man with a reedy voice that grew stronger as he warmed to his argument. "The marriage was deliberately designed in order that that it served a higher purpose," he declared. "He contributed significantly to the finances. All assets accumulated during this should go towards furthering the Order's sacred mission. Ms Spark has no claim—"

"Objection," Perseus interrupted smoothly. "This is misleading. My client had no knowledge of these arrangements. It's misleading to say they were deliberate as that was only the case for one side."

"Sustained," the judge said sharply.

Delia felt Gillian tense beside her as the Order's lawyer detailed how Jerry had supposedly always intended their life together to serve his organisation's ends. Each word seemed to wind her daughter tighter. Delia reached for her hand, finding it ice-cold.

"It's all right, love," she whispered. "He can't hurt us anymore."

Gillian's laugh was barely audible. "Oh, I'm not afraid of him hurting us, Mum. I'm afraid of what I might do to him if he comes near you again."

The tone of her voice made Delia shiver.

When Perseus rose to present their case, his presence filled the room despite his understated manner. "The Order speak of sacred missions and higher purposes," he began, "but let us speak plainly of what really happened here. A man spent decades deliberately deceiving his wife about his true identity, his beliefs, and his intentions for their shared life."

He proceeded to systematically dismantle the Order's arguments, producing document after document showing Jerry's careful construction of his false identity. "Ms Spark believed she was married to a theatre producer who shared her passion for the arts. Instead, she was being used as unwitting cover by a man who despised everything she valued. Who took the life she built through talent and hard work and twisted it to serve his own ends."

It was satisfying to hear it all laid out so clearly. Delia felt some tension unravelling within her. For months, this whole situation had wound around her tightly and now there was a deep, satisfying releasing.

Delia watched Jerry's face darken with each point Perseus made.

His fingers kept twitching, reaching for power that wouldn't come. The Order members shifted restlessly in their seats.

"The magical statute regarding marriages founded on deception is quite clear," Perseus continued. "When one party systematically deceives the other about fundamental aspects of their identity and purpose, all joint assets are forfeit to the wronged party. This prevents magical practitioners from using mundane spouses as unwitting tools – exactly what Brother Benedict did here."

"Objection!" Jerry's lawyer called. "She's a witch!"

The judge raised an eyebrow. "Indeed she is. However, that is no reason to object. It seems she was not aware of that fact at the time, so the statute on protections for mundane peoples still applies. Objection dismissed."

The judge called a brief recess to consider the arguments. As people began to move, Jerry suddenly rose and strode toward their group. Gillian was on her feet instantly, fangs fully visible now, but Ingrid and Agatha moved to flank them while Marjie's hand found Delia's arm.

"You think you've won something here?" Jerry's voice was low, meant for Delia's ears alone.

"That's close enough," Perseus said quietly, appearing beside them. Something in his tone made Jerry step back, though his eyes burned with barely contained rage.

"Time is on our side today," he said, and Delia felt a chill at his choice of words. Did he somehow know about their plans?

Delia checked her watch during the recess – less than two hours until the new moon. The timing was going to be desperately tight. She huddled with the Crones in a corner of the courtroom, speaking in hushed tones.

"They're blocking every exit," Marjie observed. "And once we leave the courthouse field..."

"We'll be vulnerable," Agatha finished. "And they know it."

"Not entirely helpless though," Ingrid said. "We're powerful."

Gillian paced nearby, her movements unnaturally fluid. "The Burks have people outside too," she said. "Just in case."

The bailiff called them back to order before they could plan further. As they retook their seats, Delia noticed more red-robed figures had somehow squeezed into the court-room. The air was thick with tension.

The judge returned, her face impassive as she reviewed a scroll that shimmered with verification spells. The room fell silent.

Delia held her breath. Beside her, Gillian had gone preternaturally still.

"Having reviewed the evidence," she began, her voice carrying to every corner of the room, "I find the argument regarding deception in magical marriage to be compelling. The statute is indeed clear on this matter. When one party systematically deceives another about fundamental aspects of their identity, particularly in cases involving magical practitioners and mundane spouses, the law must protect the deceived party. Therefore, I rule that all assets accumulated during the marriage – including but not limited to the theatre company, properties, and financial accounts – are to be transferred to Ms Spark's sole ownership. The marital contract is hereby dissolved."

A surge of triumph went through Delia's supporters. Marjie squeezed her hand while Ingrid allowed herself a satisfied smile. But Delia's eyes were on Jerry, watching as his face contorted with rage.

"This is an outrage!" he began, but his lawyer grabbed his arm, whispering urgently. The Order members were on their feet.

"Court is adjourned," the judge announced firmly, rising to leave. But no one moved toward the exits. The tension in the room was unbearable.

"Mum," Gillian whispered, "we need to get you out of here. Now."

Delia nodded slightly, her mind racing. They had to get safely away from the courthouse, open the portal. And somehow they had to get past what seemed like an army of Order members.

"Well," Delia said, trying to inject some lightness into her voice, "I don't suppose anyone thought to bring a smoke bomb?"

Ingrid's smile widened slightly as she patted her pocket. "Something rather more interesting than that, actually.

Though I do hope everyone here isn't too attached to their sense of smell for the next few hours..."

"What's this then?" Marjie asked.

"Don't breathe through your nose," Ingrid muttered. "And try to look surprised when it happens."

Perseus caught Delia's eye and gave an almost imperceptible nod. Several dark-suited figures that could only be other vampires had materialised near the less obvious exits. The Burks had indeed come prepared.

Jerry was still arguing with his lawyer, his voice rising as the Order members pressed closer, their crimson robes seeming to fill every available space. The dungeon's stone walls felt like they were closing in.

"We should have a proper celebration," Delia said loudly. "The Rose & Dragon, perhaps?"

"Excellent idea," Marjie played along. "Though mind the time – it's getting rather late."

The time. Delia's stomach clenched as she checked her watch again. The moon waited for no one. If they didn't open the portal soon...

A commotion near the judge's bench drew everyone's attention. Two Order members appeared to be having some kind of argument, their voices rising as they shoved each other. In the momentary distraction, Ingrid's hand moved so quickly Delia almost missed it.

The effect was instantaneous. A smell like a thousand rotten eggs mixed with skunk spray and something indescribably worse filled the courtroom. People began gagging and rushing toward the exits, all dignity forgotten. The

Order's formation dissolved into chaos.

"That smell!" Delia gasped.

Ingrid chucked. "You can thank me later!"

"Now!" Perseus called, and the Burk vampires moved with supernatural speed, creating corridors through the crowd. Gillian grabbed Delia's arm, her inhuman strength propelling them forward while the other Crones kept pace.

They burst out of the courtroom into the corridor, Order members staggering in their wake. But Jerry's voice rose above the chaos: "Stop them! Don't let them reach the exit!"

"The stairs to the left," Gillian said urgently.

A group of red-robed figures had recovered enough to block exits. Perseus and his vampires engaged them, moving almost too fast to see, but more Order members were recovering from Ingrid's olfactory assault.

"There!" Marjie pointed to a narrow side passage. "Service entrance!"

They ran for it, feet pounding against ancient stone. Behind them, Jerry's rage-filled voice echoed off the walls: "The power will be ours!"

Did he know what they were planning? There was no time to worry about that now. The passage twisted upward, the air growing fresher as they climbed.

"Almost past the protection field," Agatha panted. "Get ready—"

They burst through a door into what looked to have once been castle kitchens. Delia felt her magic surge back to life, fire dancing at her fingertips.

But they weren't safe yet. The sounds of pursuit grew closer.

"This way," Gillian said, leading them toward what looked like a delivery entrance. "The Burks have a car waiting, if we can—"

The door behind them exploded inward. Jerry stood framed in the doorway, his eyes blazing with unnatural light as he cleared the dampening field. The Almighty's power rolled off him in waves of darkness.

"Did you really think you could just walk away?" he snarled. "That I'd let you take everything I've worked for?"

But Delia wasn't having it. Fire rose within her as she faced the man who'd manipulated her for decades.

"You took years of my life," she said, her voice steady. "You don't get to take anything else."

"Now!" Marjie shouted. At her signal, all four Crones moved in synchronisation. Agatha's wind whipped through the kitchen, objects flying. Marjie's water spell made the stone floor treacherously slick. Ingrid's earth magic shook the very foundations, while Delia's fire formed a wall between them and their pursuers.

"Mum!" Gillian called from the delivery entrance. "The car!"

But more Order members were pouring in from other doors, their robes like splashes of blood in the morning light. Jerry raised his hands, dark power gathering around him.

"You have no idea what you're interfering with," he growled. "The power of the dragons, the ancient magic – it belongs in proper hands!"

"Oh, do shut up," Ingrid snapped, throwing something that looked suspiciously like another stink bomb.

Perseus and his vampires crashed through a side door, creating more confusion. "This way!" he called.

They ran, Delia's fire keeping the Order members at bay while Gillian and the other vampires cleared their path. The morning air hit them like a blessing after the dungeon's damp chill.

"Almost there," Marjie panted. "Just a few more—"

Jerry's power struck like a physical blow, dark energy rolling over them in waves. "Don't even bother running," he said, his voice distorted by whatever force he now channelled. "The Order will claim what's rightfully ours!"

"Choke on this!" Ingrid threw down her final surprise. Green smoke erupted around them, acrid and thick.

"What now?" Delia said, as they rushed away from the smoke.

"Rather a tight spot you're in." A familiar voice cut through the chaos. Juniper materialised in a blur of purple, looking unfairly composed in her pinstriped suit. Behind them, Jerry's dark power crashed against Ingrid's defences.

"Juniper!" Marjie exclaimed. "Thank the gods!"

"No time for that." Juniper adjusted her copper-framed glasses. "I can get four of you out of here, but we need to move now."

Delia turned to Gillian, her heart clenching as more Order members poured through the doors. "Darling—"

"Go," Gillian said firmly. "Perseus and I will handle this.

Besides." Her smile turned predatory. "I think Father could use a reminder about respecting boundaries."

They hugged quickly, Gillian's cold skin against Delia's fire-warm magic creating a strange harmony. Through the green smoke of Ingrid's last defence, Jerry's power pulsed darker.

"Be careful," Delia whispered.

"You too, Mum. Go do what you have to do."

"Ready?" Juniper's voice carried an unusual edge of urgency.

The Crones gathered close, linking hands. The last thing Delia saw before Juniper's magic took them was Gillian's face, fierce and beautiful, as she turned to face her father.

Teleportation felt like being turned inside out while spinning in several directions at once. Colours blurred, sound stretched into meaningless vibrations, and Delia's stomach attempted several impressive acrobatic manoeuvres.

The world twisted, compressed, then snapped back into focus. They stood in a forest clearing, the castle and their pursuers far behind. For a moment, everyone just breathed.

"Now I understand what Douglas Adams meant about the feeling of being drunk," Delia managed, trying to stop the world from spinning.

"Absolutely horrible," Agatha said, leaning heavily on her cane. "But what's wrong with being drunk?"

"Ask a glass of water that question," Delia said dryly.

Agatha managed a small chuckle, despite still looking slightly green at the gills. "I see what you mean."

"Yes, teleportation is rather like being swallowed in multiple gulps," Marjie said, sounding rather dazed.

"You're welcome," Juniper said brightly, straightening her jacket. "Now, I believe you have an important mission. Do hurry – the Order will be in hot pursuit."

"At least that will divert them away from Gillian," said Delia. "I know she's strong, but Jerry is...how did he get so powerful? I've never seen anything like it."

Ingrid shook her head. "He's taken it in – whatever it is that the Order worships as a god – he's imbibed that darkness."

Delia shuddered.

"Alright!" said Agatha. "No time for dilly dallying. We have a portal to open, don't we? Where's that book?"

"Here." Delia pulled the Bracewell grimoire from her bag, its pages fluttering open in the sea wind to reveal text that now glowed with inner fire. "The portal needs four points – one for each element."

"No time for rehearsal," Agatha said, already moving to take her position. Wind whipped around her, catching her robes and making her silver hair dance.

They formed a circle, positions aligned with the elements as the grimoire instructed. The wind whipped through the trees, as if in response to their working.

"Fire in the south," Delia read, her voice carrying over the wind. She channelled her magic through the words, feeling them burn on her tongue. The grimoire's pages turned by themselves, ancient paper crackling with power.

Marjie's water magic pulled at the nearby stream,

drawing it into patterns. Ingrid's earth power made the very rocks hum with deep resonance. Agatha's magic made the wind still.

The elements wove together as Delia spoke the final words.

From the grimoire, Delia read:

By FIRE AND FLOOD, *by earth and air*
   we call upon the ancient ways
   Let what was sealed be opened
   let what sleeps awaken
   Dragon's heart and dragon's flame
   We claim our birthright in the old names
   From blood of fire to blood of flame
   From ancient sleep to present wake.
   By our joined powers we command – open!

FIRE ERUPTED FROM HER HANDS, not in its usual golden streams but in colours she'd never seen before – deep crimsons and violets that seemed to bend space itself. The portal tore open like a wound in reality, its edges burning with dragon-fire.

"Now!" Marjie shouted.

And the Crones leapt through.

34

DECLAN

$\mathcal{D}$eclan paused outside Covvey's hut, scenting woodsmoke and Papa Jack's distinctive hot chocolate on the crisp winter air. Through the window, he could see the old man stirring his pot while Cedric knelt by the fire. The scene looked peaceful enough, but something in the former cleric's too-careful movements made Declan's instincts prickle.

He entered quietly, noting how Cedric's shoulders tensed slightly before relaxing again.

The man's hands remained steady as he arranged kindling – a marked improvement from the trembling wreck they'd first brought here.

"Just in time," Papa Jack said, adding a pinch of something aromatic to his pot. "The chocolate's almost ready." Steam rose, carrying scents of cardamom, cinnamon, and other spices Declan couldn't quite identify. The man had a gift for creating comfort.

Covvey sat nearby, ostensibly focused on cleaning his hunting knives, but Declan caught how his friend's attention kept returning to Cedric. The wolf-shifter's protective instincts were clearly engaged.

"The routine helps," Cedric offered unprompted, his voice calmer than Declan remembered. "Having purpose. Structure." He paused, arranging another stick with precise care. "The right kind of structure this time."

Papa Jack's quiet humming filled the comfortable silence, but underneath that peace, Declan sensed something coiled and waiting.

"Been sleeping better," Cedric continued, still not looking up from his task. "The dreams are...different now. Less about the Order. More about..." He trailed off, then added softly, "More about what might come after. About healing."

The words sounded hopeful, but Declan noticed how Cedric's fingers lingered on each piece of wood, as if needing to confirm its reality.

Papa Jack poured the hot chocolate with careful ceremony, the rich aroma filling the hut as he passed out earthenware mugs. "Marjie always said some conversations need the right atmosphere," he said, settling into his chair with a quiet groan. "A bit of comfort makes the hard things easier to bear."

Declan accepted his mug, letting the warmth seep into his hands. Through the steam, he watched Covvey set aside his knives, something troubled in the wolf-shifter's expression.

"You're thinking about what Agatha told you," Declan said quietly.

Covvey grunted. "How do you know about that?"

Declan shrugged. "Delia told me. I thought you should know."

Covvey's shoulders tensed. "Family's complicated."

"Isn't it just," Cedric muttered, then looked surprised at his own bitterness. He took a careful sip of chocolate before continuing. "The Order...they make themselves your family. Fill all those empty spaces with their devotion..."

"The Sisterhood does something similar," said Declan. "Any group that demands absolute loyalty usually does."

"How do you tell the difference?" Cedric asked, his voice small. "Between real bonds and...and conditioning? Sometimes I think I'm getting better, thinking clearer, but then..." He stared into his mug as if it might hold answers.

"The fact that you're asking the question says something," Declan offered. "Real bonds can survive doubt. Conditioning shatters under it."

Covvey nodded slowly. "True bonds flex and bend. False ones break."

"The Order's bonds already broke," Cedric said, his hands steady around his mug despite the weight in his words. "But what's left after? Who are you when all those false pieces fall away?"

Papa Jack hummed thoughtfully. "Whoever you choose to

be, I expect. That's the hard part of freedom – figuring out what to do with it."

The fire popped, sending sparks flying upward. Declan saw something shift in Cedric's expression – not quite peace, but perhaps its beginning.

"Well, well," came a familiar drawl from the windowsill. "Isn't this cosy? Like a charming little support group for the magically damaged."

Mephistos materialised fully, but his usual languid pose was betrayed by bristling fur and unnaturally bright eyes. Magic crackled visibly around him, making the hanging herbs sway without wind.

"Something's happening," the demon cat announced, tail lashing. "Can't you feel it? The Order, the Sisterhood, the Crones – all the players moving into position like pieces on a cosmic chessboard."

Declan was already reaching for his knuckle bones, a cold certainty gripping his chest. The bones clattered against the wooden table, their pattern making his breath catch.

"Delia," he said, reading the augury. "She's not at the courthouse. Not anymore."

The bones showed him distance, showed him salt spray and ancient power. Somewhere in the vast ocean, Delia's magic flared like a beacon.

"The hearing was today?" Covvey said. "Why didn't you go with her?"

"She told me to stay away," he said quietly, gathering the bones. "Said the Order couldn't know I survived. But this..."

He gestured at the pattern. "This is different. Something's changed."

"Oh pet," Mephistos purred, though his fur still stood on end, "when has anything ever gone according to plan in this little melodrama?"

"I'm going to follow them," Declan announced. "I'll make a portal to where they are. Who is coming with me?"

Covvey and Papa Jack immediately volunteered, but both cast hesitant eyes towards Cedric.

"The Crones," Cedric said, his earlier calm fracturing. "They're going to confront the Order, aren't they? Going to try to stop what's coming?" His hands began to shake, sending hot chocolate sloshing. "I need to help. I know things – about their plans, about their weaknesses."

"Easy now," Papa Jack murmured.

"You don't understand," Cedric insisted, pacing now. "Everything's connected. The Order, the Sisterhood, the breaking – it all leads to this moment. I can feel it." His voice took on an edge of desperation. "Please. I need to do something right for once."

Declan exchanged glances with Covvey. Leaving Cedric behind could be dangerous in his current state, but taking him into a confrontation with the Order...

"If you leave him, he'll try to follow anyway," Mephistos observed, examining his claws. "He'll probably cast a bad portal and get himself killed in some tediously dramatic fashion."

"I'm going to Delia," Declan said firmly, gathering his weapons. "The rest of you don't have to—"

"Don't even finish that sentence," Covvey growled, already shouldering his pack.

Papa Jack set down the pot of chocolate. "Well then. Shall we?"

Declan pressed his palm against the knuckle bones, feeling for Delia's distant magic. The connection thrummed like a plucked string, pointing toward ancient power and imminent chaos.

"I'm coming too, but please...try not to die," Mephistos drawled, dissolving into shadow. "It would be such a boring end to the story."

35

DELIA

The portal shimmered closed behind them as Delia's feet hit black sand, hot even through her shoes. Steam hissed from cracks in the volcanic rock, carrying a sulfurous stench that made her eyes water. Above them, a perfect cone of mountain pierced the clouds, its peak wreathed in ominous smoke.

"Well," Agatha said, leaning on her cane as she surveyed their surroundings, "I don't remember this particular landmark from my Cornish geography lessons."

"We're not in Cornwall anymore," Marjie murmured, her eyes distant as she tracked patterns in the steam. "Who knows where we are..."

Ingrid knelt to press her palm against the black sand, then quickly withdrew it. "This earth speaks a different language entirely. Restless. Angry." She wiped her hand on her skirt. "And considerably hotter."

"At least we know we're in the right place," Delia said, watching another steam vent explode nearby. "Though I must say, I'm not feeling confident about walking into an active volcano. Why couldn't it have been in a cave or something?"

"Because that would have been far too straightforward," Agatha commented dryly. "Why settle for a nice sensible cave when we could have a mountain that might explode at any moment?"

They began climbing the rocky slope, picking their way between steam vents and patches of ground that glowed with suspicious heat. The higher they went, the stronger Delia felt the pull of volcanic fire – wild and ancient, so different from her controlled flames. It sang in her blood, calling to something deeper than her normal magic.

"The grimoire's practically humming," she told the others, feeling the book pulse in her bag. "Like it recognises this place."

Delia felt the tension building with each step. The volcano's power thrummed through her, growing stronger as they climbed. Something waited up there, something ancient and fierce.

"Does anyone else hear that?" Marjie asked suddenly, stopping in her tracks.

They all froze, listening. Through the hiss of steam and the mountain's deep rumble, Delia caught something that sounded almost like chanting.

The chanting grew louder as red-robed figures emerged from the volcanic mist, their garments stark against the black rock. Benedict stood at their centre, power rippling off him in waves that made the very air crackle with darkness. His eyes blazed red.

"You never could leave well enough alone, could you, Delia?" His voice carried unnaturally across the distance. "Always pushing, always questioning. Years of careful planning, decades of preparation, and you had to keep digging until you exposed everything."

"Exposed?" The word burst from her like a spark igniting dry timber. "Is that what bothers you, Jerry? That I finally saw through your lies?" Fire danced along her arms as decades of suppressed rage found their voice. "Over thirty years I gave you, and every single moment was a lie."

"Not every moment." His smile was cruel. "Sometimes the indifference was real. You didn't care about me, did you? Never questioning why your husband needed so many late-night meetings, so many secret phone calls..."

The flames grew brighter, feeding off her fury. "Do you want to know what the worst part was?" she demanded. "Not the lies. Not even the manipulation. It was watching you twist everything beautiful into something ugly. I pity you. Did you ever feel anything real? Even once?"

"Feel?" Benedict's laugh echoed off the volcanic rocks. "I felt the glory of the Almighty's purpose. While you played with your petty dramas, I was serving a higher calling."

"Higher calling? You're nothing but a bully hiding behind fancy words. All your talk of divine purpose – it's just an excuse to hurt people."

She hurled a fireball that split the air.

His darkness swallowed her flame whole. "You never could understand true power," he sneered. "It got in the way of your career. You could have ruled by fear like a true leader, but you were too weak. Always building people up, always moving forwards with your pathetic attempts at meaning."

"We have different definitions of weakness," She sent another blast of fire, this one fueled by memory. "Fear doesn't usually help. But you can't see it, can you? Too busy plotting your grand schemes to understand actual human courage."

Their powers clashed in the space between them, fire and darkness meeting in an explosion that sent tremors through the volcanic rock. Delia poured everything into her flames – every sleepless night, every questioned decision, every moment of joy he'd dismissed as meaningless.

"Tell me something, Jerry." She spat his old name like a curse. "When did you stop pretending? Was it gradual, or did you wake up one morning and realise you didn't have to bother with the caring husband act anymore?"

The darkness absorbed her attack, growing stronger. "Names are power, Delia," he snarled. "I am the Crimson Shepherd. The Almighty's chosen vessel. And you..." He gathered power like a storm cloud. "You are nothing but a distraction."

His counterattack struck like physical force, a wave of cold so intense it burned. Delia staggered but kept her feet, drawing on deeper fires.

The volcano rumbled beneath them.

"Nothing?" She laughed, wild and fierce. "I'm the fire

that's going to burn your precious Order to ash. Every lie, every manipulation, every moment you made me doubt myself – it's all fuel now."

But even as she spoke, the Almighty's might pressed down like a physical weight, threatening to extinguish her flames. Each burst of fire seemed weaker than the last. She was drowning in darkness.

His power was overwhelming, centuries of accumulated darkness against her newly awakened fire. The cold pressed closer, squeezing the breath from her lungs, dimming her inner flame to embers.

"You see?" Jerry's voice seemed to come from everywhere and nowhere. "Love is weakness. Faith is strength. The Almighty—"

Ingrid glared back at him, hands on hips. "The Almighty can go play knick-knack on someone else's door." She sent a wave of earth magic rumbling through the ground, crumbling the rocks beneath his feet, but he merely rose up, floating in the air.

"You see?" Jerry's voice echoed from everywhere and nowhere. "This is true power, Delia. Not your petty flames, not your amateur theatrics. The Almighty's might cannot be denied."

"The Almighty," she spat, trying to find her feet, "or your ego?"

The darkness constricted further. Black spots danced at the edges of her vision. Even the volcano's heat seemed distant now, muffled under layers of supernatural cold.

"Still defiant," Benedict sneered. "Still clinging to your

illusions of strength. But in the end, you're nothing. You've always been nothing. Just a convenient cover for my greater purpose."

Delia gasped. Through the darkness, she could barely make out the shapes of the other Crones, similarly over-whelmed by the Order's power. They had underestimated him. All their preparation, all their newfound strength – it wasn't enough against the darkness.

36

AGATHA

*T*he wind spoke to Agatha even through Benedict's oppressive darkness – ancient currents seemed to be carrying messages from heights where the air was thin and clean.

While Delia struggled against the Almighty's crushing power, Agatha calmly opened her enchanted handbag.

"Really?" Ingrid gasped between attempts to shield them with earth magic. "You're going through your bag now? Lost your lip balm?"

"Unlike some people," Agatha said dryly, "I believe in being prepared." Her fingers found what she sought – a big leather-bound book that hummed with old magic. "Ah, there you are."

"Is that—" Marjie started, then had to duck as another wave of darkness rolled over them.

"The original Crone grimoire? Yes." Agatha adjusted her spectacles, unbothered by the chaos around them.

"That's still supposed to be at my place!" Ingrid cried.

"And you didn't even notice it was missing," Agatha said. "In the meantime, I've been studying it for useful magic."

"And you didn't think to mention this?" Delia's voice was strained as her fire dimmed further.

"We don't have time to discuss it endlessly." Agatha said. "Just like I didn't have the patience to ask permission. Besides, you'll be pleased I stole it if it can help us now."

"I hate that she has a point," Ingrid muttered.

The book fell open to a marked page.

Ancient symbols caught Agatha's eye. "Now then," she said, as calmly as if she were preparing for afternoon tea, "shall we show this pompous zealot what four properly prepared Crones can do?"

"What is that, then?" Marjie asked.

"The shield spell requires all four elements in perfect balance," Agatha said, voice steady despite Benedict's darkness pressing closer. "When I give the signal, each of you channel your power through this sigil." She held up the grimoire.

"And you're just now mentioning this because...?" Ingrid grunted, still trying to hold back the encroaching shadows with walls of volcanic rock.

"Because you lot would have wanted to practice." Agatha positioned herself precisely, compass-sure. "Some things work better unrehearsed. Raw. Real." She looked at each of them in turn. "Ready?"

"As we'll ever be," Delia managed, her flames barely visible now.

"Circle up," Agatha commanded. "Earth to the north, Fire south, Water west, Air east. Just like usual."

They moved into position, Benedict's mocking laughter echoing around them. "A shield spell? How desperate you must be."

But this was no ordinary shield and Agatha had known it from the first moment she'd seen the page – the elements were already responding. Ingrid's connection to the earth beneath them. Marjie's connection with the ocean around them. Delia's resonance with magma's ancient fire. And Agatha's own bond with the high winds that circled the peak.

"Begin," she said, and lifted her hands to summon the air.

The spell started as a whisper then Agatha began to sing the chant, her voice carrying words.

Around them, the wind began to sing. It swept upward in spiraling currents, carrying scents of ice and starlight from impossible heights. Her hair lifted in the magical breeze as the ancient words flowed.

The earth responded next as Ingrid's voice joined hers. The volcanic rock beneath them shuddered, then sent obsidian spires shooting upward – black glass transmuted by deep magic. They formed the first framework of their shield.

Marjie's water magic manifested in chains of steam and sea water that twisted between the obsidian spires, condensing into sheets of pure force. The water droplets caught light like countless tiny prisms, refracting their combined power.

"Delia," Agatha called, never breaking rhythm, "the fire now!"

Delia's flames surged upward, no longer fighting Benedict's darkness but working in harmony with the other elements. Fire raced along the crystalline structures, bonding earth and water and air into something entirely new.

The shield took shape around them – a large dome, a complex lattice of elemental magic. Obsidian and steam, flame and wind, all moving together in patterns of nature.

"Futile!" Benedict cried, hurling his power towards them. It broke against the shield. "Impossible!" Benedict snarled, hurling more darkness against their creation.

Through the faceted surface of their shield, Agatha watched Benedict's darkness rage impotently with unsuppressed glee.

Then something shifted in the heart of their protected space. A new portal began to form, different from the one they'd entered through but somehow familiar.

"Hold the shield!" she commanded as the others tensed.

But Delia's face had already broken into a smile of recognition.

"It's alright," she said softly. "I know this magic."

Covvey emerged first, his wolf magic harmonising instantly with their elemental barrier. Papa Jack followed, his quiet power settling into their space like a comfortable sigh. Then came Cedric, the wretched former cleric, looking both terrified and determined, the hood of his cloak was up high as though he was trying not to be seen.

Mephistos materialised next, somehow managing to look both bored and intensely interested.

"Well done, my pets," he drawled, examining the shield's construction. "Though the portal could use a bit more flair."

37

DELIA

*D*elia's heart recognised his magic before her mind could catch up, fire stirring in her blood at the familiar resonance.

Declan stepped through the portal, following the others, and the world seemed to pause. Their eyes met across the protected space, and everything else – the Order's attacks, the volcano's rumble – faded to background noise.

"You're supposed to be hiding," she managed, even as her feet carried her toward him. "Keeping away from the Order so you maintain the advantage of them thinking you dead."

"When have I ever done what I'm supposed to?" He reached for her.

Their kiss tasted of smoke and magic and things too deep for words. His hands tangled in her hair as hers gripped his shirt, pulling him closer, as if making sure he was real. Power sparked between them – her fire and his shadowy magic dancing together like old friends finally reunited.

"NO!" Jerry's rage shattered the moment. "Tracker! I killed you myself! This is impossible!"

Declan's smile was dangerous as he released Delia but kept her hand in his. "You should have made sure."

The Order's magic crashed against their shield with renewed fury. Red-robed figures chanted in ancient tongues as Benedict channeled the Almighty's might into waves of crushing force. The barrier trembled, its elemental matrix straining.

"How dare you!" Jerry's voice distorted with power. "How dare you defile my wife—"

"Ex-wife," Delia corrected, fire flaring in her palms. "And I'll kiss whoever I damn well please."

Darkness exploded against their shield as Jerry unleashed his rage. "You dare flaunt such perversion in the Almighty's presence?" His power crashed against their barrier in waves of cold force.

"The only perversion here," Delia shot back, "is what you've done!" Her fire surged through the shield's matrix, meeting his darkness.

Papa Jack moved with surprising agility for his age, his quiet magic creating pockets of calm in the chaos. Where his power touched, both Order members found their spells faltering, their anger draining away into confusion.

"Sometimes," he said mildly, offering a steadying hand to a dazed-looking red-robed figure, "the strongest magic isn't about power at all. It's about helping folks remember who they really are."

The Order's chanting rose to a fever pitch. Red-robed figures circled their protection, dark energy crackling between them like lightning. Their combined assault made the elemental barrier shudder dangerously.

"It's time you wake up to the truth!" Jerry cried.

"Truth?" said Delia. "Here's the truth – you're weak. You've always been weak. I survived over thirty-five years of your manipulation. Built something beautiful despite your poison. And now?" She gathered her fire, feeling it resonate with the mountain's heart. "Now I'm strong enough to stop you."

Their powers clashed again, fire and darkness meeting in explosions that shook the volcanic rock. The Order's forces pressed closer, their chanting growing louder, their combined might testing every seam of the Crones' shield.

Inside their shield, Cedric shifted uncomfortably as Jerry's attacks intensified. His hood slipped, just for a moment – but it was enough.

Jerry went completely still, his assault pausing mid-strike. "No," he breathed, then louder: "NO!"

Cedric quickly pulled his hood back up, but the damage was done. Through the crystalline barrier, they watched Jerry's face transform from calculated rage to something far more dangerous.

"My own Cleric," he said, voice vibrating with fury. "Among these heretics. These corruptions." Dark power began to gather around him, denser than before. "All my enemies, every thorn in the Order's side – gathered here like rats in a trap."

The red-robed figures around him drew back as his power built to devastating levels. Black lightning crackled between his fingers.

"Do you see?" he called to his followers. "The Almighty delivers them all to us! Traitors, Crones – every festering wound that needs cauterising!"

His laughter echoed off the volcanic rocks as darkness exploded from him. "I will pop this shield like the boil it is! Burn out every trace of resistance!"

The barrier shuddered as Jerry hurled wave after wave of dark power against it. Cold seeped through growing cracks as his assault intensified.

The Order's chanting rose again, adding their power to his rage.

Inside the shield, they staggered under the onslaught. Delia's flames fought to repair the damage while Marjie's water magic sealed the cracks, but Jerry's fury was overwhelming. Each blast of power left more fissures in their protection.

"You cannot hide forever!" Benedict's voice distorted with power. "The Almighty's might will cleanse this corruption!"

Black energy poured from his hands in an unending torrent, testing every seam of their shield, seeking any weakness. The barrier's crystalline surface began to splinter under his relentless attack.

Something shifted in the air – a ripple of new magic that had nothing to do with Benedict's assault.

A great wave rose up and Delia found herself drowning. Water filled her lungs, cold and dark and endless. She thrashed against it, trying to find air, to find fire, to find anything real.

Through the watery haze, she glimpsed her companions fighting their own nightmares. Ingrid spun helplessly in a cyclone of impossible winds. Marjie stumbled through an inferno that couldn't exist. Agatha sank into earth that moved like quicksand. Even Declan's shadows seemed to turn against him, wrapping him in suffocating darkness.

"Not...real," she heard Cedric gasp. He was on his knees, seemingly trapped in an endless maze of Order corridors, ancient chants echoing in his mind.

"The Sisterhood!" Ingrid's voice cut through their private hells. "I know this magic – this is their work!"

Papa Jack braced himself against nothing, lost in a vortex only he could see. Covvey snarled at phantom forests that closed in around him. Even Mephistos' usual grace faltered as his back arched as if fighting off an invisible foe.

Delia fought against the drowning sensation, knowing it wasn't real but unable to escape its grip. How could they maintain the shield when they could barely tell what was real anymore? Through the phantom water, she saw the Order's magic had subsided. Outside the barrier, they were in chaos. The illusions had gotten to them, too, perhaps even more so in their unshielded state. Jerry rolled on the ground, power pouring out into the air around him as he groaned.

"Focus!" Ingrid called out. "The Sisterhood's here some-where – we just can't see them. These are just illusions!"

But the illusions felt horrifyingly real. Each breath brought more phantom water into Delia's lungs. Each movement tangled her deeper in false sensations. Their shield wavered dangerously as everyone struggled against their personal nightmares.

"Remember what's real!" Ingrid's voice seemed to come from very far away. "Find your anchor points!"

Through the phantom drowning, Delia caught glimpses of reality flickering like flames underwater.

Despite her struggle against the endless depths, Delia felt a surge of satisfaction watching the Order's mighty warriors reduced to flailing and cursing at thin air. One particularly pompous elder appeared to be boxing with invisible butterflies.

Red-robed figures stumbled blindly, some swatting at invisible threats, others curled into defensive balls.

Jerry's darkness wavered as he fought whatever nightmare the Sisterhood had crafted for him. His normally commanding voice rose in something close to panic: "Get out! Get out of my head!"

"Not so righteous now, are we?" she managed to gasp between phantom waves, though she doubted anyone could hear her.

Then the air itself seemed to part.

Delia gasped.

Sabrina Bracewell descended from above, floating on threads of flame. Her silver hair writhed like living things, her eyes blazing with unnatural light. The illusions parted around her like a cloak, revealing her true form in terrible clarity.

"WHERE IS IT?" Her voice shook the volcano itself. "WHERE IS MY FAMILY'S GRIMOIRE?"

The water-illusion pressed harder as Sabrina's power joined the magical chaos. Through drowning darkness, Delia clutched the book tighter in her bag, feeling its ancient magic pulse against her hip.

"You dare?" Sabrina's fury made the air crackle. "You DARE steal our legacy? Our birthright?" Power gathered around her like a storm. "I will tear that shield apart and take back what's mine!"

38

MARJIE

Marjie felt the waves of hatred rolling off Sabrina – bitter rage and possessive fury that made her strengthen her empathic shields.

"You're nothing but a pretender!" Sabrina's voice crackled with power as she screamed accusations at Delia. "Playing at being a witch, stealing what rightfully belongs to true Bracewells!"

The raw emotion behind the words struck Marjie's senses like physical blows. Beneath Sabrina's rage lay something darker – a gnawing emptiness, a desperate need to elevate herself.

"Nobody," Marjie said quietly, stepping forward, "hurls abuse at my friends."

She reached out with her water magic, feeling the ocean that surrounded this volcanic island. Salt water answered her call, rising in a massive wave that curved through their shield's magical matrix. Before Sabrina could react, the wave struck her full force, sending her tumbling from the air.

As the Bracewell matriarch hit the ground, Marjie's power followed through. The water froze instantly, encasing Sabrina in gleaming ice that left only her head free.

"How dare you!" Sabrina thrashed against her bonds. "I am a Bracewell! We do not submit to water witches!"

But Marjie was barely listening. Through their shield, she could sense something odd about the Sisterhood's illusion magic. The patterns felt familiar somehow, like ripples in a pond she'd seen before...

"The illusions," she said suddenly. "They're based on emotion – drawing out our deepest fears and amplifying them. But through our shield..." She closed her eyes, focusing. "I can trace them back. Find where they're coming from."

"You can find them?" Ingrid asked sharply.

Marjie nodded. "Their magic leaves emotional echoes. Like following a trail of ripples back to the stone that caused them." She opened her eyes. "Who's with me?"

Through the chaos of battle and Sabrina's continued cries, Marjie felt a sudden surge of fierce joy from Delia. Her friend had gone very still, head tilted as if listening to something only she could hear.

"The fire dragon," Delia breathed. Her eyes were distant. "I can feel it."

"What can you feel?" Marjie asked.

"It's like a heartbeat made of magma...calling from deep within the volcano. It's waiting. It's been waiting so long..."

"Right then," Ingrid said briskly, though Marjie sensed

her underlying tension. "We need to split up. Some of us track down the Sisterhood while others help Delia reach the dragon."

"Sounds like a terrible idea," said Agatha, who'd now fought off the last of her illusion magic too. "The barrier has been protecting us from the full force of the Sisterhood's attack but look at the Order." She gestured to where the red robed mass lay, writhing outside. "Clearly most of us have to stay here and keep them contained."

"I'll go with Marjie," Ingrid said. Something flickered across her face – hope and fear that made Marjie's empathic senses tingle.

"Gwyneth?"

"Yes," Ingrid admitted, not meeting anyone's eyes. "Someone needs to give that woman a lesson about proper letter-writing etiquette."

"Oh my pets," Mephistos drawled from his perch on a nearby rock, "this all feels so deliciously familiar." His tail twitched. "Something about lovers and betrayal and ancient magic needing to sleep until the moment was right..."

"If you're going to be cryptic, at least be helpful about it," Agatha told him.

The demon cat's eyes gleamed. "I'm always helpful. Just rarely in ways anyone expects." He began grooming one paw with elaborate care. "Though I must say, this particular pattern does remind me of something. A rather dramatic scene involving a very powerful witch who discovered her lover's true nature. Quite the performance – betrayal, heart-break, world-shattering magic...The usual."

"Von Cassel," Declan said suddenly. "You're talking about Von Cassel and Demelza."

"Am I?" Mephistos examined his claws. "How interesting. Though I do hope this version has a better ending. The original was quite tragic. Everyone going their separate ways, powers being bound, dragons having to sleep..." He yawned delicately. "But I'm sure that's entirely irrelevant to your current situation."

"No time for the demon's riddles," Ingrid declared. "Marjie and I will track down the Sisterhood. The rest of you help Delia to that dragon or restrain the Order before they break through their illusions."

Marjie met Delia's eyes. Their friendship passed between them in that look – shared cups of tea, deep conversations, special moments of supporting each other through life's storms.

"Be careful," Delia said.

Marjie smiled. "You too, love. Try not to set anything important on fire."

"No promises," Delia replied, but her answering smile held all the warmth of a flame.

Covvey stepped forward, his wolf magic rippling around him. "I'll come with you. The Sisterhood's got some answers I need."

Marjie felt the complex tangle of emotions behind his words – hope and fear and a desperate need to understand. She nodded. Having a wolf's tracking abilities couldn't hurt.

He and Ingrid had seemed distant since the revelation of

their shared family ties, barely making eye contact. Ingrid seemed unperturbed by his offer, merely nodding.

"Right then," Marjie said, gathering her power. "Let's go end this illusion nonsense and have a proper chat with the Sisterhood about appropriate uses of emotional manipulation."

Through their shield, she could still feel the ripples of the Sisterhood's magic, leading away like a trail of tears and fears. All they had to do was follow it – preferably before Benedict's darkness or Sabrina's rage broke through.

She touched the water dragon's crystal at her throat, drawing comfort from its cool presence. Whatever waited at the end of this trail, they would face it together.

"Besides," she added, trying to lighten the mood, "I've always wanted to dramatically interrupt a secret magical organisation's ritual. Seems like the sort of thing every proper witch should do at least once."

39

INGRID

The earth sang beneath Ingrid's feet as she and Covvey followed Marjie's lead through the volcanic landscape. Every step brought messages through her boots – the mountain's ancient heartbeat, the minerals compressed over millennia, the slow ebb of tectonic plates far below. This was old earth, wild earth, untamed by human hands or magic.

Covvey walked several paces behind her, close enough to easily be protected by the protection she'd woven against the Sisterhood's illusions, but far enough away not to be a nuisance. Ingrid felt a small serving of warmth spreading towards her heart. She didn't know him well but in their limited interactions in the forest she'd always appreciated Covvey, in his gruff no nonsense manner. Over the decades, they'd occasionally met by accident while he was out hunting. He'd showed her proper respect, even in his wolf form.

It was astounding to think that all this time, he'd been her long lost older brother.

"This way," Marjie murmured, her eyes distant as she tracked emotion through the mist. "Their illusion magic leaves traces – fear and pain woven together like dark threads."

The volcanic rock grew warmer as they climbed, steam venting from cracks.

Ingrid sensed each fissure, each layer of stone, the mountain's history read like a book written in pressure and heat.

The earth here was restless, yearning toward transformation.

Rather like her own heart, she admitted privately.

Every step brought them closer to Gwyneth, and decades of carefully buried feelings were rising like magma seeking release. She'd spent so long living in the forest, tending her gardens, letting earth's slow wisdom heal what had been broken. But some roots ran too deep to ever fully extract.

"They're close," Marjie whispered, touching Ingrid's arm. "Just beyond that ridge."

Ingrid nodded, pressing her palm against the nearest rock face. The stone's song confirmed Marjie's assessment – something ahead disrupted the natural flow of earth magic, creating discordant ripples through the volcanic matrix.

"The earth doesn't like it," she said quietly. "This magic... it's an aberration. Like a splinter under the skin."

They crested the ridge and found a sight that made Ingrid's breath catch. In a natural amphitheatre formed by curved volcanic walls, wisps of steam rose like ghosts around a circle of hooded figures in white. Their chanting carried on the heated air. Ingrid shivered despite the heat.

The voices rose and fell in haunting cadence. Steam swirled around the sisters, their white robes rippling. Ingrid caught glimpses of familiar faces – Breag's stern features tight with concentration, Franwen's eyes closed in fierce focus.

But all those details fell away when she saw her.

Gwyneth stood among them, her hood fell back to reveal silver hair in waves that caught the light the way it had in their youth. Her voice rose clear above the others, carrying notes of power that made Ingrid's heart clench with remembered joy and pain. Even after all these decades, she moved with that particular grace that had first captured Ingrid's attention – every gesture precise yet flowing, like water over stone.

Time seemed to pause. The chanting, the steam, the very mountain itself – everything faded to background noise as Gwyneth's eyes met hers across the distance.

"Oh," Marjie breathed beside her, clearly catching the wave of emotions that crashed through their connection. "Oh, my dear."

Ingrid couldn't speak. All her carefully tended walls, all the protective barriers she'd built over decades of separation – they crumbled like dry earth in spring rain. Every shared moment, every stolen kiss, every whispered promise in the Clochar's hidden corners came rushing back with the force of a flash flood.

The chanting faltered. Through the steam, Ingrid saw other sisters turning, faces registering shock and outrage at their presence.

"How dare you!" Breag cried. "Sisters! Seize them!"

Several of the younger sisters stepped forward, confused and frantic. But none of that mattered. Her whole world had narrowed to Gwyneth's eyes, wide with recognition and the ache of hope.

"Ingrid." Gwyneth breathed her name like a spell, like a prayer, like something precious carried in her heart through all these years. The chanting died completely as she took a single step forward.

"No!" Breag's voice cracked through the steam. "Remember your vows, Sister Gwyneth. Remember your duty."

But Gwyneth wasn't looking at Breag. Her eyes remained fixed on Ingrid, drinking her in like a plant starved for water. "You came to find me..." she whispered.

"Of course I came." Ingrid's voice emerged rough with decades of unsaid words. The earth thrummed beneath her feet, resonating with her turmoil. "Though you might have written sooner. Say, twenty or even fifty years ago?"

A ghost of their old teasing sparked in Gwyneth's eyes. "You know me. I like to take my time with important letters."

"Enough!" Franwen stepped between them.

Covvey growled and the sisters gasped. He had transformed into his wolf and was doing an excellent job of intimidating the sisters who dared not step further forward.

But Ingrid barely noticed. All she could focus on was how Gwyneth's hands still moved in those familiar patterns – small, unconscious gestures that Ingrid remembered from countless shared moments in the herb gardens. Even after all this time, she still touched the air as if blessing it.

"Stand aside," Ingrid told Franwen, her voice quiet but carrying earth's deep authority. Steam curled around her boots as she stepped forward. "This is between us."

"There is no 'us'," Breag snarled. "Sister Gwyneth belongs to the Sisterhood. To our sacred purpose."

"Sacred purpose?" The words tasted bitter. "You mean like draining my sister's life force? Like twisting memory and truth into chains?"

Gasps echoed from the sisters. Ingrid felt a grim satisfaction at revealing this truth, though she noticed Gwyneth's shoulders tighten.

"You betrayed us!" Breag cried, pointing a finger at Gwyneth.

Gwyneth merely nodded. "I did what I had to do to serve my own integrity."

The volcanic rock trembled beneath them as Ingrid's power responded to her pain.

"Ingrid." Gwyneth's voice drew her attention back like a lodestone finding true north. "I'm so sorry. For everything. For not being strong enough then. For taking so long to see clearly."

"Don't," Ingrid started, but Gwyneth was already moving, gliding through the steam toward her with that fluid grace that had haunted Ingrid's dreams for decades.

Franwen reached out to stop her, but was brushed aside like an inconvenient speck of lint.

The distance between them closed like a wound healing – slowly, inevitably, with pain and promise. Steam swirled around them as Gwyneth moved closer, enveloping them in a private world. Mist and memory.

"I thought duty was enough," Gwyneth continued, close enough now that Ingrid could see the fine lines around her eyes, the silver threading through her dark hair. Beautiful marks of time that she'd never gotten to watch appear. "I thought serving a higher purpose would fill the empty spaces. But every full moon, I'd walk in my garden and remember how you used to say that the highest purpose was living truth, not just speaking it."

"And now?" Ingrid asked.

"Now I know you were right." Gwyneth's smile held decades of understanding. "The Sisterhood lost its way. We took sacred trust and turned it to control. Took free will and called it protection. I watched them bind Mathilda to that crystal, watched them twist her devotion into chains, and finally saw what you'd seen all those years ago."

Covvey growled.

A tremor ran through the volcanic ground as Ingrid's power responded to her surge of emotion.

"Traitor!" Breag's voice shattered their private moment. "You would betray everything we stand for? Everything we've worked towards for the great Goddess?"

"Yes," Gwyneth said simply.

The ground trembled again as the other sisters moved to

surround them. Ingrid felt their approach – thirteen pairs of feet carrying centuries of accumulated power. But she also felt something else: deep beneath them, ancient roots had somehow found purchase in the volcanic rock. Life persisting against all odds, just as her love for Gwyneth had persisted through decades of separation.

Covvey's growl turned to a whimper drawing Ingrid's attention. Breag stood near him, staring into his eyes, boring into them with her magic.

"The crystal must be fed," Franwen declared. "The power must be contained. Your sister understands this, Ingrid. Mathilda chose her duty."

"She chose what you told her to choose," Ingrid shot back. Her fingers found Gwyneth's and intertwined. The simple contact sent sparks of magic through them both.

"But we can choose a different path. Mathilda is still trapped under that crystal," Gwyneth said softly, squeezing Ingrid's hand. "We can't get to her, not easily."

"We'll figure it out," Ingrid assured her. "It may take some time, but she's a tough one, my sister. We all are in our family." She shot Covvey a meaningful look. He barked, breaking Breag's spell and lunging towards her. She cried as she staggered back.

Steam thickened around them as Marjie stepped closer, her water magic responding to the rising tension.

"There is no choice." Breag's voice carried cold fury. "The Sisterhood is for life. The vows are eternal."

"No," Gwyneth said simply. "They're not. I renounce my vows."

The other sisters gasped. Some made warding gestures while others began chanting protective spells. But Ingrid barely noticed. She was too caught up in the fierce joy radiating from Gwyneth's face.

"Run?" Gwyneth suggested, her eyes sparkling with remembered mischief.

"Oh no." Ingrid grinned, feeling the earth's power rise through her feet. "I have a better idea."

Steam billowed as Ingrid released her earth magic, letting it flow through the volcanic stone. The ground cracked and shifted, sending the other sisters stumbling as new fissures opened beneath their feet.

"You've learned some new tricks," Gwyneth observed, still holding Ingrid's hand as the earth moved around them.

"Had to do something with all that time you left me waiting," Ingrid replied, but the old hurt had lost its sting. How could she hold onto pain when Gwyneth was here, finally choosing her?

"Sisters, stop them!" Breag commanded, but her voice cracked with uncertainty as more steam vents opened, turning the natural amphitheater into a maze of mist and moving stone.

Marjie's water magic wove through Ingrid's earth power, turning steam to ice at strategic points, creating barriers that gleamed like crystal but held true strength. The other sisters' spells splashed harmlessly against these defenses, their unified power fractured by shock and confusion.

"The high ground is crumbling," Franwen warned, backing away as new cracks appeared. "We must retreat!"

The stone walls rose higher, steam curling through them like living veins. Ingrid felt every particle of earth answering her call. This was old magic, wild magic, the kind that existed long before anyone tried to trap it in crystals or bind it with vows.

"They won't be held forever," Marjie cautioned, reinforcing the barriers with sheets of ice. "Stone and steam can only contain them for so long."

"Long enough," Ingrid said firmly. She turned to Gwyneth, drinking in the sight of her – silver-streaked hair damp with steam, eyes bright with newfound freedom.

"I never truly left you," Gwyneth whispered. "Even in the deepest ceremonies, even in the crystal's shadow – part of me was always in that herb garden with you."

Their magic mingled as naturally as breath. Tiny flowers burst from cracks in the volcanic rock, wild thyme in full bloom.

Behind the stone walls, they could hear the Sisterhood's spells failing against the combined power of earth and water, desperation turning to resignation as they realised they were well and truly trapped. But none of that mattered anymore.

"Come home with me," Ingrid said softly, touching Gwyneth's cheek.

"Yes," Gwyneth breathed, and the simple word contained worlds of promise.

Their kiss tasted of steam and herbs, of decades of longing finally fulfilled. Around them, flowers continued to bloom impossibly from volcanic stone, the messy beauty of freedom bursting to life despite all odds. And the earth itself sang with the rightness of it.

"Well then," Marjie said, turning to Covvey, not quite hiding her smile as she reinforced their barriers one final time. "Shall we go and see how Delia is getting on with that dragon?"

40

DELIA

*A*round them, the Order members still stumbled through their private nightmares, red robes stark against black volcanic stone. She watched Jerry bat at invisible threats, his usual commanding presence reduced to desperate flailing.

"I'll get to restraining them. That should keep them occupied," Agatha said with grim satisfaction, leaning on her cane. "Go. Find your dragon. We'll make sure this lot stays put."

The pulse came again – stronger now, like a heartbeat made of magma, calling her upward toward the volcano's peak.

Each throb resonated with something deep in her chest.

"Ready?" Declan asked quietly.

Delia nodded, already moving. They climbed together, picking their way over volcanic rock still warm. The ocean crashed against the island's shores, salt spray mingling in the air with volcanic steam. Looking down, she caught glimpses of waves far below – deep blue meeting black stone in endless collision.

Another pulse. Stronger. More urgent.

"Can you feel it?" she asked Declan, though she suspected he couldn't. This was fire's song, which meant it was calling to her.

"I feel something," he replied, helping her over a particularly treacherous section. "Like standing too close to a bonfire. But it's distant, muffled."

Delia could sense him; his magic curled protectively around them both, offering brief respite from the increasing heat.

They reached the crater's rim as sunset painted the clouds in shades of flame. A river of lava flowed from a fissure on the far side, red and gold and mesmerising. The heat distorted the air into shimmering waves but Delia wasn't put off by the intensity, she was drawn to it.

Declan stopped at the edge of the crater. "This is as far as I can go."

Delia looked down into the crater. It was cavernous, dangerous, yet, feeling the dragon's call pull at her very bones, she felt more urgency to press forward than she felt fear.

The lava flow beckoned her. Its heat felt welcoming rather than dangerous – like slipping into a warm bath.

"That's alright," she said, squeezing his hand one last

time. "I always figured I'd have to do this part myself, what-ever it is."

His eyes held her in concern. "Be careful."

"Now where's the fun in that?" She managed a small smile, though her heart raced.

She braced herself as she approached the lava. Its heat was far from searing, still she hesitated before stepping into its lava flow, feeling its warmth wrap around her like a living thing. Behind her, Declan's presence faded into shadow as she faced her fate alone.

The lava parted around Delia's feet like thick honey, its glow reflecting off walls of ancient stone. Each step should have meant death, but her fire magic recognised this element as kin. The heat was intense but somehow comforting – like being wrapped in the world's warmest blanket.

Still, doubt crept in as she descended deeper into the volcano's throat. Every childhood fear of falling, of being trapped, of darkness rose up to challenge her courage. The walls pressed closer, the air growing thick with sulfur and steam.

"Right then," she muttered, trying to steady her nerves. "Just a nice stroll through an active volcano. Nothing to worry about. Not like I'm completely alone inside a mountain that could decide to properly erupt at any moment."

Another pulse from below, stronger than ever. The drag-on's call felt almost impatient now, as if it were saying: *get on with it.*

"Easy for you to say," she told the unseen presence.

The tunnel curved downward, following the lava's flow

into a massive chamber. Delia's breath caught at the sight. Obsidian and pumice formations studded the walls, catching the molten light and transforming it into a thousand shifting dark and fiery colours. Lava pooled in the centre in a lake of living fire that pulsed like a heart. Hundreds of feet above, massive columns of black stone hung down like teeth, ready to fall at any moment. Fear rose up but she held firm.

"No," she said, forcing herself to take another step. "I did not come this far to let a bit of questionable natural architecture stop me."

The dragon's call thrummed through her bones, drawing her forward despite her fear. She thought of everything that had led her here – discovering her magic, finding her strength, rebuilding her life, making new friends, breaking free of Jerry's manipulation. She'd faced every challenge, survived every test. She could face this too.

The lava lake's surface rippled as Delia approached, sending waves of heat rolling over her. Each pulse from below grew stronger, more insistent, until her whole body vibrated with its rhythm. The fire magic in her blood sang in response, reaching for something ancient and familiar.

"At least there aren't any spiders," she muttered, picking her way around the lake's edge. "Though I suppose they'd have better sense than to—"

The rock beneath her feet crumbled suddenly, sending her sliding toward the molten surface. Her heart lurched as she scrabbled for purchase, finding none. For one terrifying moment, she was falling...

Then her fire magic surged instinctively. The lava caught

her like a warm embrace, supporting her weight as naturally as water. She lay there for a moment, breathing hard, until hysterical laughter bubbled up.

"Swimming in lava," she gasped between giggles. "Of course. Why not? Perfectly sensible thing to do on a weekday evening."

The dragon's call pulsed again, more urgently. *This way*, it seemed to say. *Hurry.*

Taking a deep breath, Delia let herself sink into the lava flow. It felt strangely peaceful, like floating in liquid light. The magic guided her deeper, following channels within a tunnel that wound through the volcano's heart. She was relieved to find that the lava didn't stick to her, as if her magic formed a protective layer. "Like a non-stick pan," she muttered to herself, finding her skin and hair unscathed and dry.

The tunnel narrowed until she had to swim-crawl through gaps barely wide enough for her shoulders. Old claustrophobia clawed at her throat. What if she got stuck? What if her magic faltered? What if the lava flow changed direction? What if—

"Stop it," she told herself firmly. "You're the bloody Fire Crone. Act like it."

She pushed forward, letting her magic guide her through the tight spaces until finally, blessedly, the passage opened into a new chamber. Here, the lava pooled in a perfect circle around a raised platform of black stone. And on that platform...

"Oh," Delia breathed, pulling herself out of the lava pool. "Oh, that's not what I expected at all."

The egg sat in a nest of crystallised lava, deep red shot through with veins of gold that pulsed in time with Delia's heartbeat.

It was larger than any egg she'd ever seen. Its surface rippled as though flames moved beneath it.

"Well," came a familiar drawl as Mephistos materialised on a nearby ledge. "This is delightfully unexpected. Though really, someone should have a word with the decorator. All this black stone is terribly monotonous."

"How did you—" Delia started, then shook her head. "Never mind. I suppose demon cats don't have to worry about little things like lava and physics."

"My dear, I transcend such mundane concerns." He began grooming one paw with elaborate care. "It's one of the few perks of the job of being a trapped demon. Though I must say, you handled that lava swim rather well for a beginner."

The egg pulsed again, drawing Delia's attention back. As she approached, she could see something – embedded in the egg's shell was a bright red stone.

"Ah," Mephistos said, suddenly serious. "You've found your Crone stone."

Delia reached for the stone, feeling its magic call to her own. The moment her fingers touched it, visions flashed through her mind – a great dragon, wings spread against ancient skies, choosing to sleep until it was needed again. That's what she was expecting, not this...zygote.

"Are you disappointed?" Mephistos purred. "You were looking for a fully formed dragon, not an unhatched one."

Delia shrugged. "This is going to make transportation a lot easier, I suppose."

The cat yawned. "I do hope you're not expecting me to help carry that thing. These paws are made for lounging, not labour."

The egg pulsed again, more urgently. Without really thinking about it, Delia found herself opening her bag wider. "It'll fit," she said with certainty that surprised her. "Somehow, it'll fit."

"Of course it will," Mephistos sighed. "Though I must say, carrying a dragon egg in your handbag is rather gauche. Have you considered a nice decorative basket instead?"

Delia carefully lifted the egg, surprised by how light it felt despite its size. Her bag did indeed accommodate it easily. The moment both were safely stowed, the chamber's light dimmed noticeably, as if the egg had been the source of its glow.

"Right then," she said, trying to sound more confident than she felt. "I've got a dragon egg in my handbag. Now what?"

"Now what indeed," Mephistos stretched languidly. "Though I must point out, the lava is rising rather dramatically."

He was right. The pool around the platform was swelling, eating away at their safe ground with alarming speed. The volcano itself seemed to be waking up, as if the egg's removal had triggered something.

"Please tell me you know another way out," Delia said, clutching her bag close.

"My dear, I always know another way out. It's part of my charm." The demon cat's tail twitched. "Though you might want to hurry. These volcanic renovations seem rather aggressive."

A deep rumble shook the chamber, sending crystalline formations crashing down around them. The heat intensified as fresh magma poured in from newly opened fissures.

He led her through a series of increasingly narrow passages, always staying just ahead as the mountain shuddered around them. The egg pulsed steadily in her bag, its rhythm somehow comforting despite the chaos.

The tunnel narrowed further, forcing Delia to crawl through spaces barely wide enough for her shoulders. The egg's warmth pressed against her side, its pulse quickening as if it sensed her rising panic.

"Not to rush you," Mephistos called from ahead, "but this volcano appears to be having some rather dramatic thoughts about redecorating. Though I must say, the flowing lava does add a certain ambiance..."

"Less commentary," Delia grunted, squeezing through another tight spot, "more escape!"

The mountain's rumble had become a constant roar. Fresh cracks appeared in the walls, glowing with magma. The air grew thick with sulfur and steam, making each breath a struggle.

"You know," she managed between gasps, "I always thought finding a dragon would be more...ceremonial. Less crawling through volcanic death traps with only a sarcastic demon cat for company."

"I prefer 'witty' demon cat," Mephistos corrected, pausing on a ledge above her. "Though really, what did you expect? Dragons do so love their dramatic moments. Rather like myself, actually. Speaking of which..."

The tunnel ahead of them collapsed in a shower of molten rock. Delia pressed herself against the wall, feeling the egg pulse frantically.

"There is another way," Mephistos said, suddenly serious. "Though you won't like it."

He nodded toward a narrow fissure that seemed to lead straight up. Steam poured from it like a chimney, carrying the scent of open air far above.

"You're joking," Delia said flatly. "That's practically vertical!"

"Pet, I never joke about escape routes."

41

DELIA

*H*eat radiated from Delia's skin as she burst up through the steam, emerging from the volcano's depths, her handbag considerably heavier and warmer than when she'd entered. The dragon egg pulsed against her hip.

Swimming through lava had changed something in her – as if the molten rock had burned away some of her fear and uncertainty, as if tempering her in its heat.

"Well," she said, patting her bag where the impossible egg nestled, "that's one way to spend a Thursday evening."

"Your timing is impeccable." Mephistos materialised beside her, tail swishing.

Delia squinted at him. "You couldn't teleport before, could you? Are you getting more powerful?"

The cat's eyes gleamed and Delia felt an instinctive urge not to ask any more questions.

As they descended the mountain, the scene before her caught her theatre director's eye with perfect dramatic irony – Jerry and his Order members bound in shimmering magical constraints, their crimson robes stark against volcanic stone. Steam rose in artful curls around them, backlit by the setting sun like the world's most elaborate stage lighting.

"Did we actually win?" she asked, hardly daring to believe it.

"Won?" Agatha called from her perch on a relatively flat rock. "We've got them trussed up like Christmas hams. Marjie, Ingrid, and Covvey took care of the sisterhood. Got them contained."

"And we have a new friend," Marjie said softly, gesturing to where Ingrid sat with a woman in white robes who Delia vaguely remembered.

"Wonders never cease," Delia said. "I can't believe things went so smoothly."

"Like a charm," said Marjie. "Though I wouldn't mind wrapping this up soon – volcanic rock is rough on the joints."

Jerry stood apart from his followers, contained within a particularly complex web of magic. His face twisted with familiar contempt as he watched her approach – the same expression he'd worn whenever she'd suggested production changes or questioned his decisions.

"Whatever you think you've accomplished—" he began.

"Oh, do shut up," Delia cut him off. "I've had quite enough of your pompous speeches. Though, watching you fight imaginary butterflies earlier was rather entertaining.

Reminded me of your attempt at choreographing *A Midsummer Night's Dream*."

She recognised Declan's magic as it curled protectively around the prisoners, working in concert with the elemental bonds of the crones. She caught his eye, relief washing through her at the sight of him whole and unharmed.

She felt different after her journey through the volcano's heart – more settled in her power, more certain of her path.

"The fire dragon," Jerry said. "You think finding it makes you powerful? You're still just playing pretend at magic—"

"Says the man who spent thirty years pretending to care about theatre," Delia replied, surprised by how little his words meant now.

"Pet, you've developed actual wit," Mephistos observed. "How delightfully dangerous. Though I can't help feeling this is all wrapping up rather too neatly…"

As if his words were a cue, harsh laughter cut through the gathered steam. Delia turned to see Cedric rise from where he'd been sitting quietly among their allies, his eyes fever-bright in the fading light.

"Wrong!" he cried, voice cracking. "Everything's wrong. Too complicated. Too tangled." His hands moved in increasingly erratic patterns. "Needs to be simpler. Needs to burn."

The egg pulsed a warning against Delia's side as magic began to build around them like a gathering storm. Raw power crackled from Cedric's fingers, making the very air vibrate with instability.

"Easy now, son." Papa Jack's voice cut through Cedric's rising hysteria, carrying that same gentle authority that had first helped calm him at the pub. "You're not alone anymore. None of us are."

"Cedric," Covvey started, reaching for his friend, but Marjie caught his arm.

"Something's broken," she whispered, her face pale. "Something's been broken for a long time."

"Oh dear," Mephistos sighed. "And here I was hoping we could skip the obligatory dramatic twist."

But there was nothing tedious about the magic gathering around Cedric. It felt wrong – not dark like Jerry's power, but fractured, like shards of broken glass. The mask he'd worn had shattered, revealing the dangerous desperation beneath.

Delia met Declan's eyes, reading the same recognition.

Raw power exploded from Cedric like shrapnel, shattering their carefully constructed magic containing the Order members.

Delia barely had time to throw up a wall of fire before another blast hit them. Through the flames, she watched in horror as Jerry broke free, dark energy crackling around him like black lightning.

"The traitor is mine," Jerry snarled, the Almighty's power turning his voice inhuman.

"Everything burns!" Cedric's magic lashed out wildly, catching friend and foe alike. Steam vents exploded around them, turning the battlefield into a chaos of hissing white clouds.

Delia responded, strengthening her fire shield as another wave of Cedric's fractured magic crashed against it.

The other crones leapt into action, drawing upon their

elements. Delia only caught glimpses of the others fighting the freed members of the Order – Marjie redirecting scalding vapour, Ingrid raising walls of volcanic stone, Agatha's wind magic blasting paths through the chaos. But Cedric's power was everywhere, wild and unpredictable.

"I trusted you!" he screamed at them all. "Thought you could make things simple again! But you're just like them – making everything complicated, tangled, wrong!"

"Oh, darling," Delia called back, recognising the pain behind his madness. "Life is complicated. That's what makes it beautiful."

"Beautiful?" Jerry's darkness slammed into Cedric, driving him to his knees. "There is only order or chaos. Power or weakness." His next strike could have killed the former cleric if Delia hadn't deflected it with a burst of flame.

"Still trying to control everything," she said, moving to stand between Jerry and his target. "Still can't handle anything real or messy or human."

Her body trembled and power surged through her as she faced her ex-husband. Behind her, she heard Cedric's harsh breathing, felt the desperate edges of his magic still lashing out.

"Delia." Declan's voice carried through the chaos. "The portal – we need to go now!"

But she couldn't leave, not yet. Not while Jerry's darkness pressed against her fire, not while Cedric's broken magic threatened to tear everything apart.

Another blast of Cedric's fractured power sent everyone

stumbling. Behind her, she heard Declan working to stabilise the portal while the others tried to contain the chaos.

"You won't even let the mad traitor die. How disappointingly sentimental," Jerry sneered, hurling more darkness. "Always reaching for these pathetic emotional truths—"

"Says the man who spent decades pretending to be someone else," Delia shot back. "At least actors admit they're performing!"

"Oh, delicious," Mephistos commented from somewhere above. "Though if anyone's interested, our unstable friend is about to—"

Cedric's magic erupted again, this time catching Jerry full force. The Almighty's dark power met broken chaos in an explosion that sent everyone flying. Delia hit the ground hard. The dragon egg was unharmed, still radiating its warmth.

"Must destroy it all," Cedric ranted, power crackling around him like heat lightning. "Burn away the complications, make everything simple again..."

"Simple?" Jerry's voice distorted with rage as he rose, darkness gathering around him. "I'll show you simple, you pathetic traitor!"

"Delia!" Marjie cried. "Quick – reach into my bag – there should be a protection charm!"

Delia plunged her hand into Marjie's satchel, fingers closing around cool glass. She pulled out what she thought was a charm and quickly hurled it towards the former cleric.

"That's not—" Marjie started, but it was too late.

The bottle went flying as another blast of Cedric's magic

rocked them. It shattered against his chest, soaking him in water.

Cedric's eyes rolled back and tears began to pour from them.

For a moment, everything stopped.

"What was that?" Delia asked. "What did I do to him?"

"Oh love, that wasn't the charm," Marjie said. "It was the bottle of scried water from Ingrid's memories."

"You mean we've just inflicted him with the captured emotions of children running away with their mother, being separated from their brother?"

Ingrid sighed.

Covvey growled.

Cedric gasped as decades of buried pain hit him – not his own, but Ingrid's desperate need to protect her sister, their mother's impossible choice, Covvey's childhood agony of abandonment.

Delia flung some casual fireballs at Jerry to keep him distracted while the Crones watched Cedric. The emotions cascaded through him as if breaking down the walls he'd built around his own past.

"I...I..." He staggered, his wild magic faltering. "What have I done? I became exactly what I hated – trying to control everything, hurting people, making their choices for them..." Tears streamed down his face as empathy overwhelmed him.

"You understand now?" Marjie asked, moving closer despite the lingering danger.

"Yes," Cedric whispered. "Oh gods, yes. I'm so sorry. I was so afraid of complicated feelings that I tried to burn everything down instead of facing them. Just like the Order taught me..."

"And now you will perish, traitor!" Jerry said, rising up, his powers building again.

The Crones moved as one, their magic shifting from defensive to protective as Cedric's power imploded with grief and understanding. Marjie's remaining water magic wrapped around him gently while Ingrid's earth power grounded his wild energy. Agatha's wind cleared the steam, revealing the broken man beneath the madness.

"What..." Cedric stared at them in confusion as they contained rather than hurt him. "Why aren't you attacking me? Why do you keep protecting me? I tried to destroy everything!"

"Because you're not well," Delia said softly, recognising the lost child beneath his madness. "We protect. We heal. We make space for all the complicated, messy parts of being human."

"How touching," Jerry snarled, gathering more darkness. "How utterly—"

"How utterly boring you've become," Delia cut him off. "All monologues and no substance."

The dragon egg's warmth surged through her as she faced him one last time. All the fear and doubt he'd planted in her over the years burned away in pure, cleansing fire.

"Portal's ready!" Declan called urgently. "We need to go now!"

"This isn't over," Jerry warned, darkness crackling around him.

"Oh, but it is." Delia smiled. "Exit stage left, darling. You've had your final act."

With that, she threw up a huge wall of fire. Through it, she heard Declan calling them home, felt the portal's pull.

The others grabbed Cedric, still wrapped in their protective magic, and ran.

Through the chaos, Delia caught sight of Sabrina, still encased in Marjie's ice. The Bracewell matriarch's eyes blazed with fury even as frost crept further up her elegant robes. Delia felt a chill of fear, but that was a problem for another time.

42

DELIA

*T*hey tumbled onto the damp earth of Myrtlewood's town circle in a tangle of limbs and magic. The familiar scent of lawn chamomile and clover replaced the smoke and sulfur of the volcano. Delia lay there for a moment, grass cool against her cheek, dragon egg still pulsing warmly in her bag.

"Is everyone—" she started, pushing herself up.

"Mostly intact," Agatha said, using her cane to prod what appeared to be Mephistos, who had landed rather ungracefully on top of Covvey. "Though some of us could work on our dismounts."

"Eugh! I smell of dog!" the demon cat shrieked.

"Get. Off." Covvey growled.

Marjie and Ingrid still had Cedric contained in their magic, though he'd stopped struggling. He stared around with the bewildered expression of someone waking from a long nightmare.

"You saved me," he whispered. "After everything I did, you still..."

"Welcome to the family," Delia told him, remembering her own journey from isolation to belonging. "It's messy and complicated and sometimes absolutely bonkers, but it's real."

Delia felt laughter bubble up – slightly hysterical but genuine. They were alive. They were home. And in her bag was a dragon's egg!

Ingrid and Gwyneth sat on the grass, hand in hand.

"I tended the herbs," Gwyneth said softly, her voice carrying years of regret. "In the gardens at the Clochar. The same ones we used to tend together. Lavender and thyme, rosemary and sage. Every summer, when they bloomed, I'd remember how you taught me to listen to their needs. How you'd speak to each plant like it held secrets only you could hear."

"They do hold secrets," Ingrid managed, her voice rough. "They remember everything. Like the soil remembers every seed, every root, every truth we try to bury."

"Right then," Marjie said, looking at their bedraggled group. "Who wants a cup of tea?"

"Tea?" Cedric asked. "At a time like this?"

"I'm still not sure about tea," Delia admitted.

"Trust me," Marjie said, already leading them toward Delia's nearby cottage where warm lights beckoned. "Sometimes the most magical thing in the world is a proper cup of tea and a chance to catch your breath."

"About time you returned," Kitty said as Delia and everyone else crowded into the cottage, volcanic dust settling on her clean floors.

The dragon egg hummed contentedly and whisps of steam rose from it as Delia lifted it from her bag and set it carefully on the kitchen table.

Everyone crowded around to look at it.

"It's not what I expected," she admitted. "But then again, life's like that."

"Indeed it is," said Marjie, putting the kettle on.

"Well," Delia said, looking around at her gathered friends – old and new, all somehow fitting perfectly in her cosy space. "I suppose we should discuss what happens next."

"Next?" Cedric asked, taking a seat in an armchair by the fire. His eyes still held shadows, but there was something clearer in them now, like morning light after a storm.

"Well, we have a dragon egg to hatch." Delia glanced at Ingrid and Gwyneth, whose hands remained linked. "And quite a few relationships to nurture."

"And a brother to get to know," Ingrid added quietly, looking at Covvey.

He shifted uncomfortably but didn't growl, which Delia counted as progress.

"The Order will regroup," Declan warned, winding his arm around Delia's waist. "And the Sisterhood—"

"Will need to find a new purpose if they know what's good for them," Gwyneth said. "One that doesn't involve controlling minds." She shook her head sadly. "But I doubt they'll change so easily."

"Oh, is that all?" Mephistos drawled from his new perch on top of Delia's bookshelf. "Just minor tasks like hatching ancient dragons and reforming centuries-old magical institutions. How delightfully ambitious."

"We're Crones," Agatha said firmly, settling into her favourite armchair. "We're not afraid of a challenge."

Marjie emerged from the kitchen with a hot pot of tea and a knowing smile. "And we do it together."

Delia considered her journey so far, her former career, her magical awakening, all the outrageous adventures – feeling the rightness of her path settle in her bones like embers finding their home.

The cottage filled with quiet conversation and occasional laughter. Delia watched it all, this patchwork community she'd somehow gathered, and felt her heart expand like flames reaching for sky.

"You know," she said finally, "I'll always be a coffee person, but right now I think I'm ready for that cup of tea after all."

Marjie beamed. "There's hope for you yet."

A PERSONAL MESSAGE from Iris

Hello lovelies. Thank you so much for joining me and the Myrtlewood Crones. I expect to write one more book in this series (though who knows what will happen?).

I also have some **exciting news**! I've written a non-fiction book on magic - my own intuitive approach to empowerment, connecting with nature, kitchen witchery and shadow work. It's called Awakening the Wild Witch and it's coming out on April 30 2025! This book is for you if you're interested in real magic, healing and deep self-work. I can't wait to share it with you.

If you enjoyed the Crone of Arcane Cinders, please leave a rating or review to help other people find it!

You can preorder the Crone of Burning Shadows, final Myrtlewood Crones book, on Kindle. I've set a nice long pre-order, with the aim to release earlier when the book is ready (paperbacks will be out close to the release date).

If you've missed it, you might also want to check out In the Spirit, my new magical series, set in New Zealand and drawing on local mythology. It's a co-write with my dear friend Nova Blake.

If this is your first time reading my books, you might also want to check out the original Myrtlewood Mysteries series, starting with Accidental Magic.

If you're looking for more books set in the same world, you might want to take a look at my Dreamrealm Mysteries series too.

I absolutely love writing these books and sharing them with you. Feel free to join my reader list and follow me on social media to keep up to date with my witchy adventures.

Many blessings,

Iris xx

P.S. You can also subscribe to my Patreon account for extra Myrtlewood stories and new chapters of my books before they're published, as well as real magical content like meditations and spells, and access to my Myrtlewood Discord community. Subscribing supports my writing and other creative work!

For more information, see: www.patreon.com/IrisBeaglehole

ACKNOWLEDGMENTS

A big thank you to all my wonderful Patreon supporters, especially:

Linnea Johnsson

Cheryl Gawel

Cindy

Shari Yates Farrell

Dawn Dexter

John Stephenson

Danielle Kinghorn

Ricky Manthey

Elizabeth

Rachel

William Winnichuk

ABOUT THE AUTHOR

Iris Beaglehole is many peculiar things, a writer, researcher, analyst, druid, witch, parent, and would-be astrologer. She loves tea, cats, herbs, and writing quirky characters.

facebook.com/IrisBeaglehole

x.com/IrisBeaglehole

instagram.com/irisbeaglehole